Misgivings

A novel by **Anne Gibson**

Instagram: @authorannegibson

ISBN: 9798336992694 (Paperback)
ISBN: 9798336992892 (Hardcover)

Table of Contents

Prologue

Fog hovered over her mind as she tried to break through the mist. The words, *"Te quiero,"* taunted her memory. As Dee sat up, pain rushed to her head. Dizziness dispersed at the sudden movement of her body. Who said that? Racking her brain, the fog blocked any recollection. She heard those words once. She could feel it in her soul. Someone spoke those words to her, but who?

Looking around, her eyes blurred her surroundings into a messy swirl. The room smelled musty and damp. It was dark and cold. Dee tried to focus, but her eyes just burned. She tried to remember, but nothing would return. How did she end up here?

Te quiero, Dee.

Dee paused this time, trying not to rush the memory. Wanting to let it linger, she sat as still as a statue. Fresh air wrapped its arms around her. Orchid's sprung to her memory. White, red, purple and pink swirled around as she envisioned the beautiful flower. A hand gently plucked the delicate flower and tucked it into her blond braid. That hand was strong, yet tender at the same time. She wasn't a stranger to its touch. He caressed her face with that same hand, whispering sweet promises. What did his words pledge? Dee tried to force her mind, desperate to know what he was murmuring. Was he the one that loved her? She knew his hand but why couldn't she see his face? The more she struggled the thicker the fog became. His hand dropped from her face and panic entered her heart. Then the fog overtook and he was gone. But the fear remained.

"Dee!" A voice shouted. She slowly looked up. Again, it shouted, "DEE!"

The fog disappeared and pain took its place. Holding her head, Dee looked around. Darkness enveloped her and her eyes refused to adjust. Narrowing her eyes, she forced them to take in her strange surroundings. Cold, damp walls closed in around her. Her only exit was blocked with iron bars. Ropes bound her hands and feet. Despite the night's darkness and her mind's fogginess, she recognized her situation.

Her eyes swept across the tiny space searching for the man she shared her cell with. Huddled in the corner, he strained against the ropes that confined him to the opposite wall, preventing him from touching her, from holding her.

Catching her eye, he refused to look away. He stared into the depths of her deep copper eyes, investigating the amount of pain she was enduring. Once again, he yanked at his ropes, desperate to hold her and tell her how much he loved her. His desperation turned to humiliation as his emotions gave way. He tried to be the strong, brave soldier that she needed. He struggled, needing to save her. But his fear was stronger than his determination and all he could do was apologetically murmur, "Lo siento," as a single tear slipped from his eye.

She nodded her head, fully aware of his misery. Crumpling against her wall, too tired to fight against her ropes, she gave up. Darkness closed in and regret overtook her. If only he knew how sorry she really was. One day she would have to tell him the truth. Fear sank in. He would never be able to forgive her.

Dee sank back into the shadows, wishing for the fog to return. She didn't want to think about the pain she caused him. She didn't want to acknowledge the fact that the worst was yet to come.

Chapter 1

Hanging the last pew bow, Dee leaned back and observed the transformation that took place before her. She could not believe the view before her eyes, as the simple sanctuary converted into a garden of irises, lavender and flowing white tulle. Even the small stage was now a platform of cascading blossoms, illuminated by ribbons and candles. However, the beauty of the sanctuary was no match when compared to the glowing bride-to-be.

One day, perhaps. Dee couldn't help but hope. Her stomach tightened as she thought about how her Mother begged her to get married before she moved in with Mark. Her mom was a proper Christian lady, and though her step-father claimed to be a Christian, his actions said otherwise. Not wanting to belong to her step-father's hypocrisy, she rejected her mother's pleadings and her step-father's preaching. She loved Mark and knew that one day they would get married. But until that day came, she saw no reason to withhold the full extent of her love. She didn't want to be like her mother, bound to an arrogant, harsh, condescending man for the rest of her life. So, she decided to test the waters, moving in with Mark over two years ago. How could she have known two years ago that she wouldn't be married by now?

"Well, I think that about does it," said Maggie as she gazed upon the altar that she would stand before. A smile crept across her face as she envisioned the vows that would take place. Dee couldn't help but smile as she watched her friend approach the day she had always dreamed of.

"I can't believe how beautiful this place is," Dee responded. "You really have a gift when it comes to decorating."

"Well, this girl is only getting married once, so she might as well go all out," joked Jeffrey as he lovingly embraced his bride-to-be.

"Save it for tomorrow," teased Dee as the couple locked eyes and ignored her.

"I don't know about you guys," interrupted Luke, Maggie's older brother and the best man, "but all of this decorating has worked up an appetite. How about we let the pastor lock up and go for dinner."

Dee laughed at the thought of Luke working up an appetite by hanging up lace and tulle. The protective big brother had handled the flower arrangements with extreme caution, as if they were made out of glass and would break at any moment. For a big, tough soldier, he was most certainly tender and careful, ensuring that everything looked perfect for his sister's big day. With the mentioning of food, Dee's stomach rumbled. They had been too busy decorating to even think about lunch, and she was looking forward to the rehearsal dinner at Chez Martine. The loving couple went all out and booked the best restaurant in town.

"Is Mark coming?" Jeffrey asked as they started to head out.

"No. He has to work late tonight," Dee responded, recalling the late nights her partner spent in his office. She moved in with him so that they could spend more time together, but lately it seemed like she never saw him.

"On a Friday night?" Questioned Luke.

Dee shrugged her shoulders. "That's what happens when you are a CEO. If you want something done, you have to do it yourself."

Luke thought about what she said, but didn't buy it. "I always thought that CEOs hardly worked at all. You know, delegating everything so that they don't have to do anything."

Dee nervously laughed, anxious to change the subject. "Now wouldn't that be nice."

"Well as long as he's here tomorrow, that's all that matters," broke in Maggie, sensing Dee's growing discomfort.

"He wouldn't miss it for the world."

Dee checked her phone as she crossed the parking lot. Mark had promised to call her on his coffee break and update her on how late he would be, but she didn't have any missed calls. Not wanting to interrupt him with a call, she texted, "Can you make it tonight?" She was startled by the immediate response, "Working. Be home late." Disappointed by his busy schedule, she got into her car and drove away.

Luke paused before he got into his SUV. Dee crossed the parking lot, apparently fixated on typing a text message into her cell phone. Maggie and Jeffrey thanked the pastor and began walking to their car, hand in hand. Obviously not impressed with her phone's response, Dee ignored everyone else, got into her car and drove away. Luke watched as she disappeared out of the parking lot.

"You've got that look on your face." Luke hadn't noticed that Maggie had walked up to him.

"Does he always work so much?" Luke continued to stare at the spot where Dee's car had disappeared from.

"Luke, people work. Not everyone has a job as cushy as yours."

"Ya, but if I had a pretty girlfriend, I'd be making excuses not to work."

"Well, maybe you should get a girlfriend and see how well that goes for you." Luke turned and looked at his sister. He couldn't help but smile at her weak attempt to get him to settle down and marry.

"I know it's easier said then done, but I've been back for two years and I've seen the guy maybe four or five times. I've never met anyone who worked as much as he claims to work."

"You can't fix everything, Luke. How they run their relationship is none of our business."

Luke looked away from his little sister's gentle rebuke. "I know, but if Jeff starts working one too many nights, he'll be hearing from me."

Maggie smirked at his over-protectiveness. "He's already been warned. Now let's get some food. I'm starving!"

Maggie and Jeffrey had reserved a private room at Chez Martine to celebrate in. Though the wedding party was small, the family was not. Dee felt awkward and uncomfortable being the only non-family member there. Though their families were warm and welcoming, Dee felt out of the loop as aunts and uncles recounted childhood stories. As fun as it was to imagine Luke's first time babysitting Maggie, Dee wished that Mark was there with her. It would have given her someone to converse with when she felt excluded. Silently excusing herself, she slipped out of the private room.

Weaving her way through the tables, she could not help but notice the lovely couples that lingered over their food. Though old, Chez Martine was an expensive and romantic restaurant. Dee couldn't remember the last time Mark took her to a restaurant like this one. It seemed like everything changed once she moved in. She wouldn't say that the spark was gone, but things were not as romantic as they were when they first started dating. Now they were like an old married couple—except for one thing, they weren't married. Dee sighed. At this rate they would never be. She knew she had reservations about marriage, especially after witnessing her mother's strained marriage with her step-father, but seeing Maggie and Jeffrey so happily in love stirred something inside of her. She knew she ought to be content, but she wasn't and it was starting to frustrate her.

Eyeing the dramatic stairwell that was the restaurant's focal point, she made her way upstairs to the bathroom. Pausing outside of the door to the ladies' restroom, Dee checked her phone. Perhaps Mark would finish up early and be able to join them for dessert. *No missed calls.* Sighing with disappointment, she started to push open the bathroom door when she heard a familiar chuckle. Looking over her left shoulder she couldn't help but notice the perfectly tailored, charcoal grey suit and the mass of short curly black hair. She tried to remember what Mark was wearing when he left this morning, but she left before him and couldn't recall if he had dressed yet. *It couldn't be,* she tried to convince herself, yet despite her convictions she still found herself inching towards that very table.

The woman sitting across from the man in the grey suit was younger looking. She looked like she was fresh out of college, though it had only been a couple of years since Dee's college days. This girl was dark, with deep brown eyes that drank in everything the man in the grey suit said. Her eyes danced as he whispered sweet promises to her. She flirtatiously played with her necklace that dangled above the dangerously low neckline of her dress. Nearing the table, Dee made out the husky voice that mesmerized her years ago. Dee didn't want to hear anymore, yet she found her feet propelling her closer and closer, forcing her to eavesdrop.

The young girl dropped her necklace and elegantly tucked a wisp of jet black hair behind her ear. When she placed her hand on the table, the man in the grey suit seized it with both of his. Sparks danced in her exotic eyes as he leaned in and intently stared into her face. Their conversation turned serious and he lowered his voice. Unable to stop herself, Dee came closer so that she could overhear.

"You know I don't love her anymore," he confided in a hushed voice.

"Then why won't you leave her?" The young girl said. She didn't whine. Instead, she said it with such confidence that it came across as a matter of fact.

"You know I want to, but I can't. She's so weak...and unstable. I don't know what would happen to her if I..."

She interrupted, "She sounds so needy. She'll drain the life out of you. You're too young to be tied down to someone so pathetic."

"But if I don't look out for her, who will? I don't think she's strong enough to survive on her own."

Her tone was extremely confident. "Just forget her then. You have me now. Don't let her hold you back from something even better. She's making you miss out on life."

"She needs me. I can't turn my back on her."

"I need you. Will you turn your back on me?"

"Of course not," his voice sounded as smooth as velvet. "I love you more than anything. More than I have ever loved her."

With this assurance, her young brown eyes melted and she leaned over the table and kissed him. Unable to stop herself, Dee edged her way over to the other side of the table. Every cell in her body prayed that the face of the man in the grey suit did not match Mark's. Shock gave way to feelings of betrayal when she recognized his face and she could feel flames leaping through her veins. She wanted to scream and

15

hit him. She wanted to smash dishes and call him every ugly word that she knew, but words failed her and she found herself unable to speak. Instead, all she could do was stare into the face that no longer loved her.

"Dee." Mark also fumbled for words as he stood up.

She wished she had something clever to say. Something to make her seem strong, yet also inflicted pain on him for his betrayal. Yet all she could say was, "I thought you were at work." As soon as the words were out, she hated herself. She sounded like a child, not a grown woman. She sounded foolish and naive. The young girl snickered.

"I...I finished early. And since you had your party I figured I'd catch up with an old friend."

Dee looked at the girl that sat before her. She wanted to cry, but the proud smirk on the young girl's face made her indignant. Unfortunately, her indignation quickly gave way to feelings of insignificance. She stared at this girl, who didn't seem to care what Dee thought. As Dee's confidence shrank, this girl seemed to sense it and feed off of it. Her beauty was dangerously alluring. She had a great body and had no fears in showing it off. Her greatest weapon was her deep, dark eyes. Not only did they entice men, committed or not, but they trapped them. It seemed like every move she made proved her sensuality, forcing men to give her what she wanted.

Dee looked away, feeling plain. Her own natural beauty seemed ordinary and unable to compete with such an exotic beauty. Acknowledging her defeat, she turned to go, refusing to look Mark in the eyes. She forced her feet to move, not wanting Mark to see the pain that he inflicted upon her.

Though Luke loved to recount his childish ways, he could only tolerate so many stories of his reckless shenanigans contrasted against Maggie's perfection. She was always the responsible one, constantly tattling on him. Quietly ducking out of the private room, he heard a whisper, "You're not leaving me in there alone."

Luke chuckled as he found his soon to be brother-in-law following him out. "I can only take so many of Aunt Bea's stories."

Jeffrey snorted, "I'm just glad to know I'm marrying the golden child."

"Ya, she'll keep you in line all-right."

The two friends laughed as they headed towards the door for some fresh air, but their playful banter was interrupted with shouts from upstairs.

As much as Mark's betrayal hurt, the anger was beginning to outweigh the pain. Dee needed to be alone, where she could scream and break something without causing a scene.

Heading for the stairs, she could hear him calling after her. Ignoring him, she continued until she felt his grip tighten on her arm. Spinning her around, Dee could tell by the look in his eyes that he did not like being shown up in front of his date. Spite crawled inside of Dee, causing her to smile at the idea of Mark being embarrassed when she was the one who was so obviously humiliated. Such spite caused Dee to stand up tall and boldly stare him in the eyes. Suddenly she desired to defy him, wishing she knew how to humiliate him even more. She wished she knew how to play dirty. She wanted to wound him more than he wounded her.

"Let go of me," she growled, staring him down.

Mark did not like the idea of being challenged. He was a successful CEO. People didn't tell him what to do; he told them what to do. No one barked orders at him, especially his girlfriend. He dragged her towards the balcony, away from the curious eyes around them.

"I think it'd be best if you went home. We'll talk about this later." His tone was low and stern. She ignored his orders and challenged him.

"What is there to talk about? The fact that you are a liar? Or, the fact that you are cheating on me?" Her words were louder than she intended, but her growing defiance felt good.

Her challenge provoked him. He angrily pushed her against the balcony. His face heated up and he could feel a headache rising. Refusing to lose control after so many years of molding her, he threatened her. "I am not asking, I'm telling you. Go home."

Unwilling to back down and give into to his manipulative control, she hissed back, "Let go of my arm." She pushed him back, attempting to break from his possessive hold.

This final act of defiance caused a volcano to erupt inside of him. Losing all self control, he shoved her into the balcony railing with all his might. A loud crack interrupted the silence of the curiously silent restaurant and the railing broke. Before he could regain control Dee disappeared over the edge.

Just as the angry voices caused Luke to stop and turn, he saw a petite woman crash through the railing and fall from the second floor. Landing on a table beneath her, the table crumbled and crashed into the floor. Chairs broke and a vase shattered on the hardwood floor. Patrons gasped and worried shouts rippled through the restaurant. Waiters rushed over and a man in a grey suit peered over the edge and then disappeared. Luke hurried up the flight of stairs while Jeffrey rushed to the crushed table. Pushing curious onlookers aside,

Jeffrey neared the table that crumpled around the petite body. Shock seized him as he recognized the curly blond hair and the soft green dress. The manager entered the room and tried to settle down the agitated customers. Painfully, Dee tried to sit up and push pieces of the broken table aside. Jeffrey moved a broken chair out of the way so that he could kneel next to her.

"Easy Dee," he said in a calm, smooth voice. "Just lay still for a while. Don't try to get up." Looking up, he studied the broken railing that she fell through and then looked down, assessing the damaged table that broke her fall. Though it was a bad fall, it was not life threatening. However, she could have easily broken some bones. Again, Dee stirred, trying to sit up.

This time, rather than stopping her, he helped her lean forward. The restaurant manager knelt beside them and said, "The police have been called. Should we call for an ambulance too?"

Dee shook her head, mumbling, "I'm fine." Pushing rubble aside, she tried to get up. Restraining her, Jeffrey commanded her, "Sit for a bit Dee. Let's make sure nothing is broken." Turning his attention to the manager, he said, "I'm a doctor. Let's hold off on calling the ambulance for now." He then set to feeling Dee's arms and legs, checking for broken bones. He noted a small cut on the side of her head and stared into her eyes. Though full of pain, her pupils looked normal and did not indicate any signs of a concussion.

"Can you stand?" he asked. Dee nodded and immediately began moving rubble out of her way. Turning to the manager, he asked, "Is there somewhere private that she can sit?"

The manager nodded, eager to get her out of the eyesight of all his curious patrons. The sooner she was hidden and the mess was cleaned up, the sooner he could begin some damage control. Some patrons were going to be obviously upset by this unpleasant interruption. Pointing to his left, he said, "My office is at the end of the hall." Jeffrey helped Dee stand up and supported her as she gingerly stepped down the hall. The manager opened the door and pulled out a chair for her to sit on. He then closed the door and set off to find someone to clean up the mess.

Sinking into the chair, Dee groaned with pain. She held out her hand and observed how shaky it was. A waiter silently entered with some clean dishtowels and a first aid kit. He curiously observed her, enjoying the way her dress fluttered across her slim legs and her soft, creamy skin. Her golden curls served as a halo around her perfectly symmetrical face. It would take a complete fool to throw away someone like her.

As loud gasps coursed through the restaurant, Luke ran up the stairs, eager to get his hands on the man that pushed the woman off the second floor. Reaching the top of the stairs, he surveyed his surroundings and found the man in the grey suit urging a shocked young woman out of her seat. Luke rushed across the room and seized him. Whirling him around, Luke was startled to find himself staring into such familiar eyes. Sinking his fingers into the tailor made suit, Luke slammed Mark into the wall. Revenge crept into his thoughts as Luke envisioned himself pitching Mark off of the balcony. Taking a deep breath, Luke narrowed his eyes and tightened his grip. Saying nothing, he studied Mark's face. Fear flashed through Mark's eyes momentarily, immediately replaced with attempted composure as Mark tried to regain control of the situation. Putting on his business face, he gently placed his hands on Luke's firm grip, trying to escape Luke's hold.

"Luke..." he started smoothly, trying to talk his way out of this predicament.

"Shut up!" Luke hissed, pushing him back into the wall. Luke continued to study Mark as his sly smirk melted off of his face. Though he showed some fear, a confidence was so evident that it angered Luke. He knew the type: fancy, powerful men who thought that they were so smooth that they could talk or buy their way out of any situation. Luke shifted his gaze over to the young woman who stood nearby.

She no longer watched Mark, giving Luke her full attention. She took in every inch of him, sizing him up and appraising him with her dark eyes and seductive smile. She was obviously impressed by the power that Luke exerted over Mark and was not shy in expressing it. Her hungry eyes silently praised Luke and this frustrated him even more. Luke quickly glared at her and returned his attention to the real problem.

Luke's blood boiled as the reality of the situation sank in. Though Mark's lies about late nights at work upset him, what really set him off was the violence. His thoughts flew back to Dee's body, lying on the crushed table. Was she okay? He had sprung to action and chased down the man that assaulted her without stopping to check on her. Years of service in the army trained him to go for the bad guy first and think of the victims second. He sighed a quick prayer for her, thankful that Jeffrey was there to take care of her. He then averted his attention back to Mark. Mark was silently watching Luke, waiting for an opportunity to talk his way out of it.

"It's not what it looks like..." Mark began. Luke tightened his grip even more. Anger coursed through his whole body, causing him to tremble with a desire to react. Luke wanted to hit him, throw him over the balcony, anything to inflict bodily pain on him. An eye for an eye seemed fair.

Luke knew the type. He knew Mark's polished reputation would allow him to get away with nothing more than a slap on the hand. He knew Mark would talk his way out it, framing the entire incident as an accident and a complete misunderstanding. It would take a vigilante to make Mark pay and Mark would be no match for Luke's combatant training.

Sirens in the distance brought Luke back to reality, forcing him to abandon his violent desires.

"The police are almost here."

Luke watched Mark squirm. Panic swept over Mark's face. He began to search the room for exit points. Irritation clawed harder at Luke as he realized that Mark thought he would escape unpunished. If Luke hadn't responded, Mark would have snuck out the back without being stopped. Mark actually thought he'd get away with it.

There was a commotion behind Luke and he heard footsteps coming up the stairs. By the look of Mark's pale face, he knew the police had arrived. He relished in the terrified look that gripped Mark's face. Perhaps this would be enough to scare him straight, but Luke knew better than to put his hope in such an unrealistic thought. Releasing his hold, Luke backed up, allowing the police to rush forward. One officer led Luke aside and he proceeded to give his statement.

When Luke finished giving his testimony, he headed downstairs, searching for Dee. Though no ambulance had arrived, he still worried about her injuries. Having collected eyewitness accounts from various waiters and patrons, the police were wrapping things up. One officer led Mark out in handcuffs and this gave Luke feelings of both pleasure and anger. The last of the officers left an office in the back, and Luke headed that way. Entering the small room, Luke saw Dee sitting in a chair, holding a blood-soaked towel to her tear-stained face. Jeffrey rose from his chair next to her and motioned for Luke to join him outside of the room. Closing the door behind them, Luke's eyes silently questioned his doctor friend.

"She'll be ok. She needs stitches though."

Luke nodded, thankful that her injuries were minimal.

"Mark?" Jeffrey questioned.

Once again, Luke only responded with a simple nod. Jeffrey's face turned grey upon the realization that his suspicions were true.

"You should return to your party. I'll take Dee to the hospital."

"She can't go home tonight. Not if Mark's there."

Luke agreed with his friend's concern. "We'll figure something out. I'll call Maggie and let her know what's going on, once everything is all said and done."

"Maggie's going to want to go with you."

"I know, but she's getting married tomorrow. Tell her I'll take care of Dee until we can figure everything out."

Jeffrey nodded, clapped his friend's shoulder to signal an unspoken understanding and walked away, eager to join his fiancé. Luke sighed and re-entered the office. Pulling a chair up to Dee, he sat down in front of her. Tilting her head up, he was surprised by how dull her eyes looked. Usually a brilliant copper color, all hints of gold were gone and they were nothing but a diminished brown. Luke's heart ached as he tried to imagine the pain and confusion she would be feeling right now. Though he stared directly into her eyes, she avoided making eye contact with him. Keeping her eyes averted, a fresh set of tears crested and threatened to fall. Shame seemed to creep across her face as she fought to remain calm and in control. She looked like an injured bird. Luke wanted to take her into his arms and assure her that everything would be fine, but he knew that he couldn't guarantee that. He knew that this was just the beginning and that things would get messier. Gently removing the bloody towel, he checked the gash on the side of her head. Blood continued to slowly seep out of the wound. Replacing the towel, he stood up.

"Come on. I'll take you to the hospital."

Struggling out of her seat, Luke noted the pain that swept across her face. Lending her a hand, he helped her stand. Grabbing her purse off of the desk next to her, he led her out of the office. To avoid the gawking customers that remained, he led her down the hall and out the back door. Though she didn't complain, she walked gingerly beside him. Upon reaching his SUV, he helped her thin frame into his passenger seat and buckled her in. Quiet tears escaped from her eyes and streaked down her face. They glistened in the lamplight that hovered above his vehicle. Concern swept Luke as he began to doubt Jeffrey's diagnosis. Perhaps Dee was hurt more than she was letting on. Closing the passenger door, he rushed over to the driver's side, eager to get her to the hospital.

The hospital was such a bleak and depressing place to be. Waiting outside of the examination room while doctors checked over Dee's injuries, Luke offered up numerous prayers on her behalf. Glancing at his phone, he noticed his sister's continual attempt to get a hold of him. Of course she would be concerned. He wondered if Jeffrey told her the whole story, or if he omitted certain parts. As the doctor and nurse exited the room, Luke stood and entered. He would call Maggie later. Upon entering the room, he saw Dee putting a bottle in her purse.

"Painkillers?" He asked. She silently nodded, still not meeting his eyes. He hated seeing her so silent. Dee was always the one who had a clever anecdote or some sort of story to break the silence and get a conversation going. She was always the life of the party and the reason why they were having a good time. Luke groped for words, wishing he knew what would comfort her, but such words failed him and he found the direct course his only option.

"What now?" He asked, trying to sound gentle and optimistic. She just shrugged her shoulders. Realizing how confused and overwhelmed she must be feeling, Luke wished that he had a solution that would fix everything for her. Silently contemplating his thoughts, Luke searched for an idea so that Dee didn't have to think. She had enough on her mind.

"Perhaps you should spend the night with Maggie."

For the first time that night, Dee looked up and met his eyes. "No," she said slowly, "not the night before her wedding. She would worry and not get any sleep."

Luke, of all people, knew how Maggie would spend the night trying to fix all of Dee's problems. He appreciated Dee's thoughtfulness. As concerned as he was for Dee, tomorrow was his sister's big day and he didn't want anything to make it less spectacular than it should be.

"How about my place? I have a guestroom." This solution seemed to make Dee look uncomfortable. "You'd be safe," he continued.

Dee seemed to squirm as she fought for words. He could tell she was carefully trying to say the right thing. Finally, in a low voice, she responded, "That wouldn't look right." How could she explain to him that she didn't want people to think she was running into another man's arms?

"You're right," was Luke's simple response. Dee looked up surprised. She questioned his face to see if he truly understood. "Perhaps," he continued, "you should stay at a hotel. Then you wouldn't have to explain the situation to anyone. I mean, you wouldn't have to tell anyone right away."

Dee appreciated his compassion. Her voice broke as she asked the question that plagued her all night, "Did they arrest him?"

Luke studied her face and realized that she had no clue of what happened after her fall. Sitting on the bed next to her, he simply responded with a "yes."

"So then, couldn't I go home tonight, if he's in jail?"

Luke wished he knew what was going through her head. Why would she want to go back? They weren't married so she wasn't bound to him. Was it fear? Anger? Submission?

Luke was well aware of women who kept returning to their abusive partners. He wondered if Mark had hit her before. How long had the abuse lasted?

"We don't know when he will post bail. He might return home tonight. It wouldn't be safe..."

Dee cut off any further explanation with a simple nod. Still avoiding his eyes, she responded in the same, low voice. "A hotel will be fine."

Luke agreed and stood to help her up, but before they turned to leave, she placed her hand on his arm and stopped. Though she didn't look at him, her voice was thick with emotion. Her voice choked, and she hesitated over her words. "Luke," she began with a long pause, "Would you mind coming with me to my house? In case he's there...I need to get my things."

Luke's heart ached as he sensed her fear. As much as he hated to see her afraid, he hoped such fear would keep her far away from Mark. "Of course," he responded. When she refused to look at him, he tilted up her chin and forced her to meet his eyes. "I'll keep you safe," he promised. His oath caused a fresh set of tears to spring from her eyes and he wrapped his arms around her in a protective hug. He just hoped that this nightmare would soon be over.

The stop at Dee's house was silent and uneventful. He waited in the kitchen while Dee packed her things. Part of him was glad to see that she emerged from her bedroom with two large suitcases. It showed that she was prepared to stay away for a while, if necessary. He grabbed her bags and drove her to a hotel near his house. With Maggie's fiancé being his neighbour and Maggie moving in after the honeymoon, Dee would be close to loved ones and far away from Mark. He helped her check in and carried her bags to her room. As he prepared to leave, he took care of one more thing.

"I'll call Maggie and let her know you're ok. That way you can try to get some rest." Though by looks of it she would do more crying than sleeping. "How about I have Maggie pick you up in the morning? Then you can catch up a bit before you have to get ready for the wedding."

Dee nodded, thankful for his thoughtfulness. As much as she loved and trusted Maggie, she just wanted to be left alone with her thoughts. Walking Luke to the door, she thanked him. Hovering in the doorway, he looked like he had one more thing to say. Dee looked away, unsure if she wanted to hear it. Instead, he replied, "Anytime." Changing to a more serious tone, he continued, "Give me a call if you need anything." He then reassuringly squeezed her hand and walked down the hall.

Chapter 2

She could feel the bed lean as he crawled in next to her. Wrapping his arm around her, she sank into his embrace, letting his warm breath tickle the back of her neck. No longer cold and lonely, she let go of her fears. He was finally home and that was all that mattered. Her breath deepened and her eyelids drooped heavily. She was about to nod off when she felt a tightening against her throat, constricting every breath. She thrashed about, desperate to break free, but his grip was tight. Both hands overpowered her as he slowly suffocated her. Fear pushed the last bit of air out of her empty lungs, taunting her, daring her to inhale some more. She tried to breathe, but it was impossible. Then the worst of her fears came true and her body slackened underneath his lethal hold.

Dee instantly shot up, trembling and wide awake. Fumbling around in the dark, she felt the other side of her bed, checking to see if anyone else was there. Reaching over, she turned on her lamp and found her hotel room empty. She pulled her knees up and hugged them to her body, shuddering like a small child. She had fallen asleep afraid. It only made sense that her fear invaded her dreams. Fear had no boundaries. It didn't care if she was conscious or not. It didn't care anymore than Mark did.

She pulled her blankets tight, hoping that their warmth would urge her body to stop shaking. She should have known better. Going against her instincts, she provoked Mark. She had seen all the signs. Mark had to control everything. That was why work was so stressful. Rather than trusting someone else to do it, he did it himself to ensure that it was done right. She had seen the tension mounting. There was a beast prowling inside, just waiting to break free, and she was the final act that released it. It was only a matter of time before he snapped and now that he had, she feared the repercussions. Though she wasn't the entire source of his stress, she was the final straw, making her the sole target of his anger and frustration.

Turning off the lamp, Dee lay down and curled up into a ball. She begged her body to go to sleep, but fear loomed above her, making it impossible. Mark had lost it and he took it out on her. What made her really afraid was the fact that she did not know how far he was willing to go.

Dee stretched her stiff and sore body as she recalled her tumultuous sleep that night. Every joint ached, begging her to snuggle even deeper into the soft comforter. Her thoughts last night plagued her with a million fears, a few alternatives and no idea of how to handle her situation. Her emotions collided and became a tangled mess, unable to differentiate where one began or ended. Despite her fears of another violent reprisal, what really hurt was the reminder of Mark's betrayal. She wanted to hate him, but loved him. She wanted to hurt him, yet she felt sorry for him. She wondered where they went wrong. When did she lose him? When did he become the man she saw last night? She saw the stress mounting, but felt unable to stop it. Tears stung her eyes and she ached for the man who lovingly urged her to move in with him. He was almost poetic, explaining his desire to spend every possible moment with her. But that man was gone, and she didn't know if she'd ever get him back.

Rolling over, Dee forced such thoughts aside and coaxed herself out of bed. Her muscles were tight and agitated. Each step sent pain shooting up her back. Taking the painkillers out of her purse, she helped herself to the maximum dosage and headed for the shower. Perhaps some hot water would loosen her muscles and help her ignore everything that had happened. As the heat soothed her aching back, she vowed to repress her thoughts for the day. The steam relaxed her a little bit and she reminded herself that today was Maggie's big day and that was all that mattered. She would deal with things later. Forcing her mind to focus on Maggie, she made a mental list of all the things they had to do. First breakfast, then they would head to the beauty salon. Then they would pick up the flowers and head to the church where there was a room set aside for them to get ready in. Dee had to remind herself to give the boutonnieres to Luke. As well, she couldn't forget her toast to the bride. Rehearsing it word for word, Dee lingered in the shower, allowing the hot steam to soothe her. She would be okay. Today was Maggie's day and her job was to ensure that it was the best day of Maggie's life. Besides, her focus on Maggie was a welcome escape from the thoughts that loomed in her mind all night.

Towelling off, Dee wiped the steam off of the mirror. Inspecting her body, she was glad to see that none of the serious bruises would show. Though her back was tender, her dress would cover the dark shadows that revealed last night's trauma. Since her face was pale and her eyes seemed empty, Dee practiced smiling. Her smiles looked fake and apathetic but she knew that once she saw Maggie in her wedding dress, a genuine smile would take over her face.

35

Dee finished getting ready right when she heard a gentle knock on her door. Peeking through her eye hole, Dee's eyes lit up as she observed the glowing bride on the other side of the door. When she opened her door and saw Maggie's joy, Dee knew that she would have no problem pushing her thoughts aside. Squeals erupted as the two friends embraced each other. For a moment, Dee's mind was clear of all of its intruding thoughts. Letting go of her friend, she could not believe the energy that Maggie was radiating. It was contagious and comforted Dee.

"Are you hungry?" Dee asked the bride-to-be.

"I'm too excited to even think about food!"

"Well, as your Maid of Honour, it is my job to make sure that you eat. The last thing we need is the bride fainting at the altar."

"More like swooning at the sight of her handsome groom," Maggie giggled. Dee rolled her eyes, locked the door behind them and led Maggie down the hall towards the elevator. Dee could not believe how glowing and giddy her friend has become. She tried to think back to when Mark first professed his love to her. She wondered if she acted the same way.

Stopping for breakfast in the hotel restaurant, Maggie turned serious once the waitress took their orders.

"Do you want to talk about it?"

"I was hoping you'd be too excited to remember."

"I wouldn't be your best friend if I forgot."

Dee sighed. She knew Maggie would want to talk about it. Maggie wouldn't have it any other way. She was too caring, and would set her wedding thrills aside to help a loved one through a rough spot. She was way too giving.

"Truthfully, Maggie, you are my best friend so we will talk about it, but not today. Today is your wedding day and the only thing we are going to talk about is you."

"Luke said you would say something like that."

"I mean it Maggie. We'll talk about it later."

"Ok," Maggie surrendered, "and I respect that. Just one more thing." She paused and slid a key across the table.

"What's that?"

"A key to our house. We want you to house-sit while we are gone."

"Maggie, I can't..."

"Sure you can. We renovated the basement into a suite for when we have company and you can live down there until we get back."

"But you're going to be gone for two weeks."

"You're going to stay in a hotel for two weeks?"

"I don't know. I haven't thought that far ahead."

"Well, I have Dee, and it's going to take more than two weeks of grovelling for Mark to patch things up with you. It's going to take anger management classes and counselling before I let you see him again, let alone move back in with him."

"Are you sure I won't be an inconvenience?"

"The only thing that will inconvenience me is worrying about you while I am on my honeymoon. I need to know that you will be safe while I am gone. So, promise to stay at our place for at least two weeks, and when we get back we will help you come up with a plan to deal with this situation in the safest and healthiest way possible."

"I appreciate it, Maggie."

"You would do the same thing for me." She smiled her radiant smile and continued, "Well, now that we have that taken care of, on to more important matters."

"Such as," Dee teased her.

"Such as me!" She exclaimed, right as the food arrived.

As Luke approached the door of the grade five Sunday School classroom, he couldn't help but remember all the mornings he had to sit in the hall as punishment for disturbing the class. Who would have thought that such a rambunctious ten-year-old would one day grow up into a determined, responsible soldier? He smiled as he remembered Mrs. Kale getting so frustrated. While most kids preferred to angelically answer "Jesus" to every single question, he was always more interested in ruffling some feathers. He chuckled as he remembered Mrs. Kale's irritation. They were supposed to draw out their favorite Bible story. Most kids drew angels or donkeys, but he drew a picture of David cutting off Goliath's head.

Gently knocking at the door, he heard a scuttle of feet rush about.

"Who is it?" Maggie called out.

"The best looking guy in this church."

"You don't sound like Jeffrey," Maggie teased as she cautiously opened the door. She allowed Luke to squeeze in and then quickly shut the door before anyone else could get a glimpse inside of the room. Luke's face shone as he appraised his little sister in her wedding gown. She had shown it to him before, but with her hair done up and her face glowing, she looked more angelic than ever. He gave her a big hug and whispered, "I am so happy for you. You look stunning."

Releasing her, he scanned the room. Some things never changed, such as the flannel-gram propped up in the back corner. His eyes glazed over the small table with its miniature chairs and settled on Dee. With her back to him, she sat on one of the tiny chairs, busy touching up some makeup with a handheld mirror. The lilac purple dress complimented her creamy skin. Her hair, which she usually wore down in a tangle of curls, was pulled up and arranged in a perfect halo of ringlets. With her hair put up, her bare shoulders shone and much of her back was exposed. She showed no hint of bruises from last night's fall. Snapping her compact shut, she rose from the tiny chair with poise and elegance. She slowly turned to face him. Luke studied her face. Her smile was genuine but her eyes looked sad. Some things took time to heal. Luke felt a sudden urge to hold her in his arms, as he did last night in the hospital and—and what? Luke shook his head before that thought could even enter his mind.

Dee raised an eyebrow and smiled. She couldn't help but notice how good Luke looked in a suit. His large, trim figure filled it out perfectly, making him look strong and proud. Being the soldier that he was, he seemed comfortable in a suit, as if he were born to wear one.

"I came to get the boutonnieres," Luke said, stepping forward.

"Oh, yes! I completely forgot!" Dee rushed to another miniature table and opened a box. Right then Luke's mother burst into the room, squealed, and embraced her daughter. Excited chatter filled the room as his mom started to fiddle with Maggie's veil. Seeing that they were distracted, he seized the opportunity and moved closer to Dee.

Unaffected by his close proximity, she began giving instructions. "These two are for you and Jeffrey. The rest are for the parents and grandparents. This small one is for the ring-bearer and this basket is for the flower girl."

Luke picked up the delicate iris surrounded by baby's breath. He eyed it up, not to sure what to do with it.

"Here," Dee offered, "let me help you with that." Stepping closer, she removed the long pin and began attaching it to his lapel. Luke could smell something soft and sweet. He wondered if it was the flowers or Dee. As his sister gazed in the mirror and his mom continued to adjust the veil, Luke asked Dee the question he'd been longing to ask her all day. Numerous times he started to call her but changed his mind before he actually dialled.

"How are you feeling?" He asked with all the sincerity that he could muster.

Nonchalantly she replied, "I'm fine." She finished with his boutonniere and began straightening his tie.

"I'm serious Dee. How are you really doing?"

She stopped fiddling with his tie and looked over at Maggie and his mother. They were still actively engaged with the veil. Turning back, she stared him straight in the eyes. "I'm a little sore, but it's nothing that I can't handle." She squared her chin in an attempt to prove how strong she was.

Luke didn't completely buy her tough act. He continued to pry by asking, "You promise?"

Her eyes moistened and she lowered her guard a little bit. Once again, she resembled a wounded bird, tiny and scared. She hesitated before she asked the question that plagued her all night. "Do you think he'll come?"

Luke caught on to the fear that Dee felt. He tried his best to reassure her. "I don't think so, but if he does, I'll take care of it."

Dee nodded in understanding, and turned her gaze to Maggie. In a low voice, she whispered, "I just don't want a scene."

Luke touched her arm to regain her attention. "Nobody's ruining my little sister's wedding." It wasn't a promise. It was a statement of fact.

Dee smiled at his protectiveness. For a moment she wished she had an older brother who would have protected her. Perhaps he would have saved her from getting involved with a man like Mark.

Gathering up the box of flowers, Luke gave her a wink and said, "I'll see you at the altar." He then sauntered away, gave his sister and mom both a peck on their cheeks and disappeared out of the door.

Luke paused outside of the classroom door and took a deep breath. He had managed to control his feelings since he got back from Afghanistan. For the past two years, he had been able to remain in control, but seeing Dee in that gown with her hair all fixed up only reminded him that she had evolved from a skinny freshman that he met at college into a full-grown beauty. She was no longer Maggie's awkward college roommate and that affected him in ways that it shouldn't. Giving his head a shake, he pushed such thoughts out of his mind and strolled down the hall to furnish certain family members with flowers.

Having rid himself of all flowers but one, he headed to the pastor's office where Jeffrey eagerly waited. He chuckled when he saw how excited Jeffrey was. Unlike the movies, there was not a single hint of fear or anxiety in this couple. Their match was made in heaven and they knew it. The second Luke entered the room, Jeffrey jumped out of his chair and approached him.

"How'd she look?"

Luke shrugged his shoulders and responded with a subdued, "Alright."

Jeffrey playfully punched Luke in the arm and said, "Come on man!"

"You'll see for yourself soon enough." Luke liked toying with his soon to be brother-in-law and laughed when Jeffrey checked his watch for the millionth time.

Luke stood in silent awe as he watched the bride and groom take their first dance. Their endless joy promised a hopeful future. Their relationship was a solid one, unlike Dee's relationship with Mark. They were doing things the right way—God's way. His heart ached as he remembered the pain his friend had endured the last twenty-four hours. For years he had been praying for her, hoping that one day she would surrender to the Lord. He glanced at her as she stood next to him. Tears moistened her eyes as she watched the lovely couple. He wondered what she was thinking. Was her first dance with Mark as hopeful and romantic? Luke doubted it.

He was proud of how strong and determined Dee was. She really pulled through for Maggie, ensuring that this was the best day of her life. Other than this morning, Dee never mentioned Mark. As family members and friends asked about his absence, Dee gracefully dodged their questions. She held her head high and walked with pride. If Luke hadn't known better, he wouldn't have suspected that anything was wrong. Everything seemed normal. During pictures Dee and Maggie hugged and giggled endlessly, like they did when they met in their first year of college. As always, Dee filled the day with silly anecdotes and threw in numerous jokes about marriage. She greeted the family members and even showed Grandma to the washroom. She remembered what Maggie forgot and was constantly fixing Maggie's hair, pinning up a defiant strand that kept slipping loose. All in all, Dee was tough and Luke admired her strength.

When the song switched, Luke's dad walked onto the dance floor and intercepted his daughter. Jeffrey graciously handed her over and went to retrieve his mother from the edge of the crowd. Luke grabbed Dee's hand and led her onto the dance floor for the attendants turn to dance. Placing his hand on her hip, he noted how slender she was. It had been six years since her freshman debut at college but she still managed to maintain her figure. He smiled at Dee and enjoyed to see how it comforted her. He wanted to keep the atmosphere light and friendly, but he couldn't help the low, husky tone that his voice held.

"Remember the first time we danced?"

Dee blushed at the thought of her first college dance. She was a bundle of nerves, both excited and anxious. Upon Maggie's advice, she had rejected every boy that asked her to be his date. Maggie assured her that by doing so, she would be free to dance with anyone. Unfortunately, such advice backfired, for those boys found someone else to go with them and they were occupied by their dates the entire night. Luke, a senior, felt sorry for Maggie's roommate, who had been abandoned, and danced with her most of the night. In fact, he danced with Dee so much that his date got upset and left early.

When Dee nodded, he chuckled and added on, "You're not as awkward."

Dee looked down and let out a low laugh. "You know what the sad thing is," she responded, "I thought I knew everything." As they laughed together, she shook her head, "The things I now know."

Luke smiled at the thought of how much she had grown up since then. He too had grown out of his college days. Though fun and full of pranks, he knew that one day he would make a difference, and in order to do so, he'd have to buckle down. The day he graduated, he enlisted with the army. The strict rules of the army forced him to become a responsible young man, though he still managed to have some fun.

Dee smiled as she watched Luke get lost in his thoughts. She wondered if he was thinking of the good old days at college. She was shocked when she found out that Luke had enlisted in the army. She always thought he would go on to law school. Though the more she thought about it, the more it made sense. Luke was a hands-on kind of guy. He was also a man of action. He was always putting himself in the middle, protecting Maggie from stupid dates. Law was not enough for Luke. He needed to react. As her hand rested on his broad shoulder, she realized how the army had transformed him. Though he was still Maggie's fun-loving brother, he was protective and rational. He was also strong and proud, always looking out for the under-dog. Dee thought back to last night and admired how he had pulled through for her. He took care of her so that she didn't have to make any decisions. She wondered what he would have done if he saw how Mark had grabbed her arm and tried to control her. Would Luke have punched him? Fought to protect and free her? Dee began to realize how strong Luke really was. She always dismissed him as Maggie's brother and never really took account of him. If he had been there to protect her, Mark wouldn't have stood a chance.

With that thought of Mark, part of her wished that he was there. He would have been helpless, forced to stand aside and watch her dance with another man. Dee wished that Mark could see them. She would lean in and dance closer to Luke. Then Mark could feel the resentment and betrayal she felt last night. Looking up, she saw that Luke was watching her, trying to read her thoughts. She blushed, ashamed at the thought of using him as a pawn to incite Mark's jealousy. She gave herself a check and reminded herself that she was lucky that Mark didn't show up. The last thing she needed was another confrontation with him, though she knew that one day she would have to face him. She just hoped that she could put off that day for as long as possible.

Chapter 3

Luke helped Dee load the last box of decorations into her car and shut the trunk door. A maintenance worker locked up the dark and abandoned reception hall as Luke strolled around the car to the driver's side.

"I'll meet you at Maggie's?"

Dee just silently nodded and climbed into her car. She waited for Luke, who was taking Maggie's car home, to pull out before she followed him to the ritzy neighbourhood. Dee watched the large, dark houses pass by. She knew Jeffrey could afford this neighbourhood because he was a well-paid surgeon, but she couldn't understand how Luke could afford to be his backyard neighbour. This neighbourhood was made up of doctors and lawyers, not retired soldiers who now worked a desk job. Luke was always coy about his new job, dodging most questions. He'd just simply reply that he was tying up loose ends from the war. None of it made sense to

Dee, but if she was allowed to keep her secrets, then so was Luke. She dismissed the topic, acknowledging the fact that she trusted him and knew that his reasons for such secrecy must be valid.

Dee slowed down as Luke signalled and turned onto the quiet crescent that housed the newlyweds. Luke turned into the yard and opened the garage door, but parked on the driveway. He got out of Maggie's car and walked over to Dee when she pulled up. Lowering her window, he handed her the remote control for the garage door.

"I'll let you park in the garage. That way if Mark drives by he won't see your car parked outside." Dee once again nodded, thankful for Luke's thoughtfulness. She pulled into the garage and parked next to Jeffrey's BMW. The couple had taken the limo to the airport and left Luke and Dee in charge of cleaning up and returning Maggie's car home. Luke unloaded Dee's two suitcases, which were still in Maggie's car, and carried them into the garage. As the garage door lowered, he eyed the boxes of decorations in Dee's car.

"I'll take care of them tomorrow," Dee replied as she headed to the door that led to the house. When they entered the house, Luke put down the suitcases and disarmed the alarm. Dee reached for one of the suitcases, but Luke gently blocked her hand.

"I've got them," he replied. Chivalrously, he lifted both suitcases with ease and carried them downstairs to the basement suite that would be Dee's new home for the next two weeks. As Luke took the suitcases into the guestroom, Dee flicked on a lamp and flopped on the couch. As wonderful as today was, she was exhausted. When Luke came out of the room, he flipped on a few lights, well aware of the suite's layout and positioning of light switches. Though Dee had seen the suite through its numerous renovation phases, she was not as familiar to the layout as Luke was. Settling on the opposite end of the couch, Luke asked the obvious. "Long day, hey?"

Dee just silently nodded. She didn't want to seem rude, but she was exhausted. Luke hopped up, obviously not tired from the day's events. "How about some tea? Some camomile will help you sleep."

It was if Luke had read her thoughts. Dee didn't sleep very well the night before and wondered if any sleep would come tonight. Luke disappeared upstairs and soon returned with a canister full of tea bags and a kettle. Rooting around in the kitchenette, he mustered up some coffee mugs. Dee curiously watched him as he puttered around the kitchen. For a big, brave soldier, he sure didn't mind attending to domestic duties. She took advantage of his hospitality and curled up into the corner of the couch.

"I was wondering if you would like to go to church with me tomorrow?" Luke asked from the kitchen as he poured the boiling hot water into the two cups. Dee shifted uncomfortably on the couch.

"I think I'll pass," she replied politely.

"Pretty tuckered out, huh?" Luke came around the counter and handed her a steaming mug. He was used to her rejecting his invitations to church.

Dee nodded, wanting to drop the topic, but she could feel his eyes on her. "I think it'd be best if I just laid low for a little while."

Luke put his mug on the coffee table to cool and turned to face her. "Any idea of what you're going to do?"

Dee shrugged and starred into her mug of tea. The steamy aroma calmed her. "I dunno. Crawl into a hole and hide till this all blows over."

Luke tried to read her face. What was she feeling? Fear? Confusion? He thought he sensed a bit of shame, but couldn't find a reason for her to feel ashamed. He wasn't sure if she would talk, but decided to try and push the subject.

"Are you going to press charges?"

Once again Dee shrugged, but didn't look up. "I don't think that's necessary," she softly responded. It sounded more like a question with all the uncertainty in her voice.

Luke pushed further. "You don't think throwing your girlfriend off of a balcony warrants legal discipline?"

She took his bait. Gazing up from her entrancing mug of tea, she stared at him. Her eyes seemed defiant, a look he had never seen in her eyes before. "He didn't throw me off the balcony. He pushed me. It's not like he intended for the railing to break."

Luke hated seeing her defend Mark like that. "He shouldn't have pushed you in the first place."

"I pushed him first."

Luke's eyebrows shot up in surprise, but half of him wanted to congratulate her for standing up for herself.

Dee continued, "Mark's a control freak. At first, I liked it. I didn't have to make any tough decisions and he loved me more when I was compliant, so I let him walk all over me. I guess when I finally stood up for myself, he didn't know what to do. It's never happened before so he just lost it."

Luke began to see where the shame was coming from. Shame of not standing up for herself early on—for letting things spiral out of control. Luke asked the question that had been bugging him all along.

"Has he ever hit you before?"

Dee shook her head and he watched her, trying to tell if she was lying to protect him.

"It was right of you to stand up for yourself, especially when he was cheating on you."

Flames leapt across Dee's cheeks as a furious blush took over. Shame crept across her face and Luke understood the root of that emotion. She was feeling ashamed because of his betrayal. A single tear spilled over and rolled down her cheek. Her eyes remained downcast, too embarrassed to look at him.

"You saw her?" It was barely a whisper that escaped from her lungs.

Luke realized how little Dee knew. He tried to understand how confused she would have been after her fall. He had no idea that no one explained things to her.

"I saw him push you, so I went after him. When I realized it was Mark, I almost threw him off of the balcony."

A faint smile stole to her lips as Dee imagined Luke as her knight in shining armour. Dee wondered if Luke would be able to protect her now that he no longer had to protect Maggie from unwanted suitors.

"Does Maggie know about," Dee paused, "the other woman."

Luke thought about it for a second. He didn't tell Maggie about anything except for the fall. "I don't think so," he honestly responded.

"It doesn't make any sense."

"What doesn't?" Luke pushed, hoping she would keep talking and tell him everything.

"She's beautiful."

Luke remembered how the young woman had stared at him with her hungry eyes. She was appealing, but not in a healthy way.

"So are you." He tried to encourage her. Dee faintly smiled at his courteous compliment.

"But if she's what he wanted, why would he get mad at me?" Dee put down her mug and rubbed her temples. Nothing made sense. She was so confused and her heart ached way too much.

"Some guys want it all. But you can't have your cake and eat it too." That wasn't what she wanted to hear. She wanted Luke to assure her that she was Mark's true love and that he was just distracted. She wanted Luke to assure her that it was a mistake that Mark would repent of and come crawling back to her, begging for forgiveness. Just as she feared, Luke didn't say that. His blunt honesty hurt.

"What should I do?" She was afraid of what he might say, yet needed to hear it.

Luke leaned back and carefully considered his words. "That all depends." Dee looked at him with more hope than he liked to see. "If he is truly repentant, you could consider give him a second chance. But," he added sternly, "you protect yourself until you are sure that he is truly sorry. And even if he is, that doesn't mean you have to give him a second chance."

"And if he isn't?"

"You forget about him."

"I don't know if I can do that."

"I didn't say it was going to be easy."

Once again, Dee's eyes filled with tears that threatened to spill over. She struggled to regain control. Luke retrieved a box of tissues from the coffee table and handed it to her. He hated seeing her so distraught, especially over a jerk like Mark. He seriously doubted that Mark would come around. He was too selfish to care what he did to Dee. In an attempt to comfort Dee, he continued, "I never told you about the girl I liked before I went overseas."

Dee's eyes curiously peered at him from behind a mass of soggy tissues. "What girl?"

"Well, there was this girl I liked, but she barely knew I existed."

"Did I know her?"

"Probably not. Anyways, she was the prettiest thing I had ever seen. The problem was that every guy who saw her fell for her and I'm pretty sure she had a boyfriend."

"Did you tell her how you felt?"

Luke shook his head.

"Why not?"

Luke enjoyed seeing the hopeless romantic rise up in Dee. "Well," he began, "for starters, I thought she had a boyfriend."

"So!" Dee interrupted.

Luke chuckled. "Secondly, I fell for her right when I decided to enlist." Dee fell silent and he wondered if it bothered her talking about the army. Nevertheless, he continued, "what was I supposed to say, 'I love you, but I'm going to war, so if you could dump your boyfriend and promise not to date anyone until I returned, I'd be much obliged'? That wouldn't be fair for her. I didn't know how long I would be gone. I was gone for three years. I couldn't ask her to wait for me that long. Especially when she barely knew I existed."

"So, what happened?"

"I went to war and dreamed of her every night. While guys wrote letters to their girlfriends or wives, I dreamed of love letters I would write her. I barely knew her. The lonelier I became the more I thought about her. She soon evolved into this perfect memory. She was a great girl, but it would be impossible for anyone to be as perfect as I envisioned her. I dreamed of coming home one day and professing how I loved her the entire time I was gone. Thing was I didn't know her well enough to truly love her. I was just lonely and fantasizing."

"Did you tell her when you got home?"

Luke sadly shook his head. "I was gone three years. By then she had probably married. I couldn't blame her. She was the prettiest girl in town. It was only a matter of time before some lucky guy snatched her up."

Dee fell silent, disappointed with the ending.

"Anyways," Luke continued, "That's not the point. Eventually I got over her, but whenever I get lonely, I start to dream of her because she is the only girl I ever loved. It's hard to forget someone you loved. If you truly loved them, they will always creep up in your thoughts, but if they have forgotten you, you need to let go, no matter how hard it hurts.

"That's not much of a happy ending."

"Well, the story isn't over yet. One day I will fall in love and get married."

"But until then?"

"I keep on trucking."

"You think I will get a happy ending?"

"Of course. It just might not be the one you were hoping for."

Dee nodded, appreciative for his wisdom. Luke stood up and stretched. "I should get going. Is there anything you need before I leave?"

Dee shook her head and began to walk Luke to the door. "Thanks for everything Luke, I really appreciate it."

Luke genuinely smiled at her. "You're a tough girl. As long as you don't let Mark take advantage of you, you'll be fine." He turned to open the door, but paused with his hand resting on the door knob. "You sure you don't want to come to church?" Dee nodded but refused to look at him, ashamed of her cowardice.

"Ok. That's fine. I'll see you tomorrow."

"Tomorrow?" Dee asked, looking confused.

"The only way I could keep Maggie from postponing her honeymoon was by promising to look in on you everyday."

"Luke, that's not really necessary."

"I know, but Maggie will kill me if I break my promise. Besides, I'm a man of my word."

Dee smiled at the control Maggie asserted over her big, tough brother. She found it a little ironic that the soldier who faced a war head on couldn't stand up to his little sister.

"Ok, I'll see you tomorrow."

Luke smiled. "Call if you need anything," he called over his shoulder as he walked out the door.

Luke went out the back door, but at last minute changed his mind and headed for the street. Standing next to the tall hedge, Luke scanned the street to see if any unfamiliar cars were parked near Jeffrey's house. The last thing he needed was Mark spying on the house, waiting for a moment when Dee would be alone and surprised. Not a single car dotted the quiet crescent. Luke took one more look until he was satisfied. Turning around, he headed to the backyard. The yard was clean and well manicured. As he opened the gate, he heard a loud creak. No perpetrator would sneak through this gate silently. Luke smiled as he remembered Jeffrey's insistence that they put up a gate. With no back allies in the neighbourhood, the fence was the only thing that divided their properties. As Luke's friendship grew with his new neighbour, it made sense to put a gate between their yards. It saved both Luke and Jeffrey a long walk around the block, though Luke usually just climbed over the large fence. Jeffrey, on the other hand, was not so agile. How little did Luke know that that gate was really just Jeffrey's excuse to have quicker access to Maggie. As soon as Jeffrey spotted the pretty brunette in Luke's backyard, he'd dash over to make some friendly small talk. The gate saved him quite a bit of time. Before Luke knew it, Jeffrey spent more time in Luke's back yard than his own. As well, all of a sudden Maggie was visiting Luke much more frequently. Luke chuckled at their silly excuses to "come visit" him, but all in all he was glad that they found each other.

As Luke made his way across his dark yard, he noted that he needed a back light or some garden lights. He groped his way through the darkness, anticipating a collision with his patio furniture. One day he would build an actual patio, but until then the furniture lay sprawled out on his lawn.

Feeling the edge of his large bench, Luke changed his direction to avoid the rest of his furniture. Groping about, he tried to find his fence that would guide him to his front yard, where street lamps waited to greet him. Stumbling over his garden hose, he noticed a funny smell. Pausing, he inhaled deeply, recognizing the stale, yeasty scent of alcohol. He froze, scanning his backyard that was blanketed in the midnight darkness. He willed his eyes to adjust to the darkness, but they refused. He took a cautious step forward and paused. Did he hear something? His ears played games with him as silence stole through his neighbourhood. He could hear the distant traffic and heard a car approaching his street. A few houses down, a neighbour let out her dog and gently coaxed him to hurry. Though her backdoor light illuminated her porch, it was too far away to cast any light into his backyard. He listened for the approaching car, waiting, hoping that its headlights would spill into his backyard and reveal anyone that shouldn't be there. The car then stopped, a few houses short of his own, and the engine died.

Luke silently exhaled, contemplating an alternative plan. He could use his cell phone. Though small, it would cut through the darkness and illuminate the majority of his yard. The only problem was that it would give away his positioning. Luke remained frozen, convinced that the smell had grown stronger. The stench tickled his nostrils but Luke couldn't tell how close he was to whoever was intruding in his backyard. He heard a rustle, but before he could react, a strong blow hit him across his back and knocked him to the ground. The sound of wood splintering echoed in his head as he felt the effects of the board being broken over his back. Slightly winded, Luke struggled to his knees, only to be kicked. He fell flat on his face. Survival instincts kicked in and he tried to gage his surroundings. Both hits had been from behind. As soon as Luke heard another rustle, he whirled around and lunged into the darkness. He caught his assailant by surprise and tackled him to the ground. Grappling about in the dark, he managed to grab hold of a shoulder and pinned the body to the ground. Acrid scents of alcohol wafted up his nose as he held his attacker down. Wrenching one arm back, he strengthened his hold on the odorous assailant and dragged him to his front yard.

Once in the light, Luke was not surprised to see that his assailant was Mark. Pushing him to the ground, Luke pinned him with one arm and knelt on him with one knee. With his free arm, he retrieved his cell phone out of his pocket and called the police. Profanities fell out Mark's mouth in a slurred motion, but he was too drunk to successfully fight back. Trapped against the ground, obscenities continued to flow, provoking Luke to wrench Mark's arm up harder than was necessary. Mark's shouts of pain pleased Luke, but did little to satisfy him. He knew that Mark had waited for him, in hopes of finding Dee. Luke breathed a prayer, thanking God that Mark was too drunk to even consider checking Jeffrey's home. He also lifted up a prayer of protection to shield Dee from this brute. Despite his prayers, Luke still worried. He knew that Mark wouldn't stop at anything and was afraid that when Mark found Dee, he wouldn't be there to protect her.

Dee tossed and turned in her bed, unable to sleep. Anxious thoughts continued to pester her, leaving her body exhausted and her mind spinning. No matter how much she thought about it, she had no idea what to do. This bothered her. At work, solutions were simple. One would enter the numbers into the appropriate equation and not only was an answer found, but it was guaranteed to be correct. But with this situation, nothing was guaranteed to work. There were too many loop-holes and what-ifs. She had no control over the situation and this not only aggravated her, it scared her.

Curling up on her side, she tried to push such thoughts from her mind. She tried to relax by imagining the ocean, with its gentle waves carrying her further and further from the problem. She felt her pulse slow down and her breathing became deep. Her tense muscles relaxed and the soft bed coaxed her mind to sleep. Gradually sirens wafted in, mounting with an intensity that jerked her away from her sweet dreams. Her body tensed as she gripped the comforter in fear. The sirens grew louder and louder as they approached the neighbourhood. Too afraid to move, Dee cowered in her bed. The sirens hovered, refusing to pass by. Glancing at the blinds, Dee searched for flashing lights to escape through the cracks, but nothing but darkness filled the voids.

Mustering up all of her courage, she crept from her bed into the living room. Flashing lights escaped through the curtains on the back wall. Peering through the gap, she saw that the lights were coming from Luke's house. Panic seized Dee as her pulse began to race. The air felt thin as she gasped for air. She sunk to the floor and a dizziness took over. She tried to think, but her mind was congested. Taking deep breaths, she forced her heart to slow down. She needed to do something, but what? It was Mark. It had to be. But what was he doing at Luke's house? A new wave of fear gripped her as she feared for Luke's life. Had Mark gotten jealous and gone after Luke? Immediately Dee felt guilty for her previous thoughts of using Luke to incite Mark's jealousy. She had to go and check on Luke, but her legs refused to lift her to her feet. She waited and listened for an ambulance to come. The police sirens had stopped. So far, a second siren had not joined in. Perhaps an ambulance was not necessary. Luke was stronger than Mark. Perhaps he had been able to protect himself. Dee wanted to believe this, but her fears etched images of Luke's death onto her mind. An ambulance wouldn't use a siren unless it had to rush to save someone that was desperately hanging onto his last breath. If he was dead, they would arrive silently.

Dee had to know but her fears prevented her from climbing the stairs that led to the door. Like a coward, she crept towards her purse and dug out her cell phone. Dialling Luke, she was startled when he picked up on the second ring.

"Luke!" She shouted, surprised to hear his voice. "Luke, what's happening? Are you okay?"

His voice was hushed, but comforting. "I'm fine Dee. I'm sorry if we scared you."

"What happened?"

Luke paused, unsure if he should tell her the truth. He decided it'd be best left until tomorrow. "Nothing, just a drunk trying to get into my home," he lied.

Dee didn't believe him. She knew Luke wouldn't call the police over a drunk. He would only bother the police if it were a real concern.

Luke also knew he didn't sound very convincing. He tried again. "You know how it is with these cookie-cutter houses. They all look the same. He just got confused."

Dee refused to buy it, but she knew that if Luke didn't want to tell her he wasn't going to. "Are you sure you're okay?"

"I'm fine Dee. You've had a tough weekend. Try to get some sleep."

Unconvinced, Dee hung up. Despite her efforts, she knew that sleep wouldn't come. Every bit of intuition told her that it was Mark and she feared, not only for her safety but Luke's too.

After the police left, Luke went inside to get a flashlight. When he turned on his kitchen light, it lit up his backyard, allowing Luke to see the damage that was done. Numerous planks had been torn off of his fence posts, others had been kicked in. Turning on his flashlight, he headed out his patio door and searched the ground for the board that had been broken over his back. His back ached as he bent over to pick up the remains of the board. Mark had dealt him a swift and strong blow. The wood had completely snapped in half.

Canvassing the rest of his fence, he realized his neighbours wouldn't be too pleased. Hopefully they would notice the fence before they let their dog out. The last thing he needed was their Pomeranian pooping all over his back yard.

Realizing that there was nothing he could do right away, Luke decided to call it a night. Glancing over at Jeffrey's house, he noticed that lights were still on in the basement. His heart ached for Dee as he imagined her curled up on the couch, too afraid to sleep. Part of him wanted to go over and reassure her that everything was fine. The other part warned him to give her space and not get too close. Besides, a knock on her door would only frighten her even more. But on the other hand, he had a key to the house. He could just let himself in, but immediately he knew that would terrify her, causing her to think there was a prowler in her house. Convincing himself that she'd be best left alone, he headed inside.

Sinking onto his couch, Luke turned on the TV but paid no attention to the baseball highlights. His mind remained on Dee and her boyfriend who accosted him. Though Dee denied previous acts of violence, Luke remained unconvinced. This had been the second strike, two nights in a row. The last two attacks had been violent, but Luke knew that Mark was capable of more. Mark was a bomb waiting to explode and Luke feared the damage that would occur once Mark detonated. He wanted to protect Dee, but would she let him? He knew that as long as she hid the truth from him, she would never be safe. In a sense, he was thankful that Mark attacked him. Dee may be too afraid to press charges, but Luke wasn't. There was no way he was letting Mark get away with it.

Chapter 4

Sleep didn't come until the sun began to force its way between the blinds. With the sun's rays resting on her comforter, warming her, relaxation began to take over and Dee's fearful body finally succumbed to sleep. Though it only lasted for a few hours, it helped numb the pain of last night's nightmare. When Dee woke up, the sun's brilliance wrapped reassuring arms around her and she felt safe. Mark wouldn't dare try anything in broad daylight. Soon Luke would be home from church and his watchful eye would protect her.

Hopping into the shower, she allowed the steam to rise and calm her from the inside out. The stream of hot water relaxed her muscles and she revelled in the heat until her limbs began to feel like jelly. When she felt like her body would no longer support her, she turned off the water and grabbed a towel. A faint ring tickled at her ears. Rubbing the water out of her ears, she realized that her phone was ringing and raced out of the bathroom. Grabbing her phone out of her purse, Dee checked the caller ID. She didn't recognize the number. Her heart began to pound. Should she answer it? Mustering up her strength, she sank to floor and answered the call with a wobbly, "Hello?" She hated how her voice trembled, giving away her fear. She was surprised to hear the professional greeting on the other side of the phone.

"Hello, is this Dee Cairns?" Upon her confirmation the authoritative voice continued. "This is Officer McCormick. I'm just notifying you of a call we received last night regarding your common-law partner, Mark Kensington."

Luke placed his chop saw next to his newly purchased fence boards and headed back into his garage for his hammer, tape measure and a box of nails. When he came back, he found Dee gawking at his broken fence. As Luke approached, he noticed her curls were still damp and they glistened in the sunlight. Though her eyes were dark circles, her face was fresh and free of makeup.

"He sure did a number to your yard," Dee stated as she gazed at the torn up flower beds. Luke just nodded and began measuring a board. Pulling a pencil out of his pocket, he marked his cut line and began lining the board up with his chop saw. The electric saw made a loud whirling noise as it effortlessly sliced through the wood. Throwing the board aside, Luke reached for the next one and began measuring it.

One by one he cut the boards and neatly stacked them to the side.

Wanting to feel useful, Dee grabbed his hammer and began tearing the broken boards off of the railing. Placing her one foot on the fence, she braced herself and yanked. The boards were tightly nailed on, but she managed to pull them off.

Luke stopped sawing and called over, "You don't have to do that."

Dee turned to face him, trying to read his expression. "It's the least I can do," she said, baiting him. She waited to see if he would acknowledge the fact that Mark had caused all of this damage. Luke played his best poker face, looked down and began measuring another board. Dee decided to match his stubbornness and began working on another plank. This one came off a bit easier and she tossed it into the middle of the yard with the other broken one. Luke, unable to concentrate on his measurements, got up and walked over.

"You really shouldn't do that," he tried again. "You'll hurt your back."

"My back's not any worse than yours," Dee retorted, setting her focus on the bottom broken portion of a plank. She crouched and wedged the hammer behind the nails, prying them loose. When she leaned forward, Luke noticed a dark purple bruise on her back peek out from the bottom of her shirt.

Luke ran his hand through his short hair. He had wanted to tell her, but didn't know how to bring it up. He knew she needed to know, but also didn't want to scare her any more.

"You know?" He asked.

Dee nodded and pried some more at the stubborn board. "Officer McCormick called this morning and told me."

Luke crouched next to her and took the hammer from her hand. Once he had her attention he spoke plainly and honestly. "I was going to tell you today. I just felt that you had enough on your mind last night."

Dee nodded, understanding his attempt to be thoughtful. "You're just lucky your fence isn't made of PVC boards. That would have really done a number to your back."

Luke chuckled at her practicality. He enjoyed to see that his laugh was contagious, causing her to smile. "But I'm serious Dee. I don't want you hurting your back any more. If you want to help, you can see if any of my flowers are salvageable."

Dee leaned back to see if he was joking. Noting the serious expression on his face, Dee thought it would be best not to argue. Resigning, she nodded and headed towards his flower beds. Luke watched as she began rooting around, tossing some flowers out and replanting others. Part of him was glad that she listened to him. He didn't want her hurting herself. The other part of him ached for the old Dee he knew in college, the one who argued for her rights and resisted submission. He smiled as he remembered her singing in a silly voice, "Anything you can do, I can do better." He wondered if it was maturity or if her domineering boyfriend broke her persistent and stubborn nature.

Unable to answer that question, he went back to his saw and cut the remaining boards. By the time he had finished cutting and measuring, Dee had finished with the plants and was busy installing some solar-powered garden lights that he had purchased. Luke pulled the last of the broken boards off with much more ease than Dee had. He added the broken pieces to the pile she had started and then grabbed a freshly cut board. He grabbed his hammer, put a few nails in his mouth and began fitting the new board in the gap between two old boards. Dee disappeared into his garage and soon returned with a level in her hand. Luke banged the board into place and began nailing it. Dee watched with an amused smile. When Luke finished, he stepped back and eyed the job he did. Dee placed the level on top of the new board and smirked.

Luke shrugged his shoulders and nonchalantly asked, "Close enough?"

Dee laughed and replied, "Not if it were my fence."

Luke loved her taunting nature and began to roll with it. "And what would a financial advisor know about building fences?"

"Obviously more than a certain retired soldier that I know," she playfully retorted. Handing him the level, she continued, "You'll need it later on." She motioned to a large gap where five boards were missing.

"Well, if your back isn't too sore, I guess I could use the help."

Dee smiled a brilliant smile, obviously pleased to be not only acknowledged but also included. She shrugged her shoulders and replied, "No pain, no gain."

Luke smiled at her tough-girl motto and was pleased to see a bit of the old Dee shining through. The rest of the afternoon, she helped him level the planks and held them in place while he nailed. With her help, the job didn't take as long as he expected, and her effortless chatter made it much more enjoyable. Stepping back, he scanned the fence to make sure he didn't miss any spots. Satisfied, he began hauling his tools to the garage. When he came back for his second load of tools, he found Dee piling the broken boards in his fire pit. He had forgotten how practical she could be and couldn't help but appreciate her resourcefulness. Putting away the last of his tools, he locked up his garage and returned to his back yard. Dee remained next to the fire pit, stretching her back. Catching her attention, he nodded towards the kitchen and she followed him inside. Grabbing the phone, he said, "I was thinking I'd reward our efforts with some take out. How does Chinese sound?"

Dee turned on the kitchen faucet and began washing her hands and arms. She simply nodded and replied, "Sounds good."

When he began dialling the number from memory, Dee couldn't help but ask, "You have the number memorized?"

Luke shrugged his shoulders and replied, "I'm a bachelor. What do you want?"

Still scrubbing her hands, Dee looked over her shoulder and said, "Shanghai noodles."

"Anything else?" She shook her head. He wrinkled his nose at the simple request. Someone on the other end of the line picked up and Luke began rattling off a long list of dishes. Dee grabbed a towel and stared at him in amazement.

When he finished, she asked him, "Are you expecting company?"

Luke returned his cordless phone to the cradle and casually replied, "Leftovers. Then I don't have to cook for a few days."

Hanging the towel back on the stove handle, Dee snorted. "You really are a bachelor."

Rooting through the fridge, Luke handed her a Soda and motioned towards the living room. Easing herself into the couch, Dee's aching muscles welcomed the overstuffed cushions. Luke rooted through his freezer and followed her with a Soda in one hand and a bag of frozen vegetables in the other.

"What's with the veggies?" She asked when he tossed the bag to her.

"For your back." Luke settled into his armchair and propped his feet up on his coffee table.

Resting the bag behind her, Dee leaned back and enjoyed the cooling comfort it offered. Not only did it sooth her muscles, it also helped cool her down from working in the sun. For the beginning of June, it sure was a warm day.

"What about your back?"

Luke carelessly shrugged. "It's fine."

"Fine because you are a guy and you're trying to be macho? Or fine because Mark hits like a girl?"

Luke took his feet off the coffee table and leaned forward. He studied her face and replied, "Now what would you know about Mark hitting like a girl?" He waited to see if she would take the bait.

Dee's face didn't change and she talked as if it were a normal conversation. "I've known Mark for almost five years and I've never seen him go to the gym. He's not macho like," she paused, not wanting to compare him to Luke. Changing direction, she continued, "Mark's bossy, but he's not aggressive. I've never seen him act like this before."

Luke saw the sincerity in her face. He also saw how concerned she was over the change that had taken place in her boyfriend. "Do you think it could be drugs?"

Dee shook her head.

"He was pretty drunk last night."

"Mark's always been known to have one too many."

"Then perhaps stress? A nervous breakdown?"

Dee shrugged her shoulders. "He does have a pretty stressful job."

Luke nodded, fully aware of how taxing a job could be on a person's mental health. Over the years he had witnessed numerous soldiers suffer from the effects of the war. Luke pushed those painful memories aside and let the silence linger, leaving Dee alone with her thoughts. Eventually she broke the silence.

"Did he say anything?"

Luke shook his head, "Nothing coherent."

Dee seemed to understand. "I'm sorry I got you into this mess." She hung her head as a single tear rolled down her cheek. Luke got up and sat next to her. Taking her chin in his hand, he tilted her head up, forcing her eyes to meet him.

"It's not your fault," he said, trying to make his tone sound stern yet compassionate. Dee nodded but her eyes said she felt otherwise.

"It doesn't make sense. If he wanted to talk to me, why wouldn't he just call me?"

"You want to know my theory?" Once again Dee nodded but her eyes seemed to say no. Luke continued, "Mark doesn't want to talk to you. He wants to find you."

His bluntness cut deep and the tears flowed heavily. Luke let go of her chin and left her to her thoughts. He got up and retrieved a box of tissues. Handing her a few, he sat next to her, but not so close this time.

Dabbing her eyes, she asked, "Are you pressing charges?"

Luke nodded and she seemed grateful for his response. "Are you?" he pressed.

She shrugged her shoulders. "I dunno. Part of me says I should. If you break the law, you shouldn't get away with it. But..."

"But..." Luke interrupted and then caught himself.

"But if we patch things up, that will be one more thing to work through. I don't want it to haunt me later on down the road. If I press charges, I want it to be because it is the right thing to do. Not because I am angry."

Luke never thought of it like that and began to understand her train of thought. Once again Dee proved how practical she could be.

"Maybe I should call him." Dee looked up at him and searched his face for guidance. The way his eyes darkened, she knew he didn't like that option. She continued, "It's just, the longer I hide, the angrier he might get. Maybe if I call him and tell him that I still love him and that I'm willing to work things out, he might calm down and try to reconcile. You know...keep the communication channels open so that he doesn't jump to the wrong conclusions."

Luke leaned back and rubbed his chin. What Dee said made sense, but it didn't sit right with him. "A gentle answer turns away wrath, but a harsh word stirs up anger," Luke murmured in contemplation.

Dee stared at him, waiting for a response. His proverb comforted her. Luke leaned forward and looked at the floor. Eventually he responded. He continued to stare at the floor, and his voice didn't sound convinced. "I guess some communication couldn't hurt, as long as it is in a neutral setting, such as counselling. I don't trust Mark enough to let you be alone with him. Then again, perhaps a letter through your lawyer would be the best route." Luke then looked up. His face was grave and his tone became serious. "Truth be told, you didn't do anything wrong. Mark's the one that messed up and if he can't own up to it, he's not worth it."

"Mark's not some boyfriend that I can just discard the moment he upsets me. He's my partner. I love him. I've loved him for a long time."

"Was it your love that brought him to the restaurant in the first place?"

Luke's blunt words stung. She knew he was referring to the exotic woman that Mark was seeing. She didn't want to think about it, but it kept coming up. Maybe that is why he didn't call. He was content with his girlfriend. Then again, why would he hunt down Luke if he didn't care about her? Perhaps Luke was right; Mark wanted everything, but he couldn't have his cake and eat it too.

Luke's face softened as he regretted hurting Dee with his words. "I'm sorry Dee. I shouldn't have said that."

Dee shrugged her shoulders. "The truth hurts."

"But friends should word it in the nicest way possible." Dee grabbed a fresh tissue and wiped her eyes. Luke put his arm around her and pulled her close, desperate to console her. She didn't resist and crumpled in his comforting embrace. "Dee, you're not married to him. You're not bound to him. You can leave him."

Dee sighed, exhausted and confused. "It's complicated," she mumbled.

"No, it's not!" She could hear the irritation in his voice. "He attacked you. You could have been seriously injured!"

"You don't understand. You think it's so easy."

"It is easy. Boyfriends come and go."

Dee could feel her frustration mounting and had no idea of how to control it. "He's not just my boyfriend; he's my partner! My lover! I gave him everything: my heart, my soul, my body. I gave him what you "Christians" save for marriage and I didn't give it away easily. That is something that I will never get back. Mark owns it and I'm going to try my hardest to fix this because of that."

The gravity of her situation finally dawned upon Luke. It was more than a broken heart that she was trying to fix. It was the betrayal of knowing that she had given Mark a special gift that he neither cherished nor protected.

"Then perhaps a letter through a lawyer would be the best means to communicate your intentions. If you call and he freaks out on you, that's a personal attack. But if he has to communicate through a lawyer, he might try to be a bit more civil. As well, he won't know where you are staying."

Dee sat up and blew her nose. Her shoulders slumped and her eyes seemed dull and empty. "I guess that's the most practical alternative so far."

Luke nodded in agreement. He could see the wheels turning in Dee's head, searching for the most practical route to take. He felt comforted to know that she wouldn't make any hasty or irresponsible decisions. Luke rubbed her back and assured her, "Just remember you're not in this alone. You're surrounded by loved ones that will see you through all of this." He wanted to tell her more; to assure her of Christ's love, the only love that could heal her and forgive her for giving herself to Mark.

Just then the doorbell rang and Dee was thankful for the distraction. Luke handed her another tissue, stood up and went to retrieve their food. Dee got up and wandered into the bathroom. She splashed some cold water and rinsed the tears off of her face. The cold water soothed her swollen eyes. She patted her face dry and when she returned to the kitchen, she found Luke busy setting out the numerous dishes that he had ordered.

Looking up, he noted her fresh face and thought that her eyes looked a bit brighter. Giving her his biggest smile, he began opening cartons and instructed her, "You have to eat more than just Shanghai noodles." He was pleased to see Dee load up her plate and he wondered if she had even eaten yet today. With the newlyweds planning to be gone the next two weeks, there probably weren't very many groceries left in the house.

After loading up her plate, Dee looked for a place to sit. The multiple dishes engulfed the small kitchen table. Luke, with a plate in one hand and a drink in the other, slid open the patio door with his foot. Beckoning towards the outdoors he commented, "It's much too nice to be cooped up inside." Dee agreed and slipped through the door, allowing Luke to close it behind her. Settling down at his outdoor patio set, Dee's stomach rumbled.

Luke laughed and asked, "Have you eaten yet today?"

Dee shook her head and confessed, "I haven't had much of an appetite lately."

"Well, you're in for a treat. This is the best Chinese food in town!" Luke quickly said grace and they dug in.

After supper, Luke lit the broken boards and started a bonfire. Dee carried their empty plates inside and loaded them in his dishwasher. As she put the leftover food in the fridge, Luke dragged a couple of lawn chairs over to the fire. He enjoyed spending time with Dee and was thankful for her company. It was nice to hang out with her alone. Any time he saw her, Maggie and Jeffrey were always around, and Luke finally felt like he was really getting to know her. So much had changed since her freshman year at college and he was beginning to look forward to the next two weeks. Dee came back out wrapped in a blanket she had found on the couch and settled into a lawn chair. Luke was glad that she felt comfortable enough to make herself at home and he handed her a wire that had once been a hanger and a bag of marshmallows.

"You do much camping?"

Luke shook his head, concentrating on the marshmallow he was carefully browning. "Not since I got back."

"I guess three years of roughing it in Afghanistan would be enough to fix the itch to go survive in the wilderness."

Luke laughed. "Ya," he agreed, "the way they camp here seems luxurious compared to some of the nights I endured."

"You've must have seen some terrible things."

Luke stared at Dee. Her face glowed with the reflection of the campfire and her blond curls seemed to shine even more. He appreciated her compassion. "I always thought you didn't want to talk about the war.'

Dee shrugged her shoulders. "It's not that I didn't want to talk about it. I just wasn't sure if it was a subject you wanted brought up." She watched Luke's reaction, to see if she should change the topic. He didn't seem upset, so she continued. "I'm glad you didn't come back changed."

"Changed?" he asked.

"I guess I shouldn't say changed. You changed a bit, but for the better. I guess I should say scarred. Some men have come back angry or depressed. I'm glad that you're still the same old, fun-loving Luke. Just a little bit more responsible, that's all."

"Whenever Maggie wrote, she always included your salutations."

"I wanted to write. I just didn't know what to say." Luke nodded, feeling the same way.

"Maggie thought you were angry at me for leaving."

Dee grew quiet and stared at the fire's enticing flames. Her marshmallow caught on fire, but she didn't bother to blow it out. Instead, she let the flames consume it, burning it off of her wire. "I wouldn't say angry. Just hurt."

"Why?" Luke's tone was gentle, trying to ease an answer out of her. For five years he had wondered but never dared to ask her.

"I dunno. I guess because we were friends and you never told me about it. It was like this big secret and I wished you had trusted me enough to share it with me. All of a sudden you were gone, and I didn't even get to say good-bye."

"I'm sorry Dee. If I could change one thing, it would have been that. It shows how immature I was. I was afraid that if I told anyone, they would talk me out of it. Rather than facing them, I just left."

Dee's heart softened. His apology erased the hurt she felt so many years ago. "I'm glad you enlisted. The more I thought about it, the more it made sense. I was happy for you. I just missed you, that's all."

Luke's voice grew low. "I missed you too."

"I should have written."

"Me too." Dee's smile warmed Luke more than any campfire could. Luke hated how husky his voice was, but he couldn't control it. "I'm glad we cleared up this matter."

"Me too. Even if it took five years."

Luke chuckled and tossed her another marshmallow. "Better late than never."

Later that night when they had their fill of marshmallows and ran out of broken fence boards to burn, Luke walked Dee back to her place. Following her downstairs, he checked the basement suite and then headed upstairs to make sure Mark was not hiding and waiting for her. When he returned to the basement, he found Dee preparing the coffeepot for the next morning.

"All clear?" She asked.

He nodded, "All clear."

After bidding each other goodnight, Luke let himself out and headed towards his home. He enjoyed spending the day with Dee. It was good to catch up without Jeffrey and Maggie present. Their conversations became more personal; rekindling the friendship they once had five years ago. Dee's presence kept him from feeling lonely, and he was glad that she took comfort in his presence. When he left, she seemed so much more relaxed than she had been the night before. He just hoped it would be enough to allow her some rest.

Chapter 5

Putting down his coffee cup, Luke settled into his office chair and eyed the fresh stack of files on his desk. Digging through the pile, he searched for a specific one but could not find it. Giving up, he grabbed the first file on the top of the pile and began leafing through it. The mug shot was a new one and Luke didn't recognize this suspect. Staring at the unfamiliar face, Luke was surprised to see how young the terrorist was. His age was more appropriate for a child soldier, not an insurgent leader. Flipping through the file, Luke couldn't believe how dangerous this teenager was turning out to be. He should be playing soccer in the street, not ordering suicide bombings. Frustrated, Luke tossed the file back onto his desk and leaned back with a groan. Looking up, he noticed his partner, Juan, standing behind his desk, grinning at him.

"Quite the kid, hey?" Juan asked.

"He's a kid all right." Sitting back up, Luke reached for his coffee mug and took a swig.

"How was your sister's wedding?"

Luke smiled, recalling the image of his baby sister walking down the aisle. "It was great! She married a good guy."

"Now it's your turn."

Luke chuckled and reached for the next file. "I'm in no hurry."

Juan eyed him curiously, trying to get a reaction out of Luke. "You should be. The good ones don't wait around forever." Luke just shrugged his shoulders and Juan handed him another folder. "I got that file you requested. He doesn't seem like the terrorist type."

Luke reached for the file and eyed the name, *Mark Kensington*. "This one's personal."

"I'll say," Juan responded. "Sounds like you had quite the run in with him."

"You read the report?"

"Sure did. You must be getting soft, not being on the field anymore. I can't believe you let a weasel like this guy take you down."

Luke narrowed his eyes, not in the mood for Juan's teasing. "Well since you read it, anything I need to know."

Juan shrugged his shoulders. "We've got the typical slime-ball. He's flown under the radar until now. No previous misdemeanours. This is his first offence and he talked his way out of it. Walked away with nothing more than a warning."

"He pushed his girlfriend through a balcony railing."

"And would have gotten away with it if you hadn't shown up. His girlfriend made a statement but hasn't pressed charges yet. So far it looks like that will not affect his record."

"Anything else?"

"Funny you should ask." Luke looked up and found Juan looking back at him with a smug look on his face. Juan continued. "These guys are too good to be true: CEO of a software business, taking home six figures a year, etcetera, etcetera. So, I dug a bit deeper and found out that he's being investigated for tax fraud. Turns out he's been cheating the government for almost three years."

Luke's gut dropped as he thought about Dee. She worked for the government as a financial advisor. Had she done some creative bookkeeping for Mark?

"Who filed his taxes?" Luke asked, not too sure if he wanted to know.

"Some accountant from his firm who is also under investigation."

"And Dee?"

Juan hummed and flipped open the file. Pulling out her picture, he said, "She sure is pretty. This is what I mean. If you wait too long, the good ones get snatched up."

Luke glared and ripped the file out of Juan's hands. He gazed at the picture of Dee. It was a flattering picture, even if it was taken from her passport. "What about her taxes? Is she clean?"

"She filed separately. She's as clean as she gets. Did you know that when she was in college, she even claimed the tips she made from waitressing? Who does that? People work for cash so that they don't have to claim it. If you ask me, she's an angel."

Luke didn't like Juan's tone. Looking up from Dee's picture, he found Juan smirking at him. "What's her connection to you?"

"Nothing," Luke mumbled as he shoved their files into his drawer. He'd look at them in depth later.

"She's to pretty to be classified as a 'nothing'." Leaning on Luke's desk, Juan watched, waiting for a reaction.

Luke played it cool, well aware that Juan was trying to get under his skin. "I just want to make sure she's okay. Make sure she's not in over her head."

"Well, if you're not interested, maybe I'll make a play for her. Sooner or later she'll come to her senses and leave her boyfriend." Luke looked like he was ready to clobber Juan. Juan enjoyed seeing Luke get so worked up. Luke's face turned dark and he stared Juan down. Juan jumped up and faced Luke. "I knew it!"

Luke knew his face gave away more than he intended. He tried to calm down. "Knew what?"

"She's the girl."

"What girl?"

"The girl from college. The one you talked about for three years straight."

Luke remembered the endless conversations he had with Juan in Afghanistan. They were best friends and told each other everything. But this, this was too private to share with him.

"She's not *that* girl."

"Then who is she."

Luke searched for an excuse. He wasn't too sure why she mattered so much. Perhaps it was his altruistic nature. Now that he no longer needed to protect Maggie from dumb boyfriends he felt that he needed to protect Dee. "She was my sister's bridesmaid. This guy came *this* close to ruining my sister's wedding." Luke's excuse felt lame, but it was the truth.

Juan nodded. "You were always protective of Maggie. You want my honest opinion." Luke shook his head but Juan continued anyways, "I'd keep this *chica* close and her boyfriend far, far away. Because when his tax fraud comes to light, things are going to get ugly—uglier than they already are. He's just that type."

Luke nodded and rubbed his temples. Juan was right. This was just the tip of the iceberg.

"Besides," Juan continued, throwing in his final jab, "It wouldn't hurt to keep a girl that pretty close by." Satisfied with the face Luke made, Juan chuckled and walked away.

Dee stepped off of the elevator and rushed to her office. Balancing a coffee and bagel in one hand, she dug through her purse with the other, searching for her keys. Upon retrieving them, she fought with her sticky lock. Pulling her purse straps over her shoulder, she bit her bagel bag and held it with her teeth. Using three fingers to hold her coffee, she used the other two to turn the key while she used her other hand to jiggle the doorknob. The lock popped and her door swung open with ease. Hurrying into her office, she shut the door behind her and plopped onto her desk chair. Pulling it up to her desk, she logged on to the system and waited for everything to load. Impatient, she dug through her purse and retrieved her wallet. Counting her cash, she found that she had only forty-three dollars and some change rolling around in the bottom of her purse. Dee groaned, wondering if that was all that she had left.

Turning to her computer, she clicked on the internet icon, not bothering to wait for everything else to load. Because of her impatience, the internet browser took even longer to come up. She thought back to her embarrassing scenario on her way to work. Stopping to fill her car with gas, the kid behind the till loudly informed her that her card was denied due to insufficient funds. Dee blushed just thinking about it. This had never happened to her before. Thank goodness she had cash. She had no idea what she would have done if she didn't.

The internet browser finished loading and she quickly logged onto her online banking. This didn't make sense. Mark made six figures a year and she had a well paying government job. There was always plenty of cash unless...

Dee's jaw dropped as she stared at her empty accounts. Clicking on her account details, she found that everything had been transferred out early Saturday morning. She didn't recognize the account number, but knew it wasn't hers. Her head sank into her hands and her temples throbbed. Tears threatened her eyes. She knew joint accounts were a bad idea if things ever went sour, but she loved and trusted Mark. She never thought that it would happen to her. Returning to the main page, she found that their savings account was empty and her VISA was cancelled. She felt so foolish. She was twenty-four and didn't even have her own credit card. Instead, she had Mark's secondary card. What made matters worse was the fact that she was a financial advisor. If anyone should have known better, it should have been her.

Dee thought hard, trying to recall what types of investments she had. Though she was a financial advisor, Mark was the one that did all of their investing. It was a hobby for him, watching the stock market and interest rates. Calling the number on the back of her bank card, the customer service representative confirmed what she feared. Everything that she had with Mark was either closed or transferred. Nothing existed in only her name. Dee felt naive for not putting money away for herself. She heard many stories about women who would hoard money for themselves. Fifty bucks here or a hundred there quickly grew into thousands of dollars. Dee always pitied such women who didn't trust their partners enough. How foolish she had been!

A knock at the door interrupted her thoughts and her boss's head peeped through. Sitting up, Dee acknowledged her and Madge walked in. Taking one look at Dee, she said, "You look terrible. Must have been quite the wedding."

Dee scowled. Why do so many people associate a wedding with an open bar? Dee just shook her head to dismiss such a comment. Taking a seat across from her desk, Madge eyed Dee and asked, "How's the report coming?"

Dee cringed at the Tuesday deadline she had to meet. It was like pulling teeth trying to get Friday off for the wedding. The only way she could get Madge to agree to give her the day off was to promise to have the reports done and on her desk first thing Tuesday morning.

"Good, I stayed late Thursday night and got the bulk of it done. I'm just waiting for some stats from downstairs and then all I have left are some finishing touches."

Madge nodded, obviously pleased that she had stayed late to earn her day off. She eyed Dee curiously, taking in the dark circles that engulfed the usually bright eyes. "Is everything okay?"

Dee hesitated. She knew eventually people in the office would sense that something was wrong. She had just hoped that she could hide it a bit longer. "I actually have something...something to talk to you about." Dee hated how she nervously stuttered. "I had a bit of an emergency this weekend. I have some things that I have to take care of today. And I know," she rushed on before Madge could interject, "I know that the deadline is tomorrow, but I promise you that I'll have the reports done. Whatever time I spend away from the office I'll make up tonight. I won't leave until everything is taken care of."

"You care to tell me what's going on?"

Dee knew it wouldn't be that easy. How could she explain, without really telling Madge anything? Dee was private and didn't want her boss knowing her personal affairs, especially with the way that gossip travelled through the office. Not wanting to lie, she tried to evade the truth as much as possible.

"Someone got a hold of my banking information. Right now, everything's frozen. Nothing works, not my debit card or my credit cards. I have to get to the bank and open new accounts and see what's left."

Madge's jaw dropped. "I have a nephew who had his identity stolen. It was such a mess," she responded sympathetically. "Have you notified the police?"

Dee nodded. "It's just that the banks were closed yesterday, so I have to take care of this right away, before it gets worse."

Madge nodded affirmatively. "I'd like to give you a personal day off, I really would, but with this report due I can't. You take care of everything that needs to be taken care of, but if it can wait until tomorrow, make it wait, because I need that report."

Dee nodded, surprised at how understanding her boss was being. The woman was a stern, older lady and ran the office like a drill sergeant. She had never seen her with such a sympathetic side before.

"Thank you!" Dee gushed.

Madge stood up and nodded, as if to say, *don't mention it.*

"I promise to get it done. Like I said, most of it is already taken care of."

Dee grabbed her purse as Madge walked to the door. Before she went out, Madge stopped and turned to face Dee. "Just don't let the others know."

Dee nodded to convey that she understood and Madge winked and walked out the door.

The numbers blurred together as Dee stared at her computer screen. She rubbed her aching eyes and checked her watch. The night was getting late, but she had to finish the report. Forcing her eyes to focus, she concentrated on the stats that she just entered. She stared at the large numbers and envied them. Her appointment at the bank had not gone so well. Mark had cleaned out every single account that she had signing authority on. Even their investments were either closed to transferred to investments in his name only. Dee had to open an account, which currently had a balance of zero, and was forced to apply for a line of credit to tie her over. She hated the thought of debt. She had never borrowed money before. It embarrassed her. To make matters worse, she despised the way Eileen, her co-worker, looked at her when she asked for a cash advance on her pay check. She wanted to slap the smug little smile off of Eileen's pretty face, but she couldn't get mad at Eileen. Dee had gotten herself into this mess and she would have to face the consequences. Even if that meant asking for a cash advance to tie her over until her line of credit was approved.

Her meeting with her lawyer was just as discouraging. He was more interested in a financial settlement than he was about communicating reconciliation. All she wanted was for him to send a letter she had written the night before. She didn't see why he needed to know who owned the house. And she most definitely did not need his pity when she explained her empty bank accounts. She felt frustrated and exhausted and all she could think about was the pile of work waiting for her at the office.

Once again, Dee struggled to focus on her report. She input her final figures and was glad to see that it finally worked out. She had spent hours trying to make it balance. She should have been home by now, but her lack of concentration was causing her to make silly errors. She saved it and pressed the print button. As her printer hummed, she watched the numerous pages pop out, all carrying various charts and graphs. The rhythmic hum caused her to relax and her eyes began to droop.

The gentle vibration of her phone startled her out of the printer's hypnotic trance. Checking the caller ID, she was surprised to see Luke calling at such a late hour. Answering the phone, Luke's frantic voice startled her.

"Dee, he shouted, thankful that she answered. "Where are you?"

"I'm at work."

"Work!? It's past eleven."

Dee propped her phone up to her ear with her shoulder and began binding the report together. "Yeah, I know. It's just been one of those days and I had a report that I had to finish."

"You should have called."

"Why?" The question popped out before Dee could have stopped it, and she regretted her grumpy tone. The long day was taking a toll on her.

"Why?!?" Dee could hear the frustration creep into his voice. "Because I was worried. I checked in on you and you weren't home."

Dee was tired of being told what to do. She was tired of having ridiculous expectations thrust upon her. "You're not my father Luke. I don't have to report to you."

Luke tried to smooth his tone. The last thing Dee needed was another man bossing her around. He couldn't help being concerned. It was getting late and Dee hadn't shown up.

"I'm sorry Dee. You're right. I was just worried."

"Well don't be. I'm a big girl. I can take care of myself." Luke was startled at how antagonizing she was becoming.

99

Usually so easy-going, he had never seen her lose her temper before. Part of him wanted to let her scream and kick. The other part wanted to hold her tightly until she calmed down.

What he should have said was, *I know you can take care of yourself, but I want to help.* Instead, his pride crept through and he found himself saying, "I promised."

This really set Dee off. She wanted to scream and throw her phone against the wall. Her face became hot and her body shook with rage. "This isn't Afghanistan, Luke!" She retorted. "It's not your job to protect me, so just leave me alone!"

She jabbed at her cell phone as hard as she could. She hoped her aggressive hang up wouldn't be lost on Luke. Luke stood there, with the silent phone to his ear, shocked at her outburst. Her last remark cut at his pride and he could feel resentment rising up inside of him. Why couldn't she see that he was just trying to help? Why did she have to be so stubborn? The way she unappreciated his concern reminded him of his arrival in Afghanistan. Civilians were outraged whenever he showed up. They threw rocks at him and quite often when he tried to help them, they just spit on him. His anger rose as he remembered how unwelcome they made him feel. He flew half way around the world and was risking his life for them, yet they still resented his presence.

Luke lowered his phone and hung up. His blood boiled at the thought of her rejection. Fine! If she didn't want his help, she wouldn't get it.

Chapter 6

Dee checked the clock and gladly called it quits for the day. *TGIF,* she thought as she filed away some folders and cleaned off her desk. Logging off of her computer, she looked forward to going home and taking a long, hot bath. It had been a long week, full of ups and downs. Eileen had agreed to give her a pay check advance, but then took the rest of the week off because her children had the flu. With no one else able to approve such a request, Dee would have to wait until Monday and hope that Eileen would be back. Her bank had hiccups of its own and her line of credit application had taken longer than expected. Though the bank had guaranteed her that her funds would come in tonight at midnight, she would have liked it sooner. Her forty-three dollars didn't last long. She got a few groceries to tie her over for the week, but her car was running low on gas. She just prayed that she had enough to make it home. She just had to make it until tomorrow.

Locking up her office, she headed for the elevator and waited. She hadn't heard from Luke for the rest of the week. She felt bad for how she had spoken to him, but wasn't sure if she had calmed down. With how stressful her week had been, she was afraid to apologize to him. What if she tried but just blew up at him again? She was hoping that her Saturday would be event free. That way she could relax, clear her head, and apologize to Luke with the right state of mind.

Entering the elevator, no one else joined her and it remained empty until she reached the main floor. Alone with her thoughts, she realized how much she missed Luke's company. He had been both a comfort and a distraction. She wished she hadn't lashed out at him. It wasn't his fault. She knew that he had good intentions. Why did it always end up being the innocent who took the brunt of the blow when stress piled up too high?

Getting off the elevator, Dee thought of all the times Mark came home from work stressed. He always took it out on her, and like a good girlfriend, she endured it. With that thought, Dee began to despise herself. What Mark did to her, she did to Luke and she realized how unfair she had been.

Walking outside to her car, the sun's warm sunrays cheered her up and encouraged her. She had a feeling it would be a good weekend. She just hoped Luke would be as forgiving as she hoped he would be. Getting into her car, she tossed her purse on the passenger seat and opened her sunroof. Putting on her sunglasses, she pulled into the heavy traffic. If seemed everybody else was leaving work early to enjoy the nice weekend. Traffic slowly rolled along, but Dee was in no hurry. She liked driving. The gentle hum of her car relaxed her and the cool air that blew through her window was refreshing.

Looking ahead, Dee realized why traffic was moving so slow. Up ahead, the police were conducting a stop check before traffic could merge onto the freeway. This didn't surprise her. With higher rates of accidents on the weekend, the police often did stop checks, especially with summer approaching.

Putting her car in park and letting it idle, Dee dug through her wallet and retrieved her drivers licence. Rummaging through the glove compartment, she searched for the car's registration. Turning up nothing but old receipts, she began digging through the console. Looking up, she noticed that the car in front of her had driven ahead. Pulling up, she lowered her window and pulled down her visor. When she flipped open the mirror, numerous papers fell out, but none of them were the current registration. Just then an older police officer approached her door.

"Heading home for the weekend?" The police officer politely asked.

"Yes Sir." Dee mustered up her best smile and handed him her driver's licence. As he looked it over, she dug through the pocket on the driver's side door.

"Do you have the registration?"

"I'm looking for it. I'm not too sure where it would be tucked away." Dee began flipping open pockets that she never paid attention to. Each one remained empty.

"Is the car registered in your name?"

"I'm not too sure. I know it's registered in my partner's name. I'm not too sure if he added me as a secondary registrant."

The police office simply nodded. "I'll just run it through our system and see what it turns up." Walking to the back of the car, he wrote down the licence plate number and went over to his car. Sitting in the driver's seat, he punched in some numbers on his laptop. Then he radioed in a request. Minutes later he returned to her door.

"Miss, I need you to step out of the car."

Dee looked up at him startled. "Is there a problem?"

"This car has been reported stolen." His tone was flat and even and his face was serious.

"Stolen! That's impossible. This is my car."

"It's not registered under your name," the officer stated impatiently.

"It's registered under Mark Kensington," Dee offered.

"I know. The car is registered solely in his name and he reported it stolen earlier this week. I need you to step out of the car."

Dee's stomach stilled as she realized what Mark had done. Turning off the car, she reached for her purse and climbed out. Looking behind her, she could see the occupants of the waiting cars watch her curiously. She could feel her face heating up as a blush crawled up her neck. The police officer looked at her sympathetically and led her to his car. While he radioed for a tow truck, Dee waited by the police car's back door. Tears threatened her eyes, and she looked down at her feet ashamed. She worried that this would make her look guilty, so she forced herself to stand tall and look straight ahead. The police officer had kind eyes that wrinkled when he gestured to the passenger side door.

"I won't make you sit back there. You don't look like a criminal."

Dee appreciated his kindness and let him escort her to the other side. Opening the door for her, Dee sat down inside. As he carefully closed the door, Dee looked around. She had never been in a police car before. She was amazed at how many gadgets consumed the dashboard. With no room for the laptop, it sat on the console, securely fastened down with a chain.

The police officer got in on his side and as soon as he sat down, he began punching numbers into the computer. Looking up every now and then, he gently explained. "Normally there wouldn't be a problem, but your name is not on the car's registration. Since your partner reported it as stolen, we have to impound it and take you to the station to file a report."

Dee nodded and put on her seatbelt as he started the car. Staring at her white knuckles that gripped her purse in her lap, she asked, "Are you going to press charges?"

"That's up to your partner." Trying to comfort her, he added, "I'm sure it's just a big misunderstanding. We'll see if we can get it sorted out."

When they arrived at the police station, the police officer led her to his desk. Taking a seat across from him, Dee watched as he typed on his computer. Satisfied with what he found, he printed off a file and picking up his phone, he dialled a number off of the papers he just printed. Dee sat there watching, too overwhelmed to try to problem solve. Fear gripped her as she wondered if she'd have to spend the night in jail, just like Mark had to a week ago. Would she have to pay a fine? Dee thought about her empty bank account and her head began to throb. She rubbed her temples as the officer hung up the phone. Turning to look at her, he offered her a box of tissues, and left his desk without a word. Dee sat there perplexed, not too sure if she was supposed to follow him or remain seated. He soon returned with another officer, who was much younger than him.

The younger officer held out his hand and introduced himself in a professional voice, "I'm Officer McCormick. I spoke to you the other day."

Dee stood and shook his hand, nodding when she recognized the name. He gestured for her to take a seat and pulled up a chair next to her. Sitting down he looked her squarely in the face and said, "We have a bit of a situation here, don't we?"

Dee nodded, not too sure of what to make of his tone. It was so serious that she wasn't sure if he was playing the good cop or the bad cop. She looked at the kind, older cop for help. He smiled gently and returned his attention to Officer McCormick.

Officer McCormick continued. "Let's start with how you obtained the car."

It was a statement, not a question. Dee felt overwhelmed, not too sure how to respond. "It's my car. I mean, it was given to me as a Christmas present."

"By your partner?"

Dee nodded. Officer McCormick began jotting notes down on a pad of paper.

"How long ago was that?"

"A year and a half ago."

"But you never transferred the registration into you name?"

Dee shook her head. "I always assumed I was on there somehow. As a secondary owner or something."

"Have you been home since the incident last Friday night?"

Dee nodded. "I went home that night to get some things."

"Such as the car?"

"No. I went home to get clothes and toiletries. I had the car all along."

"Are you the only one in the household who drove that car?"

Once again, Dee nodded. "Mark has his own car. Whenever we would go somewhere together, he'd drive his Mercedes. It's more of his style."

"So, you've had that car since Friday night?" Dee nodded. He jotted down a note and continued. "Any idea why he would wait until Tuesday to report it stolen?"

Dee shook her head. Her mind swam with confusion and she had trouble concentrating. He continued. "Have you spoken to him since the incident?"

Dee looked up and turned to the older officer. She felt comforted by his gentle, wrinkled face. "I wrote him a letter and had my lawyer send it to him."

"To your knowledge, has he received the letter?"

Dee nodded. "My lawyer confirmed that he received it Tuesday morning."

"What did this letter communicate?"

"Um...a desire for reconciliation."

"Did you issue him an ultimatum?"

"No," Dee paused unsure of what all of the questions meant. "I did request counselling."

"And did he respond?"

Dee shook her head and tears welled up in her eyes. It hurt remembering the disappointment she had felt when her lawyer called her. She had laid it all on the line and Mark rejected it. She reached for another tissue and dabbed her eyes. Officer McCormick flipped through the file and began scanning the lines for a certain piece of information.

"According to this file, your husband reported the car stolen Tuesday afternoon."

Dee's heart sank upon the realization that this was a form of Mark's retaliation to her letter. Her shoulder's sagged and she felt like she had an incredible load on her back. She wondered what else he could do to hurt her.

Gathering up her courage, she responded with as much strength as she could. "If I had known that there would have been a problem with the car, I would have left it at home. Like I said, I thought I was on the registration."

Officer McCormick merely nodded and continued to write notes. She looked to the other officer for help. He looked at her sympathetically.

"Quite often," the older officer spoke up with a tone that was milder than McCormick's, "in the case of a domestic dispute, a partner may cut off all resources in an attempt to force the fleeing partner back home. In this case, Mark may not have intended for you to be arrested. He may have intended for you to wake up and find the car missing so that you'd be forced to call him for help. Would this explain why he did not respond through your lawyer?"

Dee felt numb as she simply responded, "he drained our bank accounts."

Officer McCormick looked up from his notes and leaned forward. "Did you have any personal funds set aside?"

Dee felt embarrassed to admit how naive she had been. Shaking her head, she explained, "I've been waiting for a bank loan to be approved."

"And until then?"

Dee shrugged her shoulders. "I'll make do."

The older officer leaned forward and gently asked, "Do you have anyone you can call."

A single silent tear stole down her cheek as she thought about how alone she was. With Maggie gone, Luke was the only person willing to help her and she burnt that bridge already. Once again, Dee shrugged her shoulders. "I'll figure something out." Looking at Officer McCormick, she asked, "Do I have to stay here until you've sorted things out with Mark"

"Normally, yes. But in this case, we'll let you go. However, if he does decide to press charges, we will have to bring you in and book you."

Dee nodded, thankful for their leniency. She feared Mark's anger and worried that he would press charges.

The older officer added, "Even if he does decide to press charges, I wouldn't be surprised if the case is thrown out in court. Truthfully, it's already a domestic dispute that doesn't look kindly on him. This will only make him look worse."

His words comforted her. Looking up, she asked, "Could you not call him, until I leave. I just don't want him following me. He doesn't know where I'm staying."

The older officer offered her a gentle smile and responded, "Just let us know when your ride is here."

Officer McCormick then gestured to the hallway where some pay phones were. Leaving the office area, Dee stole into the silent hallway and sunk onto the bench nearby. Burying her head into her hands, she wept as she tried to figure out what to do. Her head throbbed as she thought about her empty wallet. She couldn't even afford to take a cab home. She wished Maggie were home already. Maggie had a knack for making all of Dee's worries go away. Leaning her head back against the cold, cement wall, Dee tried to concentrate. She knew there was only one person she could call, but what if he was still mad at her and didn't answer. Her only other option was Mark and that wasn't an option at all. Wiping away her tears, Dee took a deep breath and tried to calm down. Digging through her purse she retrieved her cell phone. Pulling up Luke's number, she sighed. Breathing a quick prayer, Dee mustered up all of her courage and hit the call button. It was now or never.

She was surprised by Luke's cheerful voice when he answered.

"Hey Dee! I'm glad to hear from you."

Dee stopped, caught off guard. She was expecting him to tear a strip out of her. She thought she would have to beg for forgiveness, and here he was, acting as if nothing had happened. It took a big man to burry the hatchet.

"Uh, hi Luke." Words failed her and she hated how stupid she sounded.

"Are you okay?" She could hear the concern in his voice.

"Um, yeah," she lied. "Luke, I just wanted to call and apologize for how I treated you Monday night."

She was about to begin her well-practiced speech when he cut her off. "Hey, no problem. I'm sorry I acted like a nagging wife."

Dee couldn't believe the difference that existed between Luke and Mark. Mark would have made her grovel before he spoke a word to her. She would have to spend days highlighting his attributes and pointing out her faults. It took weeks of damage control and sometimes she tip-toed around him for months, afraid he would bring up the past. Not only was Luke dismissing the problem, he was taking ownership for part of it.

Dee could feel her headache retreating and his words encouraged her. Smiling, she responded, "More like a caring father."

Luke laughed light heartedly and Dee relaxed, thankful for how well this was going.

"Are you home yet?"

"No," Dee paused wondering how she could ask for a favour after he had been so understanding. "I'm still downtown."

"I'm just leaving the office. Do you want to meet somewhere and get some grub?"

"Actually, I was calling because..." Dee paused, afraid to ask. Luke sensed her hesitation and wondered why she sounded so nervous.

"Is everything alright?" His tone was gentle and compassionate. Dee could feel his concern and she began to cry. "Dee? You still there?"

"Ya." Dee wiped her eyed with her soggy tissue. "Um, Luke, I'm in a bit of a bind. I was wondering if I could get a ride home."

"Of course." His reply was immediate. Could such a giving nature come so naturally? "What happened to your car?"

"It got impounded."

Luke's jaw dropped as he wondered what type of accident she was in. "Are you hurt?"

Once again, Luke's caring nature caused tears to escape from Dee's eyes. "No. There's just a problem with the registration, that's all."

Luke had a feeling that the problem had something to do with Mark. He listened as Dee gave him the address of the precinct she was at.

"Don't you worry about a thing," Luke tried to reassure her. "I'll be there in twenty minutes."

After Luke hung up, Dee stared at her phone, stunned. What had just happened? After spending so much time bearing Mark's moods, she was shocked that people like Luke existed. Images swarmed in her head, causing it to ache. She leaned back and rested her head on the cold wall. She tried to ignore memories of Mark screaming at her, but her mind was too exhausted to disregard them. Last time he lost it was due to ten minutes of tardiness, but that was all that it took. His words were vehement and his attacks were personal and piercing. She knew how nasty Mark could get, but it was always with words, not actions. He knew how to really hurt her, always targeting her desire to marry.

She remembered how the tears flowed and she apologized over and over, as if begging him to stop. Yet the daggers flew and his words stabbed at her soul. *"How do you expect me to marry you if you can't even pick me up on time?"*

She tried to defend herself, explaining the heavy traffic, but he wouldn't hear of it.

"If you really loved me, you would have thought of that and left earlier!"

He would rant and rave, telling her that a good wife would win him over by complete submission. She submitted to the point that he walked all over her. She tried her hardest to be the partner that he needed. Just because she couldn't predict the future didn't mean that she would be a bad wife!

That attack was over a month ago, and she still tip-toed around Mark. She knew that if she did one little thing to set him off, he would bring it back up. Combining the present fault with numerous past faults, he would prove that she couldn't do anything right and completely crush her spirit. Then she would go out of her way to make him happy. She would put in the extra time to wait on him hand and foot, as if to prove that she could be the wife that he needed.

Dee sat up and wiped away her tears. For a slight moment, Dee wondered what it would have been like if she had fallen in love with someone else. After enduring so many attacks, she forgot that people didn't normally function like that. Taking in a deep breath, she dared to dream what a marriage with Luke would look like. With Mark, ten minutes of tardiness meant two weeks of grovelling. With Luke, she had lost her temper and directly attacked him, yet he put it in the past before she even apologized. Not only did he forgive her, but he even apologized for nagging! If she had married him, would he always apologize for his mistakes, or would that eventually wear out? Would a man like Luke eventually play the submission card and drain the life out of his wife? Would men like Luke last, or would they eventually turn into someone like Mark?

When Luke arrived at the police station, he caught sight of Dee immediately. She looked like a small child, sitting on the bench all alone. The way her shoulders slumped and her head hung low reminded him of all the times he had guiltily waited outside of the principal's office. She nervously toyed with the buckle on her purse. Luke hated to see her looking so dejected. She used to walk with the air of an athlete, strong and confident, but as she sat there, she looked broken and uncertain.

Dee looked up and caught Luke watching her. Standing up, she hooked her purse over her shoulder. She walked over to Luke and stopped a few steps away from him. Hesitating, she adjusted the weight of the purse on her shoulder. She looked like she wanted to say something but couldn't. Luke had never seen her look so lost or helpless before. Closing the gap, he put his hand on her shoulder and asked, "Are you okay?"

Dee nodded, but her eyes filled with tears. Closing his arms around her, Luke drew her in. Dee didn't resist and he was surprised to find her nestling against him. Her stiff, rigid demeanour collapsed into his chest. Sobbing, she cried, "I am so sorry."

Lifting one hand to stroke her soft curls, he hushed her in an attempt to soothe her. "So am I," he whispered, causing her to sob even harder. He held her for a few more moments before she finally straightened up. Pulling herself away, she madly wiped away at her tears. She felt embarrassed for losing her composure, but felt better at the same time.

"I appreciate you checking in on me. I was just mad at Mark and I took it out on you. I really am sorry!" The tears still flowed, but at a slower pace. Despite how lost and alone Dee felt, she was grateful that Luke pulled through in a time of need.

"No problem," he replied nonchalantly. He acted as if it was no big deal, but to Dee, it was. In a gentle voice, he added, "Let's get you out of here."

Dee nodded and turned to the office area. Through the windows she could see the older officer watching her. Waving goodbye, he nodded in approval. Re-slinging her purse over her shoulder, Dee stood up as straight as she could and turned to the door. Luke followed behind her, admiring the effort she made to regain her composure.

Settling into his SUV, Dee relaxed and leaned her head back. As Luke started the engine, he turned to her and asked, "Are you hungry?"

Shaking her head, she replied, "I just want to go home, take a bath and go to bed."

Luke nodded in a way that said he understood and pulled out of the parking lot. They drove in silence until he reached the freeway. Turning down the radio, Luke leaned back and looked over at Dee. "What kind of problem was with your registration?"

Dee looked like she didn't want to talk about it. Pushing the matter, Luke asked, "Did Mark want the car back?"

By Dee's reaction, he could tell that he was on the right track. Her cheeks blushed and once again her eyes filled with tears. Focusing on the freeway, Luke switched lanes. He was surprised when Dee spoke up. He thought he'd have to pry it out of her. "He reported it stolen."

Luke gripped the wheel. He never imagined Mark could stoop to something that low. Glancing over, he noted that Dee listlessly looked out the passenger window. Propping her elbow on the doorframe, she rested her chin in the palm of her hand and watched the cars zoom by. The passing cars quickly blurred together and confused her tired eyes. As she rubbed them, Luke once again noticed the dark circles that engulfed her usually bright eyes.

"What are you going to do?" Dee shrugged her shoulders but didn't turn away from the window. "Could you buy a new one?"

The thought of Dee's lack of funds caused her to draw away from the window. "Maybe a used one," she contemplated. "Funds are a little tight right now."

Luke wondered what she meant by that. Though Mark was the main provider in their relationship, Dee worked for the government and had a decent paying job. Pushing the matter, he asked, "How so?" He had never seen Dee with anything low-end, let alone used.

Once again, Dee began toying with the purse that sat in her lap. He could see a blush rising up her neck, spreading into her cheeks. "He drained out accounts." Her tone was low and ashamed. Luke was surprised at her lack of anger. If it were him, he'd be outraged.

"Did you have an account in only your name?"

Dee's blush deepened and he wondered how bad it was. Looking up, she stared straight ahead and avoided his eyes. Defending herself, she began, "I know Luke. It was stupid of me..."

Luke cut her off. He hated seeing her cut herself down, when obviously she was the victim. "I don't think it's stupid. When I get married, I hope my wife will trust me enough to share all of our finances. In fact, I'd be really hurt if she was secretly stashing funds."

Dee's jaw dropped and she stared at him. Luke could see her blush disappearing. Was it him, or was she sitting up a bit straighter? Luke wondered how far a bit of encouragement could go and decided to give it a try.

"As far as I'm concerned, you were a good girlfriend. It's just too bad that Mark's taking advantage of you."

"I never thought of it like that."

"You should." Luke knew he sounded blunt, but it was true. Shoulder checking, he signalled and merged into the next lane, taking the exit into their neighbourhood. Slowing down, he was glad to see that he was able to cheer her up a bit. "You could borrow Jeffrey's car until they get back. I'm sure they wouldn't mind."

Dee shook her head. "I had a bit of a mishap driving my step-dad's car in high school and I vowed to never drive anyone's car ever again."

"What happened?"

"I was waiting at a red light, when a car came behind me and rear-ended me. He was going so fast that he pushed me into the oncoming traffic. When all was said and done, six cars piled up and my car was a crushed tin can."

"Were you hurt?"

Dee nodded. "The Jaws of Life had to cut me out. I spent the last few weeks of my sophomore year in the hospital and the rest of the summer recovering."

"Thank God you weren't killed."

"That's what I said. My step-dad never saw it that way though."

Luke looked over. "I knew you didn't get along with your step-dad, but you never said why. Was he mad?"

"Furious."

"Why? Cars can be replaced. Daughters can't be."

"It wasn't insured."

Luke let out a low whistle. "Then I would be furious. At myself though."

"It takes a big man to own up to his mistakes. He never was that type of man. He never let it go. I couldn't wait to move out. That's why I rarely went home even though my parents lived in the same city."

"I always wondered why you preferred to spend Thanksgiving in an empty dorm building rather than at home."

"I remember the Christmas after Mark and I moved in together. He convinced me to take him to my parents' place for the holidays. Sure enough, my step-dad starts ranting about how much I cost him when I crashed his car. Mark got fed up and asked how much it cost to repair the car. When my step-dad told him how much, Mark wrote a check right then and there for that amount. He slapped it in my step-dad's hand and said he never wanted to hear about that matter ever again. It was the first time anyone stood up to him."

"Felt pretty good, hey?"

"Felt great! When we got home that Christmas, there was a Lexus sitting in our driveway. Mark handed me the keys and told me that it was my car and I could do whatever I wanted. He said I could even enter it in a demolition derby and he wouldn't care, because it was mine."

"Yet he took it back?"

"Kind of ironic, isn't it?"

Luke turned and pulled into his driveway. Parking his SUV, he turned off the ignition and stated, "Not ironic, just sad."

Dee slowly nodded as the reality sank in. Getting out of his car, Dee turned and headed for his backyard. Stopping she turned and faced Luke who was standing next to his car watching her. "Luke, thanks for everything. It feels really good to know someone's backing me up."

Her smile was genuine and her eyes brightened a little bit. "Anytime, Dee. I mean it." By his tone, Dee knew that he was serious. Nodding, Dee accepted his offer and headed home. After all that she had gone through, she was ready for a long, hot bath.

Chapter 7

Dee woke up to the beautiful melody of birds chirping outside of her window. The sun's bright rays broke through the thin slits between her blinds and stretched out across her bed. Rolling over, she was surprised to find that it was almost noon. Dee couldn't remember the last time she slept in so late. She knew she was exhausted, but she never would have imagined sleeping in that late.

Dee sat up and stretched, glad to find that her back wasn't as stiff and sore as it had been earlier in the week. Crawling out of bed, she peeked through her blinds. Across the street, the neighbour's children ran through the sprinkler and squealed with delight. The rose bush next to her window stretched towards the sun and the blooms were fully extended, sharing all of their soft pink glory. *Today's going to be a good day*, Dee thought to herself. Turning from the window, her stomach growled. Last night's long soak in the tub relaxed her, but also reminded her of how exhausted she was. Dragging her weary limbs out of the comfortable tub, she collapsed on her bed and fell asleep without eating any supper.

Pulling on her robe, Dee wandered into the kitchen. Pulling open the fridge door, the empty shelves stared back at her. Forty-three dollars didn't go very far, but it didn't bother Dee as much as it did yesterday. Grabbing a jar of peanut butter from the cupboard, she opened a bag of bread and withdrew the last two slices. Though it was not exactly a feast, Dee was surprisingly content. Sitting at the kitchen table, she turned on her laptop. As she ate her breakfast, Dee checked her bank account and was glad to see that true to their word, her loan came in last night. With how much she was approved for, she wouldn't have to even worry about a cash advance at work. Maybe she could buy a car. With that thought in mind, Dee finished her sandwich, logged off her computer and headed for the shower with an extra bounce in her step. Already today was looking up!

Allowing the shower to fully wake her up, Dee got dressed and headed for Luke's house. Feeling refreshed and energetic, she knocked on his back patio doors. Peering inside, she saw him sitting at his table looking over a file. When he looked up, she let herself in. Closing the file, Luke set it aside and stood smiling. He noted how bright her eyes looked and breathed a prayer of thanks for that. When she plucked some grapes from the bowl on the counter, he couldn't help but comment, "Looks like someone got a good night's sleep."

Dee smiled and sat down at the table. "I completely passed out last night. I just got up." Luke looked at his watch and smirked when he realized the late hour. Motioning towards his file, she asked, "Are you busy?"

Luke shook his head, "Just looking over a file to kill some time."

"You need to be outside."

Luke chuckled at her enthusiasm. The Dee he knew in college was beginning to shine through. Unlike the depressed and dejected woman he drove home last night, Dee now seemed confident and optimistic.

"Any suggestions?"

"Well," Dee said, standing up and helping herself to more grapes, "If you're not busy, I was going to see if you wanted to come car shopping with me?"

"Car shopping?" Luke was surprised, but glad to see that she was taking last night's incident head on. "Anything in mind?"

Dee shrugged her shoulders and popped a grape in her mouth. "I dunno. Something cheap and economical. I was hoping I could rely on your expertise."

"What do you consider cheap?" He had seen the house she lived in and the previous car she drove.

Once again, she shrugged. "I can afford up to five thousand."

Luke contemplated what they could get. Anything under five thousand would look like a tin can compared to what she used to drive. "That is cheap."

Dee tilted her head to the side and casually replied. "I'm not vain."

Luke nodded in agreement. Though she wore nice clothes and had a rich boyfriend, she was the most down to earth person he knew. "We drove past a used car dealership yesterday. They had a cute little Yaris for sale."

Dee scrunched up her nose. "Cute?"

"You said you weren't vain." Dee made a face and threw a grape at him. Laughing, Luke caught it and ate it. Standing up, he grabbed his keys and commented, "At least it isn't a mini-van."

Dee giggled and followed him out the door.

Dee couldn't believe how successful her afternoon was. Only having to visit two dealerships, Luke found her a great deal. Leveraging the price of a car at one dealership, Luke helped her coax a car salesman into lowering the price of a Civic at a different dealership. Though it was used and the miles were high, the car was in decent condition. Despite the cheap price, Dee felt like a million bucks. As she followed Luke back home, Dee inhaled and revelled in the new car scent. It was the smell of independence and Dee felt proud of her new purchase.

Parking her new car in the garage, Dee headed over to Luke's. By the time she got there, he was already firing up the barbeque. Turning, he faced her and smiled. "I think celebrating is in order. How does steak sound?"

Dee appreciated his generosity. After helping her buy a car, she ought to be taking him out for supper. She couldn't believe how humble he was. Mark on the other hand...

She stopped there. She didn't want to think about him. After all that she had gone through this past week, she just wanted to enjoy her one small victory: her car. Officially the first car that she ever owned, she didn't care if it was used or "economical" as the salesman kept saying. Mark wouldn't be seen with such a car, but Dee didn't mind. It made her feel strong. She made a decision all on her own. Though Luke helped her find it, he left the decision up to her and she appreciated it. Mark would have tried to change her mind. Being the control-freak that he was, he would just buy a car without her opinion and she would have to accept it.

Sitting on the garden bench, Dee watched as Luke came out of his kitchen, balancing a plate, a couple foil packages and two Sodas in his hands. He looked like a waiter as he expertly slid the patio door shut with his foot. Handing Dee a Soda, he returned to the barbeque. Lifting the lid, a sweet, smoky scent escaped and mingled with the gentle smell of apple blossoms. Dee inhaled deeply, enjoying the smell of charcoal. Putting all the food on the grill, Luke closed the lid and sat down next to Dee.

Cracking open his Soda, Luke sat back and said, "I don't want to brag, but we found a great deal today."

Dee smiled at his use of "we". He encouraged the idea of teamwork and didn't take full credit. In reality, it was Luke who found the car and bartered the price down. Unlike Mark, he wasn't saying, *I found you a great deal and now you owe me big time.* Luke was genuinely glad to help and showed no desire for compensation.

Dee observed a dragonfly as it settled on a nearby flower. "It feels good to own something of my own."

Luke nodded and played with the tab on his Soda can. Dee continued. "My step-dad was such a control freak. He controlled all of my decisions. Then I met Mark and he slowly weeded out any attempt to do things my way. I can't believe I fell for someone just like my step-dad. I really am my mother's daughter."

Luke thought of the picture of Dee's mom in her old dorm room. Dee truly was the spitting image of her mother. "Was Mark always like that?"

Dee shook her head and placed her can on the ground. "When I first met him, I admired how bold he was. He was a go-getter and didn't let anything stand in his way. When he wanted something, he got it and I loved that about him. I loved how resolute he was. Now it drives me crazy. Nothing stands in his way, not even me."

"I seem to recall you being pretty stubborn in college."

"We were identical. That's what drew us towards each other. Unfortunately, we were like magnets with the same charge. Rather than connecting, they repel from each other. In order to connect, one had to change its charge. In order to save our relationship, someone had to give."

"And that person was you."

Dee's eyes turned sad as she nodded. "I thought I was doing the right thing, swallowing my pride and going along with his desires."

A silence lingered between them as her shoulders began to drop with the weight of troublesome memories. Luke's heart thumped as he imagined taking her into his arms and telling her to forget about such a jerk. Would such an action comfort her? Would his loving arms help her to forget or make her long for Mark even more? Keeping his hands to himself, he played with the tab on his can. His eyes remained on the can, but his deep sigh caused Dee to pull away from her thoughts. Looking over, she wondered what caused Luke's face to look so grave. Perhaps it'd be best if she didn't talk about Mark and all their problems. Dee racked her brain, trying to think of something to say that would change the subject, but Luke continued on the subject. His voice was low and serious and it caused Dee to stare at him. "There's a fine line between submission and oppression. It's not your fault Mark crossed the line."

Dee's heart warmed, thankful that someone understood. "Then you don't think I'm weak and cowardly for letting myself get walked all over?"

Luke looked up and the sadness left his eyes. Instead, something powerful flashed through. Was it anger? Rage? His words were blunt and his tone was so serious that it surprised Dee. "It takes a strong woman to give up everything, especially her pride, in order to show how much she loves someone."

With that being said, he got up and checked the food in the barbeque. Flipping the steaks, he closed the lid but lingered next to the barbeque. He hated the words that came out of his mouth. He wished that he could tell her to forget about Mark. To tell her that he was a better man—that he would love and respect her more than Mark ever could. But he couldn't tell her any of that. Five years ago, when he left for Afghanistan, he left trusting that the Lord would take care of everything. He left before he tried to take matters into his own hands. He couldn't love Dee to the Lord. He had to trust that she would find her own way to believing and understanding Christ's love. Though he had hoped that she would find the Lord while he was gone, he never thought that he would come back to find her living with Mark.

Luke knew that he loved Dee, but he also knew that she wouldn't understand. He had to keep waiting, trusting that one day she would find Christ and that God would reward his patience with a godly wife.

Dee's words broke him away from his thoughts. "It's my fault you know."

Luke turned and stared at her. Their eyes locked. Her eyes read regret, his eyes shouted anger. Why did the victims always take the blame? Dee knew what he would say and continued before he could. "I knew better than to move in with him. But I did it anyways."

Luke groaned and returned to his seat next to her. How could he refute that? As much as he hated to admit it, she was right. All along she knew better. Now she had to endure the consequences of her disobedience. A forlorn tone took over her voice. "Luke, when you fall in love, do it right."

"*If* I fall in love."

133

Dee chuckled. "Luke, there's no denying it. One day you will get married. I've seen the heads turn when you walk by."

Luke smiled. He had felt the eyes following him at church. If the young women were discreet, their mothers were not. Getting up, Luke once again checked the barbeque and determined that the food was done cooking. Heading inside for some plates and cutlery, Luke casually called over his shoulder, "Supper's ready."

When he came back outside, he found Dee standing next to the patio set smirking at him. As he set the table, he tried to avoid her scrutinizing gaze. Turning to the barbeque, he slid the steaks onto a clean plate and silently handed them to her. He then retrieved the two foil packages and placed them on the table. Even when he took his seat, Dee continued to look at him with the same expression.

"What?" He asked.

Dee laughed. "For a big, tough soldier, you sure do get squirmy talking about your love life."

Luke looked up, feeling his ears turn warm. "I wasn't squirming."

"No, you just changed the subject."

"I thought that conversation was over." His voice sounded innocent but the expression on his face said otherwise.

"It's fine if you don't want to talk about it." Dee's tone was light-hearted and teasing. "We can talk about something else."

"I wasn't changing the subject." Luke's tone was defensive and Dee enjoyed seeing him so embarrassed. "What more can I say? You think I should get married. One day I will probably get married. Until then, there's not much to say. It wouldn't make a good story."

Dee leaned over her plate. "You're telling me that in the two years that you have been back, not a single girl has caught your eye?"

Luke's mouth turned dry and he took a long swig of his Soda. He continued to chug until he emptied the can. Dee smiled at his discomfort. Luke had negotiated his way out of numerous crises before, yet here he was stumbling for words. He hated how flustered he was becoming. "That's about it," he replied, trying to make his voice seem casual and at ease.

But Dee refused to back down. "How about Sarah?" She asked, mentioning a friend of Maggie's from church.

"Too young."

"Ok. How about Martha?"

"Too old."

Dee shot him a look. "Luke, she's the same age as you."

Luke coughed as he searched for an answer. "She looks older," he mumbled, embarrassed that he couldn't come up with a better excuse.

"Ok, how about her sister that just moved here."

Luke shook his head. "I don't know her."

"So, get to know her!"

Luke coughed again. He desperately needed something to drink. "I think we should pray before the food gets cold." Dee narrowed her eyes, but bowed her head when Luke bowed his. He rattled off a prayer and then jumped up. "I need a drink, are you good?"

Dee laughed at his discomfort. "I'm good." Before she finished the word "good" Luke raced into the house. Opening the foil packages, Dee helped herself to some potatoes, asparagus and steak. When Luke still didn't return, she filled up his plate. Closing the foil to keep the vegetables warm, Luke emerged with two more cans in his hands. Sitting down, he began cutting his steak and refused to look up.

"I'm not done with you yet," Dee stated.

Luke shrugged his shoulders and forked a piece of steak into his mouth.

"I've got all night." Luke looked up and studied her face. She was serious.

"You know that many single girls?"

Dee chuckled. "More than you know!"

Luke groaned and pointed towards her untouched plate. "Your food is getting cold."

"Fine," Dee said. She picked up her fork and knife and began slicing her steak. "Tell me about your job."

Luke groaned and leaned back. There were two things he didn't like to talk about. His love life, or the non-existence of his love life, and his job. He tried to act like this new subject didn't bother him. He would bore her with a description of a monotonous day and she would never ask again.

"What do you want to know?"

Dee swallowed and asked, "Well, what do you do?"

"I work for the government."

"Ok," Dee said slowly, "that tells me who you work for. It doesn't tell me what you do."

"I'm just tying up loose ends from the war."

"Such as?" Luke really wished she would let it go.

"Such as closing files and following up with soldiers as they re-integrate back into society."

"And that causes you to mysteriously disappear for weeks at a time?"

Luke looked up and saw that she was staring him down. She wasn't buying it. He once again shrugged his shoulders and cut off another piece of steak. "Sometimes I travel to other bases and work from there."

Dee put down her fork and leaned in. "Other bases call you away in the middle of the night?"

Luke stopped chewing and looked at her. She refused to break eye contact. How did she know about that? Jeffrey must have noticed more than he thought. He really didn't want to lie, but what he did was confidential. "Sometimes there is an emergency." He spoke slowly and seriously. "Sometimes a crisis prevents a soldier from re-integrating into society properly."

Luke's tone was getting cold, conveying that this subject was off limits. Though Dee wasn't convinced, she didn't want to push it. The last thing she needed was him getting upset at her.

"Well, whatever you do, I hope that you're safe." Her face read concern and Luke appreciated it. He knew that Maggie worried about his job. Of course she would vent her concerns to her best friend. Luke smiled in an attempt to reassure her. Changing the subject, he said, "So tell me about your job."

"Oh, you know," Dee toyed with her Soda can, "I work for the government. Pretty much the same thing that you do."

Luke laughed, glad that she understood his desire to change the subject. It felt so good to watch her relax and tease him. Her carefree laugh reminded him of when he met her in her freshman year. Endless times he would find

Maggie and Dee rolling on the floor in uncontrollable fits of laughter. He didn't care if the joke was immature or lame, he was just glad to see them so carefree and happy. Sometimes it was even entertaining to watch, like two small puppies playing at his feet.

Leaning back in his chair, Luke breathed in the clear air. The night was starting to cool off and it was refreshing after the hot afternoon. Dee, finishing her last bite, also leaned back and took a sip of her Soda. The look on her face was so serene that Luke wished he could capture it with a photograph. She conveyed such peace and contentment that one wouldn't have guessed the turmoil she recently endured.

"You look like you've found some peace," Luke commented, watching her face to see if it would become anxious.

Dee remained relaxed. "It's amazing what a hot bath and a good night's rest can do for a person."

"And some serious contemplation?" Luke pondered.

Dee nodded. Though her face became serious, it remained content. "I had an epiphany last night."

"And what did it reveal?" Luke gently asked, willing to coax everything out of her.

"That just because things are done Mark's way doesn't mean it's the right way." Dee reached up and brushed a stray strand of hair away from her face. Tucking it behind her ear, she continued, "I've been so busy trying to please Mark that I've forgotten what really matters. Right now, I need to take care of myself and hope that everything else will work out."

"What if Mark asks you to come back home?"

Dee smiled. "That's the beauty of it. He hasn't! All week I've been focusing on all the things that he has done to me. By concentrating on the negative I've missed all the blessings. I know Mark's trying to force me to return to him by cutting off all of my resources. Meanwhile, I have managed to withstand his assaults. I've been so worried about what to do if Mark asks me to come home, but he hasn't!"

Luke enjoyed seeing her so optimistic, yet his heart ached with a desire for her to know that those blessings were from God. He longed to tell her, but he was afraid that she would dismiss him, much like she had in the past. "Let's hope he doesn't ask, because I like having you for a neighbor."

Once again, a carefree giggle escaped from her mouth. "You're only stuck with me for one more week."

"You mean you wouldn't stay? I know it's not my house, but I wouldn't be surprised if Maggie and Jeffrey offered to let you stay a bit longer."

"I know for a fact that Maggie will insist that I stay longer. That's just how Maggie is." Luke nodded in agreement. "But they are newlyweds and deserve some privacy. Besides I'm a grown woman. I need to get an apartment of my own."

"You should look for an apartment in this neighbourhood, because with Jeffrey being a newlywed, I have a feeling I won't see him much and I could sure use the company."

Dee smiled sympathetically. Numerous times she had spent the night alone, waiting in an empty house for Mark to get home from work. "If you had a girlfriend, you wouldn't have that problem."

Groaning, Luke stood up and gathered the empty dishes. "We're not starting that conversation again." Dee laughed, gathered the leftover food and followed him inside.

Chapter 8

Dee applied a fresh layer of mascara to her eyelashes and studied herself in the mirror. Her eyes were bright and sparkled with hints of copper. Her face looked fresh and worry-free. The past few weeks had been extremely therapeutic. After Maggie and Jeffrey returned from their honeymoon, Dee spent a long night crying with Maggie. As she confessed everything that had happened with Mark, her friend soothed and comforted her. Dee didn't hide anything from her best friend and exposing her dark secrets helped alleviate some of the pain. It felt good to be truthful.

Maggie was a lifesaver and comforted her in ways that Luke couldn't. Immediately Maggie insisted that Dee stay and rent their basement suite. Although Dee was originally apprehensive about intruding on the newlyweds, their generosity was exactly what she needed. They respected her space as much as she respected theirs and this gave Dee a sense of independence. Using the back door as her private entrance, Dee seldom saw them. Rather than coming downstairs to check on Dee, Maggie would phone from upstairs to make sure a visit was all right. It was as if Dee still lived halfway across the city. Things were working out perfectly.

Luke served to be not only a great neighbour but also an enjoyable distraction. When the newlyweds were too busy to socialize, Luke's company was appreciated. Though he mysteriously disappeared for a few days after the happy couple returned from Fiji, he was more than glad to hang out with Dee. As he distracted her from her loneliness, she kept him from missing Jeffrey's usual visits.

Dee stood back and studied her face in the mirror. Hearing some noises upstairs, she assumed Jeffrey was home from work. Checking her watch, Dee realized she would be late if she didn't hurry. Putting on one more coat of mascara, Dee checked her make-up and fluffed her hair. Satisfied with how she looked, she hurried out of the bathroom, surprised to find someone standing in her living room.

Mark curiously eyed her simple suite and turned when she came out of the bathroom. He looked at her with a smug expression.

"M...Mark," Dee stuttered. "What are you doing here?"

"Well 'hello' to you too," he replied saucily.

Dee hated how comfortable he looked when her own heart raced. He looked overly confident as he took off his coat and laid it on the couch.

"How are you?" He asked, allowing his eyes to follow Dee's form from head to toe.

"Late," Dee replied, reaching for her purse on the kitchen counter. She didn't want to be rude but she felt nervous and uncomfortable with him in her living space.

Mark walked over to her, and with each nearing step Dee could feel her blood pressure rise. Fear crept up her spine as he seemed unfazed by her comment. His face remained smug and his tone was arrogant as he spoke.

"I want to talk." It was a statement rather than a suggestion. His eyes lingered longer than Dee liked.

Dee looked away and dug through her purse. "I'm sorry, but I have to go." Retrieving her keys she looked up, "Perhaps we could set up a time with a counsellor."

Dee watched his face for any signs of anger. He took another step forward and closed the gap between them. "Dee, Dee, Dee," he repeated. He took hold of her hands. His were cool and calm. Dee hoped he didn't notice how her own hands trembled. "You're the love of my life. We don't need a counsellor to work things out."

Taking the purse out of her hands, he put it on the counter and led her to the couch. Sitting down, he roughly pulled her down next to him. As he comfortably lounged, Dee sat up and inched over, increasing the gap between them. Mark seemed to notice her discomfort but didn't mind. In fact, it seemed to make him even more confident.

"I really do need to get going," Dee started. She hated how her voice trembled and faltered, exposing her anxiety. Mark just smiled and ignored her comment. He let his gaze linger on her figure.

"I've missed you." His voice was smooth and it gave her the chills. Dee felt anger rising up amidst her fear. His cool composure annoyed her. Frustration gripped her, detesting the way he just sauntered in after weeks of silence.

"You could have called." Dee wished her voice sounded as cool as his. Instead, it betrayed her and conveyed the hurt that his silence invoked.

"I wanted to give you space. Give you a chance to calm down and think." His words were smooth, but free from emotion.

Dee started to get up, but he grabbed her arm and pulled her down. Reaching over, he brushed her hair away from her temple. Dee cringed at the touch that usually caused her to melt into his embrace. "You said you wanted reconciliation. I'm here to reconcile."

Dee pulled away, hating how he used her words against her. It was true. She did want to reconcile, but not like this.

She wanted to meet in a neutral location where she could call the shots, not here in her home where she felt vulnerable.

"I do want to reconcile, but..." he cut her off before she could say, *not like this.*

"No buts," he murmured. "Let's put the past behind us."

Dee stood up, angry at how light heartedly he was handling such a serious situation. "It doesn't work like that," she exclaimed, exasperated.

Mark stood up and his tall height towered over her. His eyes became serious and determined. "It can, if you just let it."

"What about the other woman?" Dee almost shouted, losing all control. Why couldn't Mark see how serious things were? His indifference infuriated her.

"She's out of my life." He said it so nonchalantly. Dee studied his face to see if he meant it. She didn't know what to make out of his smug smirk. He once again stepped forward and sunk his hands into her hair. "I'm here to make things right with you, not her. Isn't that enough?" He then gazed at her lips expectantly. Dee wanted to resist, but before she could pull away, his mouth closed over hers.

His kisses used to calm her and assure her after a lonely night. This time it hurt and annoyed her. Dee grew stiff and frustrated, pushing him back.

Mark grew angry at her resistance. This was the second time she pushed him away, denying him. Never had she fought against his advances, until now. Furious at her growing defiance and the lack of control that he was experiencing, he gripped her arms tightly and kissed her hard. Though she struggled, his grip empowered him. Determined to gain control, he kissed her again.

Throwing all of her weight into him, she knocked him off balance, causing him to release her and stumble back a few steps. Livid, his eyes blazed. Dee had never seen him with that look before and nervously backed into the wall. Stalking towards her, Dee cowered against the wall that trapped her.

"Mark, please, don't..." she begged.

Once again, he gripped her arms so tightly that it hurt her. "You became mine on that sophomore night and you will always be mine," he snarled. Dee squirmed, desperate to break free from his hold, but his anger overpowered her fear.

"Hello?" Luke answered his cell phone.

"Luke!" His sister shouted, "Where are you?"

"I'm at home," Luke responded, curious of Maggie's frantic tone. "Is everything alright?"

"Yes," she said, though she didn't sound convincing. "No. I don't know. Dee hasn't shown up for our girls' night and I'm worried."

"She's probably just running late."

"I know, I know. I'm trying to be rational, but Dee never misses and I can't get a hold of her. She's not answering her phone."

"Did you try her at work?"

"Yes!" Luke couldn't believe how worked up his little sister was getting. "Can you check the house? See if she's there and make sure she's okay?"

"Yeah," he said, getting up from his computer chair. "I'll check."

"And call me as soon as you know something!"

"Yeah, yeah," Luke mumbled hanging up on his overreacting sister.

Luke knocked on the back door that Dee used as her entrance, but no one answered. Peering inside, the house seemed quiet and empty. Walking around the garage to the front of the house, he was surprised to see her car parked in the driveway. *She is home.* Turning around, he went back to the back door and knocked again. Still no answer. *Perhaps she's in the shower. Or wants to be left alone.*

The last thought didn't sit right with him. The last few weeks had been drama-free for Dee and he could see that she was healing and moving forward. Though Mark refused to contact her, he hadn't struck back at her since the car incident. Common sense told Luke that it could be anything, such as a bad day at work, but his gut said otherwise. Not being one to ignore his intuition, Luke dug out his keys and let himself inside. Standing in the doorway, Luke listened. He could hear movements downstairs. Peering down the steps, he called out her name. The lights were on, but Dee did not answer.

Luke didn't want to intrude on her private space, but concern gripped him. Flipping open his cell phone, he called her. He could hear her cell phone's muffled ring from somewhere in the basement but she didn't pick up. Something wasn't right. Dee wasn't the type of person to screen her calls. If she didn't want to talk, she'd politely say, *now's not a good time.*

Luke called out her name one more time, but when she didn't appear at the bottom of the stairs he headed down. He found her stuffing an armful of bedding into the washer. She was casually dressed in a pair of black yoga pants and an oversized t-shirt. Her hair was wet from a recent shower. By the looks of it, she had no intention of going out. Slightly turning to her left, she picked up a sheet off of the floor and threw it in the wash. She saw Luke out of the corner of her eye but ignored him, wishing that he would just leave.

"Dee," Luke paused hesitantly. "Are you okay?"

Dee reached up and pulled the laundry detergent out of the overhead cupboard. "I'm fine," she muttered with an edge to her voice. She poured out enough soap for a few loads of laundry. Closing the lid, the washer began spinning the linens and Dee willed the rhythmic sound of the washer to push away her thoughts. A single tear broke free from her eye and rolled down her cheek. Biting her lip, she tried to control herself.

Luke watched as she stood at the washer. Her back remained turned to him, but her shoulders slowly began to shake. Her posture slumped and nothing about her stance resembled the confidence that Dee was slowly developing over the past few weeks. Luke walked over to her and put his hand on her shoulder. Dee cringed and folded her arms, closing herself off from him. When she refused to acknowledge him, Luke grabbed both of her shoulders and gently turned her so that she was facing him. Her face, though freshly scrubbed, was stained by the streaks her tears left behind.

She bit her lip, in an attempt to stop its trembling. Luke tried to meet her eyes, but she looked away. He glanced at her folded arms that fended him off and noticed the red dots that were slowly turning into bruises. Taking her hand, he tenderly turned her wrist so he could see better and found the fingerprints that remained from a harsh grip.

"Mark?" He asked in a low voice. Taking into account the bedding that she was so desperate to cleanse, Luke understood the nature of Mark's visit. Anger rose inside of him. Dee's quiet sob confirmed what he suspected and she trembled so hard that he thought she would collapse. Pulling her close he wrapped his strong arms around her and supported her as her body grew weak. Sinking one hand into her soggy curls, he let her tears soak his shirt and he murmured into her ear. When the tears refused to subside, he led her to the couch, sat down and pulled her close. She caved into his embrace and Luke held her like a small child. Brushing her curls aside, he studied her eyes and ached at how lost she looked. All the confidence that she had gained over the past few weeks had been wiped away and replaced with hurt and shame. The tears flowed and her shoulders trembled. Luke let her burry her head into his shoulder and he rested his cheek on her damp curls.

Luke's concern outweighed his anger and he gently stroked her cheek, willing his touch to sooth and comfort her. The sobs disappeared, but the tears continued to flow, followed by the occasional gulp or hiccup. His cell phone vibrated in his pocket and Luke remembered his concerned sister. Lifting his hand from Dee's soft cheek, he sent Maggie a text message: *She's fine. Just a late night at work.* Turning his ringer off, he then tossed his phone onto the coffee table and wrapped his free arm around Dee in a strong embrace. He wouldn't blame Dee if this was a secret she would want to keep from Maggie. Some things were too personal to share.

Luke held her for what felt like hours. Eventually her tears subsided and he could feel her body relax. As her breathing deepened, Luke found her sleeping in his arms. It took true pain to cause a person to cry herself to sleep. Wriggling his left arm free, Luke carefully slid away. Easing her head down onto the couch, Luke stood up and searched for some clean linens. Finding a sheet and a comforter in one closet, Luke went into Dee's bedroom and made up her bed for her.

Returning to the living room, Luke gently gathered her into his arms and carried her to the bedroom. Easing her out of his arms and onto the bed, he tenderly pulled the comforter up and tucked her in. He leaned forward and kissed her forehead, praying over her. As much as Luke wanted to help her, he felt helpless. Some scars ran so deep only God could heal them and Luke prayed that God would help her when he couldn't.

Getting up, he left her bedroom and switched the laundry from the washer to the dryer. Perhaps that would ease the pain if she didn't have to deal with the laundry and its horrific reminders. Turning off all of the lights, Luke let himself out and locked the door behind him.

As he headed towards his backyard, Luke saw Maggie pull into the driveway and prayed that she would leave Dee alone for the night. Luke went inside his house without his sister even noticing. He didn't want to talk to her. Maggie was too perceptive and would immediately realize something was wrong.

Crawling into bed, Luke knew he wouldn't sleep. When he was in Afghanistan he came into contact with many victims of the sex trade. Though he was disgusted with the men who sold their sisters, daughters and even wives, none of it affected him so personally. Dee's attack really hit home and made him realize how vulnerable she was. This wasn't a war-torn country. This was the United States of America and she was someone he truly cared for.

Luke's anger grew and he got up and stalked across his room. His temples throbbed and he thought about going to Mark's house and avenging Dee. He would...would what? In Afghanistan he was trained to shoot and kill any terrorist threat. Here Mark was, terrorizing his girlfriend in a free country where Luke was not allowed to harm Mark in any way.

Luke crawled back into bed and tried to calm his thoughts. He thought of Dee, peacefully nestled in her bed. Her trauma induced sleep unconsciously set her free from today's pain. She would be safe until she woke up. Then the memories would continue to haunt her.

Luke's body longed to go back and hold her, to ensure that no nightmares interrupted her rest. He thought of how her damp curls and soft skin felt in his hands. He wanted to kiss every bruise that slowly developed on her arms. To kiss away her tears and tell her how much he cared. But she was vulnerable and didn't know the Lord, so he kept such desires to himself.

Luke rolled over and stared at the clock. Five AM. Sleep had evaded him most of the night, and by the looks of it, this early morning would be no exception. Stretching, his stiff muscles were evidence of the tossing and turning that took place last night. Luke had spent hours racking his brain, trying to come up with words that would make Dee see that only God could help her. Yet no ideas came. No matter how hard he prayed for wisdom and advice, he was still lost and confused. He didn't know how to help, let alone if he could help. Usually the one to rush out and save the day, Luke's helplessness made him feel useless and it frustrated him.

Dragging his stiff body out of bed, Luke threw on some shorts and a long sleeved t-shirt. Tying up his runners, Luke set out on a long run through his neighbourhood. The dew was fresh on the ground and the streets were quiet and sleepy. Nobody was out this early on a Sunday morning and Luke embraced the solitude. He sprinted, hoping the exercise would clear his mind. So many thoughts were spinning at the same time and he didn't know where to start. The cold air stung as his lungs panted against the fast pace and Luke slowed down to a brisk jog. Thick clouds blocked the sunrise from showing and Luke was glad. The grey sky matched his mood.

Luke ran for an hour. As his legs strained against the hard pavement, his mind remained congested and confused. Turning home, Luke was disappointed to find that the run did not help. Though it worked his muscles, it did not ease his brain's overload.

Stopping on his front lawn, Luke sank down into the wet grass and as he stretched, he prayed for guidance. In Afghanistan, the Lord was with him, constantly guiding him through numerous conflicts. No matter how chaotic things got, Luke always seemed to know what to do because God was there leading the way. But today the Lord seemed too far away to hear his prayers. No answers came and Luke was unaccustomed to such silence.

Pulling himself up, Luke headed inside. Maybe a hot shower would help.

Dee woke up to a soft knock at her door. Sitting up, she felt disoriented. Crawling out of bed, she reached for her robe, only to realize that she was still wearing her clothes from the night before. As memories of the previous night accosted her, Dee stood there numb and confused. Though she remembered the terror, she did not remember going to bed. Again, a gentle knock sounded from behind her door.

Opening the door a crack, she was surprised to see Luke waiting on the other side. Turning to view her clock, she was surprise to read 6:09 AM. "Luke," she started, "It's..."

"I know," he interrupted. "It's early. But I wanted to talk to you before Maggie does. I'm making us some coffee."

Dee could hear the coffee pot gurgling in the kitchen. She nodded and closed the door. Rooting through her closet, she pulled out a sweater. As she slid her arms through the sleeves, she couldn't help but notice the dark bruises. The nightmare returned as she remembered Mark's aggressive grip. The rest flooded into her mind and she shook her head, trying to erase the memories. She had taken a scalding hot shower in an attempt to purge her skin of Mark's hostile touch, but the bruises served as haunting reminders that lingered on her skin. She also tried to scour her bed of any reminders by washing her bedding, but the images in her mind remained. Tears rose but she then remembered Luke's gentle embrace. He had held her until she could cry no more. She didn't want anyone to know, but as always, he was there. Rather than zipping up her sweater, she pulled it around her tightly and pushed her thoughts aside.

She found Luke pouring coffee into two mugs on the kitchen table. He motioned for her to have a seat and then returned the pot to the coffee maker. Taking a seat, he studied her face. Dee stared into her mug, trying to avoid his scrutinizing glance. He noticed how swollen and red her eyes were, thought the dark circles had faded a little bit. Taking her hand into his own, he pulled up the loose sleeve of her sweater. The bruise on her wrist had deepened and grown. Four large dots exposed the handprint that Mark had left on her forearm. Did she fight back? Did she kick and scream? Or did she cry and beg him not to? Luke pulled down her sleeve and hid the incriminating evidence, but still held her hand.

"I wish none of this happened."

Luke's tone was so sincere it made Dee cry. Why couldn't she trust Mark like she could trust Luke? All of Mark's lies swirled around in her head and she felt ashamed for falling for them. His most recent lie hurt the most. Shame crept up as she remembered the glimmer of hope she felt when he said he was no longer seeing his girlfriend. She was a fool for believing him. After the deed was done, she had lied in bed, vulnerable and violated. She cowered beneath the sheets feeling degraded and dishonoured. His phone rang and he got up to answer it. His tone was cold and angry, but soon warmed up. She overheard his all too familiar words, "Your apology is accepted." Before he hung up, he affectionately murmured, "I love you too. I'll see you soon." Gathering his clothes he left without saying another word, leaving her dejected and ashamed. She was nothing but a pawn, used to incite jealousy and an apology from his disobedient girlfriend.

Luke stroked Dee's hand, pulling her away from the painful memory. Taking a sip of the hot coffee, the strong beverage warmed her from the inside out.

Luke tried again. "Just because he is your boyfriend doesn't give him the right."

Dee nodded and spoke before he could continue. "I'm going to take care of it." Her words surprised Luke. "I'm not going to let him come into your sister's home. I'm not going to put Maggie at risk."

He appreciated Dee's desire to protect his baby sister. He just wished that she would do it for herself. Luke squeezed her hand and this drew her eyes from her coffee mug to his own eyes. "I'll help you," he assured her.

Tears filled the eyes that had bravely fought them. "You already have," she whispered.

Luke's cell phone vibrated, interrupting their private conversation. Looking at the caller ID, Luke frowned. Getting up, he walked into the hallway before he answered. His voice was low and quiet. Dee wrapped her hands around her hot mug and willed her mind to go blank. Looking at the clock she was surprised that someone would call so early on a Sunday morning. Minutes later Luke returned with a frown on his face. Though he took a seat, he sat on the edge of his chair as if he were to get up immediately.

"I'm sorry, Dee, but I have to go." His face was genuine and full of remorse.

"Duty calls?" Dee asked, referring to his mysterious job. Luke nodded. Why would he be called in so early on a Sunday morning? Dee searched his face for answers, but she was too tired to question him.

"Maggie was worried about you. I told her you had to work late. That's your cover story in case you don't want to tell her."

Dee nodded, thankful that Luke would keep this a secret, even from his sister. "Thank you," she whispered in a wavering voice. His simple nod seemed to convey *you're welcome*. Getting up, he headed for the door. Dee got up and followed him. Opening the door, a cool breeze wafted inside.

"It'll be cool today. You can wear a sweater to cover your bruises," Luke noted. Dee nodded and rested her hand on his arm before he left.

"Be careful, Luke." Her words echoed her suspicions of his "desk" job. Luke wrapped his arms around her and buried his cheek into her soft curls.

"You too," he murmured. Stepping back, he took one more look at her and disappeared out the door.

Wandering back downstairs, Dee finished her coffee. The house was silent as the newlyweds slept in. Dee was thankful for their generosity, putting in an extra effort to focus on the good. Though yesterday's attack had been devastating, Dee had much to be thankful for. She hoped that by focusing on such blessings she would make it through the next few days.

Finishing her coffee, Dee got up and went to go finish last night's laundry. She cringed at the thought of having to touch the sheets that she was violated in, but thought it would be best to get it over with. Opening the washer, she was surprised to find it empty. Even more surprising was the fact that the dryer was also empty. Walking over to the closet, Dee found the linens folded and neatly stacked. Had Luke finished her laundry in an attempt to spare her some pain?

Wandering back into the kitchen, Dee filled her coffee cup and sank into the overstuffed leather couch. Luke was such a mystery to her. He didn't fit the stereotype of a big, tough, emotionally-detached soldier. Instead, he was kind and compassionate. He was even domestic, going out of his way to do her laundry. Dee wondered how long he had been in her suite. He must have gotten up especially early to finish her laundry, make coffee and squeeze in an early morning chat. Or had he spent the night, standing guard? Dee thought of the bed she woke up in, sheeted and blanketed. Had she fallen asleep? Did Luke make her bed and then carry her to her room? Dee slowly began to realize not only how sensitive Luke was, but also perceptive. He seemed to think of everything, even the conversation that would soon follow with Maggie.

Chapter 9

"How was the trip?" Juan asked, making the cold, desolate mountains of Afghanistan sound like a resort.

Luke frowned as he recollected the disappointing mission. He had spent months working with intelligence, surveying and watching resistance groups that existed in Afghanistan. When satellites pinpointed a camp, the special tactics unit had hoped to find some soldiers who had been taken prisoner during the war. By the time his team made it there, the camp was abandoned and all they found were the corpses of some locals. For two years Luke had been organizing and executing missions that liberated American prisoners and rescued hostages. Very few missions failed and it had been a long time since they turned up a dead end. Luke felt discouraged, wondering how many prisoners would survive much longer. His thoughts traced back to his comrade, Lieutenant Wayne McCabe. Having disappeared near the end of his tour, Luke took on this job with the sole purpose of liberating his mentor and friend. Luke had felt so close and the failed mission frustrated him.

"You didn't miss anything but dirt and dead bodies." Juan accompanied Luke on most missions but opted to stay home this time and serve as analysis from the base.

"Things heated up here while you were gone."

Luke raised his eyebrows. Since all that they had found was a dead end, Luke and his team had spent a lot of time tracking, trying to pick up a lead. Though most missions only lasted a few days, this one carried on for nine. With the nature of Luke's job, quite a bit could happen in the course of one week. Juan's statement perked his interest. "How so?"

"Well," began Juan, enjoying the spotlight, "Whenever I pull up a file for you, it is red-flagged, alerting me every time the file is updated."

"Which file are we talking about?"

"The Kensington one."

Luke's mouth went dry. Every night that he was away he fell asleep wondering about Dee. He thought of the bruises on her arms and the emotional damage she was suffering through. He had hoped she was healing. Had things escalated while he was gone? Things would have to be pretty bad to be any worse.

"How bad?" Luke feared the response but had to know.

"That *chica* of yours in one tough cookie." Juan's words made Luke imagine Dee lying in the hospital in intensive care. Had she survived the wrath of Mark's temper? Juan continued, "And brave. She finally pressed charges against ex."

Luke wondered if he heard right. Ex? Did Dee finally make a break? "What were the charges?"

Juan opened the file and read, "Two counts of aggressive assault, one count of sexual assault."

Luke was proud of Dee for acknowledging the fact that Mark had raped her. Many women would be too ashamed to admit it. "Did he retaliate?"

"I'd say." Luke's eyes grew large. So, the worst was yet to come. He braced himself, afraid of what news Juan might share. "He threw everything of hers on the front lawn and lit it on fire. The firefighters and police were called in and he was given a hefty fine."

"That's it?" It seemed like a nothing compared to all Dee had been through. Perhaps he would finally leave her alone.

"Dee's communicating through her lawyers, trying to recover her lost finances. Hopefully she will get it back before he gets charged with tax evasion and fraud." Luke took the file from Juan and read the police report Dee had made. Maybe it was a blessing in disguise. Luke's thoughts travelled back to Dee, wondering how she was coping. He had a feeling she would be devastated, even though she deserved to be free from someone as dangerous as Mark. A smile crept across his face as he imagined her newfound freedom. Dee could finally start all over.

Juan sat on the corner of Luke's desk and faced him. Folding his arms, he struck a casual pose and asked, "Since this *chica* is a friend of yours, I was wondering if you would introduce me to her? You know, with her being single and all. She's going to need a shoulder to cry on."

Luke narrowed his eyes. Though Juan was his best friend, there was no way he would let him make a pass at Dee. Juan laughed, thoroughly enjoying the fact that he had gotten under Luke's skin. Standing up, he patted Luke on his shoulder and said, "Just think about it." Luke knew his friend was taunting him, but the idea of Dee with another man bothered him. He just hoped Juan didn't notice.

Chapter 10

The snowflakes gently swirled by as Dee opened her trunk. She couldn't believe how much snow DC had gotten. Already a good inch of snow blanketed the ground, making a soft crunch underneath her boots. The delicate flakes melted as they hit her face. Though it was snowing again, the weather was mild and comfortable.

Luke appeared from the backyard as Dee tossed her suitcase into her trunk. It was December 23, and Dee raced out of the office as soon as lunch hit. Hurrying home, she packed and was now ready to spend the holidays alone, in a cozy cabin in Shenandoah National Park.

"You sure you want to spend the holidays all by yourself?" Luke asked again. Numerous times he had invited her to join him and his parents in Alexandria. Though she considered the Bardens to be like family, she was looking forward to some isolation. Since the break up six months ago, Dee revelled in her newfound independence. It wasn't like she was sitting in her basement suite all by herself while

Maggie and Jeffrey vacationed in Hawaii for Christmas. No, she was going to enjoy nature and the solitude it had to offer.

"My mom makes a great turkey..." Luke continued his campaign of persuasion.

Dee shook her head. She knew what a good cook his mom was and that made it awfully tempting. "Christmas with you and your family would be a lot of fun, but I need to be alone. Do some soul searching over the holidays."

Luke's face grew sombre and he nodded in understanding. "You've handled everything so well. Sometimes I forget how hard the past few months have been on you." He looked down and noticed the snowshoes carefully packed in her trunk. Raising one eyebrow, he gave her a questioning glance.

"If it keeps snowing like this, I'll be able to do some snowshoeing. It's been too brown the past couple of years."

"Won't be any tours over the holidays," Luke commented.

Dee smiled, "That's the beauty of it." She was off until New Years and had full intentions of avoiding as many people as possible.

Luke knew she was athletic because she was on the college track team, but he never would have imagined her being a snowshoe enthusiast. Yet, now that he thought about it, it made sense. It seemed like everyday he was learning something new about her and he loved it. With Mark out of the picture, she was really opening up and blossoming into a strong, determined woman. She was also opening up to discussions about faith and numerous times Maggie was able to share the gospel with her.

Dee closed her trunk and walked over to the driver's side door. Opening her door, Dee turned to say good-bye. Luke casually leaned against her car. His face was serious and reaching into his jacket he withdrew a package. Handing it to Dee, he gently said, "Merry Christmas."

Dee smiled and took the package, pulling back the wrapping paper. In her hands laid a well worn Bible. Flipping through it, she could see notes scribbled in the margins. "For all your soul searching," he murmured and she gave him a quick, friendly hug.

"I'm going to miss you."

His voice was low and husky and affected Dee in a way she needed to figure out. Over the past few months, she had spent an increasing amount of time with Luke and would miss his company. But if Maggie was right, she needed more than just another man's love. She needed this holiday and some privacy to figure things out and to see if Maggie was right. She nodded back, knowing that she would be thinking of him quite a bit over the holidays. Getting into her car, Luke leaned in to say his final goodbye.

"If you get lonely, or start to go stir crazy, the invitation is always open."

Dee put on her seatbelt and smiled. "Thanks Luke. Have a Merry Christmas."

"You too. Drive safe." Luke then closed the door and watched her as she backed out of the driveway and drove out of sight.

Dee's heart warmed at his protectiveness. It didn't smother her. Instead, it just showed how much he cared. As much as Dee would have liked to spend the holidays with him, she knew she needed some time away to figure out her feelings for him. She cared immensely for him, but was it as a friend, a brother figure, or something more?

Dee focused on the roads as the snowflakes danced in her headlights. One thing for sure, Luke affected her in a way she never expected, especially so soon after her break up. She thought trust wouldn't come easily, but after the circumstances that he had helped her through, she couldn't help but trust him. He was so different from Mark; so gentle and caring. As well, he was respectful and considerate. Mark was too arrogant to be such things, yet Luke was more of a man than Mark would ever be.

Dee momentarily squeezed her eyes shut and then focused on the road. She didn't want to have bitter thoughts of her ex-boyfriend. She also did not want to throw herself at

Luke just because he was everything that Mark wasn't. She looked forward to her days of solitude. She intended on spending it in search of guidance, and if God provided her a sense of direction, then she would know that He really wanted her to be part of His family. She didn't want to rush into a relationship. As well, she wanted to do it the right way this time. In order to do so, she would be patient and silent, waiting until she knew what to do.

As soon as Dee got to her cabin, she lit a fire and watched as the snow flew furiously outside. The last few miles of driving were treacherous as the snow thickened and flew in all directions. It was as if it couldn't make up its mind and Dee smiled at that thought, letting the snow relate to the way that she felt.

Pulling herself away from the window, she grabbed Luke's Bible and pulled the chair closer to the fire. Settling in, she absentmindedly flipped through, reading the private thoughts that were jotted down in the margins. She marvelled at his unswerving faith. He was so sure. Dee had grown up in a Christian home—her Aunt and Uncle were even missionaries—but she never heard someone talk to God on such a personal level. In the margins, Luke talked to God, thanking and praising Him and occasionally asking Him questions.

Dee knew that Maggie and Luke loved the Lord and longed for her to know Him as they did. In a way she wanted to know Him the same way. She was tired of hypocritical Christians, such as her step-father, and she found Luke and Maggie's faith authentic and refreshing. The problem was the Church had a long list of sins and many of them Dee committed, especially after she met Mark. Yet, Maggie was adamant that God forgave all sins, big or small. Dee knew that she couldn't get her virginity back, let alone her innocence, but if Maggie was right, she could get forgiveness and perhaps that would make things better.

Dee flipped to a random page and read, "Husbands, love your wives, just as Christ loved the church and gave Himself up for her." In the column Dee read Luke's personal thoughts, "Lord, let me be a shining example of your love. Every time my wife looks at me, let her see Your love." Dee thought about what Luke's love looked like. He protected and cherished his sister. Dee had her rotten moments, yet he showed her nothing but kindness, compassion and forgiveness. She admired everything about Luke. If he was mirroring God's love every time he interacted with her, then she wanted the real deal. She wanted true love and forgiveness, not just an example of it.

Then it hit her. With tears streaming down her cheeks she begged God for His forgiveness. She asked Him to love her, like Luke had but more, and promised to love Him in return. As she confessed her inequities a huge weight lifted from her shoulders. Her mind seemed clear and the dull ache in her heart was replaced with a burning joy. Immediately she knew that she made the right decision and poured into Luke's Bible; wanting to know more, wanting to know everything.

Dee helped Maggie put out some treats in preparation for their New Year's Eve party. New Year's Eve: the day before Dee's twenty-fifth birthday. She felt a little odd, feeling too old to be single, yet too young to be in a serious relationship. Either way, Dee felt confident and eagerly anticipated the year to come. Maggie had returned from Hawaii absolutely glowing and Dee suspected there was a small one growing inside. Dee, in turn, returned from the mountains feeling refreshed and at peace, knowing that God was in control. As long as she let Him remain in control, she knew that things would work out.

As Dee sliced cheese and layered it on a platter, she listened to her friend gab about the guests who would soon arrive. Maggie gushed on and on about Dylan, a friend of Jeffrey's from the hospital. Dee had met him a few times and had to admit that he seemed like a nice enough guy. However, Maggie was not subtle about her intentions of setting them up. Though Dee felt comfortable hanging out with the newlyweds and Luke, she felt awkward when the foursome included Dylan instead of Luke. Despite the fact that Maggie thought the world of Dylan, Dee did not know him well enough to trust him yet. Without trust, she had no intentions of building an intimate relationship with him.

Dee remained silent as Maggie continued to gab, switching subjects every few minutes. She enjoyed seeing her friend so happy, basking in the love that Jeffrey provided her. Dee couldn't remember being like that when she was with Mark. Her relationship with Mark was so serious, so goal driven. It was more like a business transaction, constantly trying to maximize all of its potential. She wondered what it would have been like if they were more like Maggie and Jeffrey, with God as their foundation.

Dee heard voices at the door and assumed that Jeffrey was home from work. Though they were not expecting guests for another hour, Dee wondered who was with him. Was it Luke? Sometimes it seemed like he spent more time in their house than in his own.

Maggie wiped her hands dry on a tea towel and quietly squealed in Dee's ear, "That must be Dylan!"

Dee rolled her eyes at Maggie's obvious attempt to set them up. As Maggie rushed out to greet them, Dee cowered in the kitchen. She didn't want to seem rude; she just didn't want to seem interested. She wasn't going to lead him on, only to find out he's not what she was looking for. She didn't know what she was looking for. She didn't even know she was looking!

Dee sighed and continued cutting a pile of cheese. Dylan came into the kitchen as the newlyweds remained in the front room, murmuring about their day. As his eyes traveled from her head to her toe, silently appraising her, his not-so-subtle approach annoyed her. She knew she looked good. She was tall, slender and attractive, but that didn't give him the right to blatantly ogle her. She was dressed modestly and wished that he would be modest with his stares.

Though she acknowledged his presence with a nod, she turned her attention to the pile of cheese and pretended to be interested as she layered them on the tray. Dylan sat on the other side of the island and watched her.

"How was your Christmas?" His tone was earnest and seemed genuinely interested. It didn't sound like he was asking just to be nice.

Dee tried to be friendly, though she felt awkward and uncomfortable. Even though Dylan was a Christian, she didn't feel close enough to share the joy of her newfound faith. It was too intimate to share with him. Other than telling Luke, Maggie and Jeffrey, she kept it to herself. "It was great," she replied nonchalantly. "It snowed the entire time! How was your holiday?"

Dylan proceeded to tell her about his timeshare in Florida. She tried to be interested, though she was not impressed. Dylan reminded her of Mark when it came to material wealth. He drove a fancy car, had a fancy top floor condo and had no qualms when it came to bragging about it. She wondered what he would think about the tiny cabin she stayed in. He probably assumed she stayed at the resort.

Maggie came into the kitchen and beamed when she saw them chatting. She interrupted them by saying, "Dee, I hope you don't mind but I ran out of room in my fridge and put some stuff in yours. Would you mind bringing it up?"

Dee shrugged her shoulders nonchalantly. Of course she didn't mind. Technically speaking, it was Maggie's fridge. Heading for the stairs, Maggie turned to Dylan and said, "Would you be a dear and give her a hand?"

Dee winced at her friend's conniving plan. She continued to walk out the kitchen as Dylan followed her. Being tricked into going on "double dates" was one thing, but inviting Dylan into her personal space bothered her. Her basement suite was supposed to be her refuge from men, especially men she didn't want hanging around her. Though Luke was more than welcome to visit her, she felt uncomfortable being alone with Dylan.

Heading straight for the fridge, Dee felt cold and rude. She would be much more relaxed if Maggie didn't meddle so much. Opening the fridge, Dee saw a couple trays of sweets. That was all. There was so little that one person could manage. Dee felt frustrated and worried what Dylan would think. Would he think that she planned this with Maggie so that she could be alone with him? She could feel a blush rising up her neck. Hoping that the fridge would cool her down, she handed Dylan a tray. Grabbing the second tray, she closed the fridge door and turned. She found Dylan standing right behind her. Having set his tray on the counter, he took the tray out of her hands and placed it next to his. Dee hated how close he was standing and inched along the counter. He stepped closer, blocking her escape route and smiled expectantly at her. She distrusted the look on his face. It resembled Mark so much, with its smug confidence.

"We should probably head upstairs," Dee said, desperate to duck out of this uncomfortable situation.

Dylan didn't move. He continued to gaze at her. "I was hoping we could talk." By the look on his face, he *expected* to talk. Dee wondered if a girl had ever turned him down before. She seriously doubted it.

"I've enjoyed getting to know you over the past while," he continued.

"I...uh..." Dee stuttered, unsure of what to say. If she told him she didn't want to have this conversation, would he listen?

He inched closer and Dee felt her hands tremble. She wished he didn't notice, but immediately he placed his one hand over hers in an attempt to calm her. It made things worse.

"I know you just got out of a messy relationship. I won't rush things. I just want to get to know you better." His speech was smooth and well rehearsed. Dee wanted to believe that he would take things slow, but the way he stared expectantly at her lips said otherwise.

What would he do if she said no? Would he back off? Or would he grip her tightly? What if she pushed him away? Would he strike her? The last thought caused her whole body to shake. She bit her lip and wished that her heart wouldn't race so anxiously. She knew the type: conceited and arrogant. They didn't handle rejection well. She had a feeling he wouldn't respect her boundaries.

He let go of her hand, but rather than backing off, he sunk both hands into her hair. She winced at his intimate touch, something that she did not initiate nor welcome.

"It's okay," he murmured, confident that his tone would soothe her. A single tear rolled down her cheek. Rather than being alarmed, he gently wiped it away and gazed even more

177

intently at her. Dee wanted to scream, but her breath stopped and choked her. He slowly leaned in, but Dee pulled away as far back as she could.

She heard footsteps come down the stairs, halting at the base in the living room. Dylan moved back and Dee breathed a prayer of thanks for this timely interruption. Looking over his shoulder, she found Luke standing there, obviously embarrassed for walking in on their private moment. He looked as if he were going to head back upstairs, but when he caught the upset expression on Dee's face, his glare said enough. Picking up on Luke's protectiveness, Dylan grabbed the trays of goodies and headed upstairs without a word.

As Dylan disappeared, Dee slowly exhaled. She had no idea how long she had been holding her breath. Feeling lightheaded, she sunk to the floor and the tears began to flow. She felt embarrassed, but she couldn't gain control of her emotions. Pulling her knees up, she sank her head into her knees, wanting to hide her humiliation.

Luke walked around the corner and eyed her as she sat on the floor. Her shoulders quivered. Was it from anger or fear? He approached her and sat on the floor next to her. Putting his arm around her, he drew her close. Dee surrendered and curled into his comforting embrace.

"It's not the first time a guy has tried to kiss you." Luke thought back to the freshmen that practically lined up to ask her out.

"I know I should feel flattered."

"But you don't." He said it as a statement, but his tone seemed to question why.

"I feel like such a coward." Dee leaned forward and wiped away her tears. Luke stroked her back in a soothing manner. "It was his approach. He was so arrogant! As if he expected me to swoon at his feet. And he knew I was uncomfortable, but he kept pushing my limits." She switched her tone to a mocking one, "To divide and conquer...he's so much like..." she cut herself off. It wasn't fair to compare him to Mark. Though Dylan was conceited he was nowhere near as bad as Mark.

Luke could feel the anger rising as her back tensed. He knew where she was going with that thought. No wonder she panicked. Just like Mark, he was forcing himself onto her, only this time it was in a PG manner. Luke tried to derail that train of thought. "He's not your type," he offered.

"Arrogant jerks?" She snorted sarcastically, "No, they are not my type, yet I seem to attract them easily enough."

"Dee, you attract anyone that comes into your sight." Luke's low tone caused Dee to suck in her breath. She looked at him, trying to figure out of it was a compliment or a come-on. Luke averted his eyes and tried to change the subject. "What is your type?"

Dee shrugged, unsure of herself. "I dunno, someone nice."

"Nice is too general. Come on Dee, something specific. Something you can't find in any guy."

Dee laughed. She felt like Luke was interviewing her for a dating service. "How about a professional athlete? Does that narrow things down?" She joked.

Luke narrowed his eyes and became serious. "How about trust?"

Dee grew quiet and pondered his words. "Trust doesn't come so easily anymore."

"What about me? Do you trust me?"

Dee sat up and leaned her head against the cupboard door. Looking at Luke, she ignored his stern gaze and exasperatedly exclaimed, "Luke, if I can't trust you then there is no hope for this world."

Luke tilted his head back and gazed at the ceiling. "You know what my greatest regret is?" Luke's nervous tone caused Dee to turn her head and stare. Always being so confident and strong, Dee was surprised to see him so unsure of his words. He turned and met her eyes. When she shook her head, he continued. "My greatest regret is never telling that girl from college how I felt before I enlisted. But worst of all, I never told her how God felt about her."

Dee watched him as he spoke. He averted his eyes and stared at nothing. His words wobbled with his discomfort. "The last few years have been full of so many thoughts that started with 'if only'. If only I had told her, maybe she wouldn't have dated such a jerk. If only I had told her," he paused, taking in a deep breath, "maybe she wouldn't be sitting on this kitchen floor, afraid to trust another man. If only..." His voice caught and he stopped.

Dee stared at him, caught off guard by his unexpected confession. She knew he cared; they were such good friends in college, but she had no idea that he cared this much, silently, for so many years. Luke stopped staring into space and turned to meet her gaze. His eyes were intense with passion and regret. "If only I wasn't such a coward."

The Luke that she always knew began to fade. She had always known him to be strong and confident. He was the bravest person she knew, yet when it came to relationships, he was unsure and afraid of rejection. Nonetheless, here he was, facing his fear and confessing his true feelings. The look in his eyes showed his vulnerability as he searched her face for a reaction.

Dee smiled and blushed. For weeks she had been contemplating her relationship with Luke. Now that she

Anne Gibson

knew God's love, she wanted a Godly man like Luke for a husband. Since Christmas she had spent hours praying, asking God what she should do with her growing feelings. God remained silent and she determined that if it was meant to be, God would make it happen, and here it was, happening right before her eyes.

Refusing to look away, Dee spoke in a soft whisper. "I don't know if I could have handled such a revelation five years ago, but I'm glad you're telling me now."

"I should have shared the gospel with you sooner." Dee could see the regret in his eyes.

"Luke, everything in your life screamed Christianity, yet I didn't listen then. Perhaps it was God's timing. Perhaps he didn't want you to give me your Bible until now. I might not have listened if it weren't for everything Mark put me through."

Luke smiled, still unable to believe that the woman he loved finally surrendered to the Lord. For five years he prayed and finally God answered his prayers. With Dee complete in Christ he loved her even more.

"I just thought it would be easier." Dee broke into his thoughts. "God took so much pain and fear away when I was in the mountains. I thought it would last. But here, with Dylan..." she sighed, frustrated with how afraid she had become.

"The Bible doesn't promise that it will get easier. In fact, quite often it gets harder."

Dee's eyes grew large. "But why? If God loves us..."

Luke cut off that thought. "It's because there is a war between good and bad. You made a huge decision and the enemy hates you for choosing the right side. Quite often the enemy tries to make life harder in order to scare you away from your initial decision."

"Then why do people remain Christians?"

"Because life is hard either way. It's just much harder without Christ."

It made sense. Life was tough with Mark. It still was tough, but Luke was right. With God's help she found healing and He gave her courage to face the rest.

"Have you really been praying for me for five years?"

Luke's smile affirmed that he had. Instantly, his confidence returned, pushing aside his fear of rejection. An honest pride replaced his vulnerability and Dee admired the strong man that sat next to her. Slowly he leaned his head towards hers. He wasn't hesitant, just cautious, watching to see her reaction. If she pulled away, he'd back off. Instead, her gaze deepened, anticipating his advance. He leaned in more, only to be interrupted by footsteps hurrying down the stairs.

"Dee," a shrill voice called out.

Luke squeezed his eyes shut and pulled back annoyed by their interruption. Dee's eyes stared at him, as if urging him to kiss her quick before his sister appeared around the corner. Luke gave it a second thought, but before he could lean in Maggie's head popped over the counter.

"Why are you guys sitting on the floor?" She asked incredulously.

Luke leaned back and tried to act casual. "Oh, you know, just hanging out."

Maggie put her hands on her hips. "Well, the party is upstairs. Go hang out upstairs!"

Luke was content sitting on the floor, but his sister stared him down. Groaning, he gave into his sister's demands. Standing up, he offered Dee a hand and helped her up. When Maggie turned for the stairs, he pulled Dee close and whispered in her ear, "We'll finish this conversation later." Dee blushed at the touch of his warm breath on her cheek. She felt like a teenager, all giddy inside. Nodding in agreement, she wished he wouldn't pull away. Maggie stopped at the stairs and stared at them.

"What are you whispering about?" She demanded to know. Dee giggled at how oblivious Maggie was to their intimate proximity.

"Wouldn't you like to know," Luke teased as he sauntered by. His little sister swatted his shoulder as he headed up the stairs. Giving Dee one last bewildered stare, she shooed Dee up the stairs and followed them.

Maggie's list of company was an enjoyable combination of church friends and colleagues. Dee enjoyed mingling with the mixed crowd, but anxiously waited for an opportunity to finish her conversation with Luke. Later that night, she spotted him outside talking on his cell phone. Hurrying downstairs, she grabbed a cardigan and wrapped it around her shoulders before she went outside. She stood in the driveway waiting for him to finish his call. Ruptures of laughter drifted from the house. Occasional snowflakes drifted from the sky but melted as soon as they hit the pavement. Though winter had begun, the weather that night was mild. Luke snapped his cell phone shut and turned to Dee. He smiled at the fact that she had sought him out. It showed that she was as eager as he was to finish their conversation. If only work hadn't called and interrupted the party.

"Important call?" Dee asked as he walked up to her.

Luke solemnly nodded. "Work," was his single word reply.

Dee looked up at him and tried to read him face. She knew there was more to his job than he was telling her, but what was it? "It's New Year's Eve!" She exclaimed, "The

185

beauty of having a government job is that you don't have to work holidays!"

Luke groaned, "Not with my job."

"Are you going out of town?"

Luke nodded and the disappointment was evident in his face. He took Dee's hand into his and he looked her in the eyes. She looked sad and he regretted his urgent departure. "I'm sorry, Dee." The way he murmured her name caused her back to tingle. "I really wanted to talk to you. There's so much I want to say, but not enough time."

Dee nodded her head in an attempt to show she understood, but deep down she was disappointed. "How long will you be gone?"

Luke sighed. "I wish I knew. A few days, maybe a week. I never know until the job is done."

Stepping forward, Dee wrapped her arms around him and leaned her head against his strong chest. "Just be careful," she whispered. Though she didn't know the exact nature of Luke's job, she suspected that it was dangerous. Why else would he be so secretive about it? Luke wrapped his arms around her and held her for a few moments. He liked the fact that they could stand there in silence and not be uncomfortable. Gathering his courage, Luke tilted Dee's chin up. Leaning in, his warm lips met hers. His kiss was soft and gentle, not forceful or demanding. When Luke started to pull back, Dee leaned in and kissed him deeper and longer. He gently caressed her cheek, longing for this moment to last forever. When she finished kissing him, he allowed for her to pull back and he stared into her eyes.

"I've wanted to do that for over five years," he murmured. His voice was deep and husky, causing Dee's spine to tingle with excitement. He continued to stare at her, unable to tear his eyes away from her beautiful face.

"I'm glad you finally did." Luke loved hearing Dee flirt back. It reminded him of the girl he met at college, rather than the broken hearted and downtrodden woman he observed over the past year.

Pulling back, Luke gathered both of Dee's hands into his own and stared into her copper eyes that sparkled in the lamplight. "I wanted to take you out for your birthday, but I'm afraid it will have to wait."

The way Dee's eyes lit up at the mentioning of her birthday proved how happy she was that he remembered. He wondered if Mark did anything special to celebrate. He was probably too hung over from the previous night's festivities to do anything special for her. But she was no longer Mark's girlfriend, and Luke would see to it that she got the royal treatment.

Dee looked at him hopefully. "Would it be a date?"

"A real date," he promised, "just you and me. No longer will I be invited along so that you won't feel like a third-wheel."

"I was kind of hoping Maggie and Jeffrey could come." Dee teased.

Luke taunted back, "If that's what you want...although our conversation might make them feel a bit uncomfortable."

Dee leaned closer, "Hmm...I wouldn't mind having you all to myself."

Luke took a deep breath. Her flirtatious behaviour was having a dangerous effect on him. His watch beeped as it turned to the eleventh hour, reminding him that time was passing and he needed to leave. "I have to go," he murmured, wishing he could stay there forever.

Looking up at him, Dee openly invited him to kiss her good-bye. Luke picked up on the longing look she gave him, but knew if he kissed her again, he would never leave. Leaning in, he gave her a quick peck on the cheek. Before he walked away, he whispered in her ear, "Make sure Dr. Jekyll doesn't try to kiss you at midnight. If he does, he'll have me to deal with later." Luke then pulled away and left, leaving Dee standing on the driveway, laughing at his referral to Dylan.

Mark hung up his phone, ready to explode. Cyril promised to provide him with false receipts before the holidays, but it was already New Years Eve and he was nowhere to be found. Mark needed them! The auditors were beginning to breathe down his neck. Though the documents were not legit, they would buy him enough time to secure some funds and get out of town. He paced the length of his room. If Cyril didn't show up, he'd be in hot water. Not only would the fines wipe him out, he'd do some serious time! He looked in the mirror and smoothed his tie. He wore power suits, not orange jumpers.

His cellphone vibrated, but he ignored his girlfriend's call. He wasn't in the mood to party. He needed to vent. His thoughts raced back to Dee. He couldn't help but suspect that she had something to do with this. It was too much of a coincidence that the second she caught him cheating, he was being audited. She was good with numbers and figures, and as naive as she was, she must have suspected something. He should have known better. The second he tossed her to the side, she ratted him out.

Clenching his teeth, he grabbed his coat and got into his car. Enough was enough! She was ruining his life and this time he would make her pay!

Chapter 11

The party went on into the wee hours of the morning, but Dee didn't mind. After connecting with Luke, she felt refreshed and giddy. When the guests left and Maggie and Jeffrey headed to bed, Dee forced herself to go downstairs, though she didn't feel the least bit tired. Walking into her empty basement suite she felt lonely. She wished that Luke didn't have to leave. She imagined what it would have been like if he could have stayed. They could have stayed up all night, reminiscing about their past and dreaming about their future. Dreamily, Dee sunk into her couch and imagined that Luke was there holding her, murmuring sweet nothings into her ear. Glancing at her coffee table, she noticed a journal bound with a big pink ribbon. Sitting up, she reached for it and pulled a note out. She read:

Dee,

You deserve more than flowers or chocolate; you deserve the truth. I hope this makes your birthday a special one.

Luke

Undoing the bright ribbon, Dee stared at the journal. Loose papers and a couple of envelopes fell out. The first envelope carried her dorm address and a return address. She hadn't lived there for years. Some even had stamps on them, but they were never mailed. Dee studied the return addresses. The first one was Luke's parent's address in Alexandria. A couple were from a training base in Fort Belvoir. The rest were from various locations in Afghanistan. Ripping open the first envelope, a picture fell out. Picking it up, Dee eyed the snapshot that captured her dancing with Luke at her first college dance. She couldn't believe how young she looked. She was only nineteen. Luke also looked young, with his shaggy hair and tight t-shirt. Though Luke had always been buff, he was no where near the build that he is today. Dee smiled as she remembered the first time they danced. They were so carefree, having the time of their lives. So much had changed over the past six years. They both had grown up and learnt many things the hard way.

Opening the letter, Dee laughed at the cartoons that Luke had drawn in the margins. Either he was bored or extremely nervous when he wrote this.

Dearest Dee,

Dee smiled at the thought of hearing such tender words roll off of Luke's tongue.

There were so many things I wanted to tell you as the end of the school year neared, but I never found the right opportunity to do so. I know the plan was for me to study law in the fall, but to be honest, such plans never sat right with me. I don't want to waste a few more years of my life hitting the books when I can be doing something much more meaningful. I've enlisted with the army. In a week I will go to Fort Belvoir for my training. After that, I hope to be shipped out to Afghanistan.

Dee, I wanted to tell you about these plans for a long time, but was too afraid to. I was afraid that you wouldn't understand or would convince me to stay. I am a 100% certain that this is what God wants me to do, so I have to do it. I must admit, I am really excited about it.

The only thing that I am not excited about is not being able to talk to you or see you. Your friendship means more to me than I think you realize. I care about you so much. Some days I think that it might even be love, but what do I know? I'm only 22. What I do know is that what I feel for you I have never felt for anyone ever before. The first time I danced with you, I knew that you were one of a kind and that a girl like you doesn't come along very often. I don't know if this might come as a shock to you. Perhaps all along you just thought of me as Maggie's big brother, but I need you to know I longed to be more.

When I realized how deep my feelings were for you, I wanted to tell you, but I knew it wouldn't be fair, because deep down inside I knew that one day I would enlist. Who knows how long I might be gone. Six months, a year, ten years? I might not even come back. That's why I need you to know how I feel. No matter how long I am gone, I will love you. Nobody will be able to replace the spot you have in my heart.

Dee, I'm not asking you to wait for me. That wouldn't be fair. I'm just asking you to consider how you really feel for me. When a boy asks you out, and I know there will be many, ask yourself, "Do I care for him more than Luke?" If the answer is yes, then I wish you complete happiness. We started as friends and we will always be friends, no matter what.

193

I will miss you the most while I am gone. Please keep me in your thoughts. I pray that one day I will see you again!

   Love,
   Luke

Dee wiped away her tears, recalling how timid Luke was when he told her about his feelings in the kitchen earlier that evening. For almost six years he had affections for her but was too afraid to tell her. Dee wondered how her life might have been different if she had known. He was gone for three years. Would she have waited for him? Would letters and tokens of love been enough to make her wait three years for him? She was young, immature, and a terrible flirt. Though she spent many nights crying, worrying about her friend in Afghanistan, she eventually pushed aside her thoughts about him. Though she never forgot him, she soon replaced him. The next year she met Mark and as she fell in love with Mark, her thoughts about Luke lessened. But with the way things turned out with Mark, she wished she had known and tried to wait for Luke. Now that she was older and wiser, she could see that Luke was well worth the wait.

Opening his journal to the first page, she saw that the date matched the date on his letter. Reading his private thoughts, she soon understood why he never mailed the letter. His words were prayers, confessing to God his love for Dee but knowing that he couldn't be with her until she loved the Lord. He begged God to help him; to give him patience. He asked for strength to wait for he knew it would be wrong to tell Dee his true feelings. Dee felt the power of God, knowing that God answered Luke's prayers. If He hadn't, Luke would have mailed her his letters. Page after page Luke prayed for Dee, begging for her to find Christ. He prayed for her protection and earnestly asked God to give him a chance to be her husband. Dee admired his unswerving faith and yearned to be as devoted.

Opening a few more letters, she soon realized that they were written out of moments of weakness. Each one professed his love and his desire to be with her immediately. God must have intervened, giving Luke the strength to wait. She couldn't imagine the patience and self-control that Luke would have exhibited. She wondered if her faith would ever be so unswerving that she would wait almost six years for an answer to her prayers.

Dee spent the rest of the night pouring over Luke's letters and journal entries. She embedded his words into her memory. She laughed as he joked about his training camp experiences with friends named Juan and Wayne. Here and there his letters were interspersed with terms of endearment written in Spanish. Some of them were romantic, the rest

195

were silly. Positive that Juan had dictated them to Luke, she wondered if Luke knew what he was actually writing. She cried as he shared his fears, as well as the pain he endured watching an innocent country be torn apart by terrorism. She couldn't believe how brave he was. He was also transparent, not wanting to hide anything from her. She smiled as she read his dreams of telling her how he felt about her. He wrote about desires of coming home and sweeping her off her feet while he proclaimed his love. Dee never realized that Luke was such a romantic at heart. For a tough, brave soldier, he could get pretty sappy.

The letters stopped in December of his last year overseas. It was also Dee's last year of college and the end of her semester she had moved in with Mark. Luke returned in July. Did he know? Had Maggie written and told him? Had Dee broken his heart and that is why he no longer wrote? Though he never mailed these letters, there was no letter recording his knowledge of her relationship with Mark. Perhaps those letters were too painful or too bitter for him to share with her. His journal entries changed, asking God what he should do with his life. He stated his obedience to do whatever God commanded of him. Though he continued to pray that Dee would find God, he stopped praying for God to bless the love that he felt for her.

Dee ended up crying herself to sleep on her couch that night, clutching his journal, well aware that she had broken his heart. And for what? A failed relationship with Mark! She had broken his heart for nothing! Ashamed at her immaturity, she cried, wishing she could have taken it all back.

The next morning Dee woke up on her couch. The letters were scattered around her, proving that such words of love were not a dream. Dee sat up and stretched, feeling refreshed and rejuvenated. Though she had wasted years with Mark, rather than Luke, she felt grateful for a second chance. She prayed for Luke, asking God for his safe and swift return. There was so much she needed to tell him. There was so much on her heart that she wanted to share with him. There was so much they needed to catch up on!

Getting up, Dee headed for the shower. Though it was only eight, and despite the fact that she had a late night, Dee felt a desire to get her day started. No longer would she lie in bed, wishing for the day to be over. Today was her birthday and Luke had given her the greatest gift! She couldn't wait for her birthday party. Some girlfriends were taking her out for dinner and she couldn't wait to gush about this new man in her life. She would keep his name a secret, until things were official. Dee wondered if even Maggie would be able to figure out who her mystery man was. She had been pretty oblivious the night before. Running the hot water, Dee climbed into the shower. If one day Luke decided to marry her, Maggie would be her sister-in-law. Already Dee's day was looking better!

Dee stared at herself in the mirror and couldn't believe how radiant she looked. Twirling around, she admired her slim figure accented by her black cocktail dress. If only Luke could see her! She dreamed of his reaction as she tucked a curl back. She spent the last half hour taming her wild curls and it was well worth it. Even Luke wouldn't be able to resist sinking his hands into her beautiful hair.

A knock at the back door brought Dee back to reality. She wasn't expecting anyone, and normally guests went to the front door. Being her private entrance, Dee was the only person who used it, except for Luke who was too lazy to walk around to the front door. Her heart skipped a beat. Could it be Luke? Had he gotten out of the task that was taking him out of town? Flying up the stairs, Dee eagerly opened the door, disappointed to find Mark standing there.

As always, he stood there with a smug expression. His gaze travelled from her head to her toes and his smile approved. Pushing his way past, Mark walked inside and headed downstairs without asking. Dee closed the door and sighed. She no longer cared. She was over him and moving on. If he wanted to try anything, Maggie and Jeffrey were upstairs sleeping. If she screamed, they would come to her rescue. She followed him downstairs and stood in the middle of the living room.

Mark gazed at her and smiled. His eyes looked funny, sort of glazed over. Dee wondered if he was hung over from the night before, but she couldn't smell any alcohol. "You look nice." Again, his eyes appraised her, but his tone sounded bitter. As if he were baiting her, he asked, "Going on a date or something?"

Dee folded her arms. "The girls are taking me out tonight." Not that it was any of his business.

Mark's eyes flashed and grabbing Dee with one arm he shoved her into the wall. Tightening his grip, he leaned in and growled, "Don't lie to me!" Dee squirmed but couldn't break free. She had seen him angry and aggressive, but she had never seen him like this. He was edgy and unpredictable. She checked his eyes. Could it be drugs? Or just rage? Fear began to rise inside of her. If it was drugs, who knows what he would do?

"I'm...I'm not," she stammered, afraid that she would provoke him even further.

"I saw you," he hissed. His breath was hot on her face and stunk. "I saw it all!"

Dee trembled, unsure of what he meant. He was so angry that he wasn't making sense. Was he having a breakdown? Would he go nuts and...and what? Dee pressed her eyes shut, trying to stop her thoughts from going in that direction.

He pushed her back into the wall and began to disjointedly rant. "I came last night. I came to talk to you. And I saw you. I saw you with him." Tightening his already firm grip, he continued, "I saw everything."

It was his tone that unsettled Dee the most. Though he was angry he didn't yell. His voice remained low and eerily controlled. She wished he would scream at her. It was his flat voice that reminded her of psychopaths and that was what scared her the most.

Dee wished she had an explanation. She wished it was all a big misunderstanding, but it was what it was. She felt angry as she recognized the double standard. He could cheat on her, but she couldn't move on, despite the fact that they broke up months ago! She wanted to yell at him and tell him how unreasonable he was being, but he was too unstable. What if he lost it?

"How long have you been seeing him?"

"We're...we're not." Dee wished she had a more believable answer, but it was the truth. Nothing was official yet. She watched for a reaction and cringed as his face boiled.

A vein in his forehead throbbed and Dee knew she was treading on thin ice.

Grabbing both of her arms, he threw her to the ground. Crawling on top of her, he grabbed her shoulders and shook her. "Don't lie to me!" He snarled as he shook her, "Don't lie to me!"

Dee trembled and her tears choked her. She fought for her words. She no longer cared how afraid she looked; she had every right to be terrified. She tried to push him back and cried out, "It's not like that!" She knew she had to lie. The truth would only make things worse. "You broke my heart! You spent the holidays with your girlfriend and I was all alone. And with New Year's and my birthday...I felt lonely. It was just an impulse. I thought it would take the loneliness away. But you saw what happened, he walked away. He wasn't interested."

Mark stopped shaking her shoulders and sat up. For a second, Dee thought that he had calmed down. Instead, he reached into his jacket and pulled out a gun. Dee stared at him horrified. The worst of her fears had come true. Mark had lost it. She prayed that it would be quick and painless and that he would leave Maggie and Jeffrey alone. She also prayed that Luke would stay out of town for a while. Her tears ran so fast that they blurred her vision, but she could feel the cold barrel of the gun press down onto her throat.

"I don't believe you," he hissed.

Her heart pounded so hard she was afraid he would hear it. She fought for words, and begged, "Please, Mark, you have to believe me. It's the truth!" Sobs erupted and she could say no more.

"But he kissed you!"

Dee trembled. How could she talk her way out of this? She prayed for words, even if they were lies. "I...I think he felt sorry for me, so he let me kiss him. But after, he told me he didn't feel the same way. He understood how lonely I was, but he wasn't interested. You saw it Mark, you have to believe me! He left! He didn't take me home with him. He wasn't interested!"

She felt him relax, though the barrel of the gun still pressed down on her throat.

"And you?" He snarled, "Were you interested?"

Dee closed her eyes and slowly shook her head. "I was just lonely," she moaned. She silently begged for him to believe her.

Instead, he pushed the gun into her throat even harder and leaned forward. He whispered into her ear, "There are eight bullets in the chamber of this gun. I only need one to finish you off. If I catch you with him again, the other seven are going in him!"

When Dee paled at his ultimatum, he sat back satisfied. Turning off all emotion, he got up and walked out of the door as if nothing had happened. Dee curled into a ball and sobbed. No one could help her now. No restraining order would stop him. He had lost it and wouldn't stop at anything. The only thing she could do was ensure that Luke never saw her again. She thought of his wonderful journal and sobbed even harder. Perhaps if she hadn't been so immature, they would have had a chance. But now, it could never be.

Dragging herself off of the floor, Dee knew what she had to do. Mark wanted Luke's blood more than he wanted hers. It was one thing to gamble with her life, but another's? Going into her room, Dee pulled out her two suitcases and packed her meagre belongings. Other than her clothes and her laptop, she didn't really have anything of value, except for Luke's Bible and his sweet journal and letters. Gathering them up and tying them together with the pretty pink ribbon, Dee gently packed them between layers of clothing. She knew that rereading them would only cause her more pain, but she felt selfish and refused to sacrifice them. Other than her memories, they were the only thing she would have to remember Luke. Like he had claimed in his letter, he too held a place in her heart that no one else could fill. Unfortunately, he would never have the chance to fill it either.

Zipping her suitcases shut, Dee dragged them into the hallway. Scribbling a quick note for Maggie, Dee quietly let her self out, threw her bags into the trunk of her car and drove away.

Chapter 12

When Dee stepped off of the plane, the hot, muggy air of Colombia hit her. The plane's airconditioned cabin no longer kept her cool and as she crossed the tarmac, the still air caused her to start sweating. In DC it was snowing, but here the sun bore down on her and there was no present breeze to relieve her. Following the mob of people, Dee climbed onto a tiny bus that would shuttle her to the airport terminal about a quarter of a mile away. With no seats remaining, Dee stood and held onto the railing. People crowded around her, blocking any path of fresh air. She felt like she would suffocate and wondered if coming here was a good idea.

Her thoughts flooded back to the previous night that she spent in a hotel. She had no idea where to go or what to do. All she knew was that she couldn't stay in DC. The only place she could think of was Saravena, Colombia, a tiny city that was her refuge in her teen years. As a child, her family often came to visit her father's sister and her husband. Having no kids of their own, they started up an orphanage called Hope's Haven. When Dee was in grade five, her father died and the annual visits became unaffordable. When Dee's mother remarried in her grade eight year, her step-father saw no need to visit relatives that he wasn't related to, and the idea of restarting these annual visits was banished. However, when she was sixteen, Dee managed to convince her mother to let her come one last time. Hope's Haven became a bit of a haven for herself. It was the only place where she could escape her belligerent step-father and lovingly embrace the few memories she had of her father. As well, Saravena was the farthest place she could think of where she still knew someone.

She remembered her tearful conversation as she asked her aunt for permission to visit the orphanage. As usual, her aunt was delighted, until she realized that the length of Dee's stay was indefinite. Not wanting to go into details over the phone, Dee knew she was in for a long conversation on the drive home. Having a six hour layover in Bogota, Dee tried to figure out what she would say and how she would say it. She thought she had it all figured out, but when she stepped off of the plane in Arauca, the hot air smothered her, forcing her to forget her well rehearsed speech. Though the drive from Arauca to Saravena wasn't long, Dee knew that her aunt would try to pry out every possible detail.

When the shuttle pulled up to the terminal, Dee allowed the mob to push her off of the bus. Not too sure of where to go next, Dee decided to go with the flow and followed the crowd. She soon found everyone stopping and waiting at a luggage area. Dee took a seat and pushed a sweaty curl off of her forehead. Endless chatter filled the small area, but Dee wasn't interested in listening. Though it was years since Dee studied, let alone spoke Spanish, she still picked up the odd phrase here or there.

When the luggage began to appear on the conveyor belt, the mob crowded around. People pushed and shoved, impatient to retrieve their belongings. Dee remained seated. She didn't care anymore. So what if someone stole her bags? She felt empty inside and knew that her meagre belongings wouldn't fill that void. She sat there feeling dejected and wondered if she would ever return to her old self? Luke had warned her that it would be tough. But this—with Mark—it was too much. She thought of a verse from Luke's Bible, "'For I know the plans I have for you,' declares the Lord, 'plans to prosper you and not to harm you, plans to give you hope and a future.'" When she read this at Christmas she believed it, but now she had her doubts. She wished that she could fully trust God, but truth be told, she was too afraid. Would she ever heal and move on? She wished that she had Luke's unswerving faith. With the thought of Luke, she wondered if she would ever heal and move on. Would the needs of Saravena allow her to forget, or at least repress her pain? Last time she came to visit she was optimistic and excited. Now she felt used up and hopeless.

When the crowd began to dwindle, Dee stood up and joined the few stragglers. Retrieving her bags, she headed for the doors. A small boy offered to help her, but she gently turned down the peddler. Stepping outside, the muggy air was consumed with exhaust fumes. Struggling to breath, Dee found her uncle waiting next to an old VW van. Dee smiled when she realized that he was driving her home instead of her aunt. Being a man of few words, she knew he wouldn't pry. For the first time in two days, Dee felt encouraged and thanked God for this small blessing. As much as she loved her aunt, she wasn't looking forward to the interrogation.

Hugging the tall, lanky man, he silently threw her bags in the back and helped her into her seat. Closing the passenger door, he leaned his entire weight into the door, ensuring that the door actually latched shut. He pushed until a loud click satisfied him. Heading around to his door, he awkwardly slid in and slammed his own door shut. Putting on his seatbelt, he coaxed the engine to start and smiled at the noisy roar that came out of the old engine.

Dee silently stared out of her window and observed the transformation. Last time she had visited, about ten years ago, Arauca was busy rebuilding. New buildings took over the one side of the road, and there was no sign of bombed out ruins. Nearby, some US soldiers patrolled outside of their barracks. Their presence did little to make her feel safe and chills ran down her back.

Noticing her shiver, her uncle spoke up. "The USA has set up quarters here and in Saravena. Though things have settled down, it's still not safe. There are still guerrilla camps nearby."

Dee nodded. Many of the children in her aunt and uncle's orphanage were orphaned because of guerrilla attacks. Dee always thought it was ironic, in a sad way, that those same children eventually grew up and joined the rebel movement that killed their parents. It was unfortunate that it seemed like the only option for young men.

Her uncle continued, "Lots of young boys have left the orphanage and joined the movement. As much as Janet and I regret seeing them leave, they have indirectly offered the orphanage a level of protection. They respect your aunt and I, and leave the place alone. We haven't been raided or vandalized for years."

Dee never realized what a big risk her aunt and uncle took in setting up an orphanage so close to such turmoil. Dee continued to take in the setting, observing the crowded buildings that slowly grew into the rural farmland.

"Janet mentioned that you might be staying for a while." His tone was gentle and hesitant, as if to say she didn't have to talk about it if she didn't want to.

Dee nodded and looked at her lap. "Mark and I broke up."

Her uncle didn't say anything for a while. When he did speak up, Dee was surprised at his words. "And you think coming to Colombia will fix everything?" For a man of few words, they sure were blunt ones.

"I just need to be somewhere where Mark can't ruin my life." Such words made Dee feel like a coward, but she knew that she couldn't stand up to him.

"Things are pretty ugly back home?"

Dee nodded. Ugly was such an understatement. Eager to change the subject, Dee asked, "Why didn't Aunt Janet come along?"

Her uncle smiled. "She's out of town for a few days. Went on a retreat with some missionaries. Looks like you can hide for a little bit."

Dee couldn't help but smile. For a quiet man, he was really introspective.

Luke sighed and hung up his cell phone. Every time he dialled Dee's number, he got the same recording, "*The number you have dialled is no longer in service. Please try again.*" For the entire flight home, Luke anxiously waited for the plane to land in DC so he could call her and talk to her. Now he couldn't get a hold of her and this frustrated him. It also worried him. Why had she disconnected her phone? Pulling into his driveway, Luke hopped out and headed straight for his neighbour's house. He didn't care how rough he looked from his long flight. He needed to see Dee right away.

Luke knocked at the back door and waited. He knocked again, louder this time. Maggie soon appeared and looked perplexed.

"Luke, why are you knocking? You never knock."

It was true. He was always welcome in their home and always let himself in. If the door was locked, he had the key, but this was Dee's entrance, and he wasn't going to intrude on Dee. If she lived anywhere else, he would knock first.

Luke ran his hand through his hair and awkwardly replied, "I came to see Dee." He wondered how much his sister knew. Had Dee told her about their conversation? By her blank look, obviously not.

"Dee's gone." It was a simple statement, but Maggie said it with such sorrow.

"Do you know when she will be home?"

Maggie shook her head. Her eyes became sad as she explained. "Dee moved out."

Surprise and shock took over Luke. Why would she do that? "Where'd she move to?"

Maggie shrugged her shoulders and tried to act like she wasn't concerned. "I don't know. She just packed up and left. Didn't even say good-bye. Just left a note."

Luke felt like he had been sucker punched in the gut. His breath stopped and blocked his windpipe, suffocating him. "Can I see the note?" He forced out.

Maggie nodded. Letting him inside, she headed downstairs. She left the note exactly where she found it, too devastated to throw it out. She worried about her friend. It wasn't like Dee to just disappear. She wondered what had happened. What could be so bad that Dee couldn't even talk about it to her best friend? Luke picked up the note and read it.

Maggie,

I'm sorry to leave like this, but I just needed to get away. Things have spiralled out of control and have become too much for me to handle. I'm sorry for not saying good-bye in person. I need you to know that I appreciate everything you have done for me. You truly are my best friend.

Dee

P.S. I won't be coming back, so feel free to rent out your suite to someone else.

Luke dropped the note onto the counter and went to her old room. Opening her closet, he found it empty. Going to her dresser, he opened each drawer, only to find them bare. He sunk down onto the bed. The room wasn't just empty, it was hollow and meaningless. A lump grew in his throat. He stared at the bedspread and thought of the night that he carried Dee to bed and tucked her in. How badly he wanted to lie down next to her and hold her all night, making her feel loved and protected. Had he pushed her away? Did he come on too strong? He thought about their kiss, how she had leaned in and welcomed it. She seemed happy and content. She showed no sign of fear. Luke groaned. He should have known better. Though she was strong, her wounds were deep. He came on too fast, too soon. She wasn't ready and he scared her away.

Maggie came into the room and sat next to him. A tear escaped and she leaned her head on her big brother's shoulder. "She seemed so happy." Another tear followed.

Luke put his arm around his sister and sighed. He understood her pain. His matched, perhaps even surpassed hers. An ache grew inside, worse than the one he felt when he found out that Dee was living with Mark. His first regret was leaving without telling her. Now he regretted the fact that he told her everything.

His sister continued, "Why would she leave like this?"

Luke's thoughts turned to his letters. Though gentle and loving, they were genuine in his pain and regret. He had wanted her to see the depth of his love. Perfect love drives out fear, so he went on a limb and exposed his true feeling. He had no idea he was dropping a bomb that Dee wasn't ready for. If only he had waited. He had already waited for almost six years. What was another year or two?

Maggie sniffled and wiped her nose with the back of her hand. "Do you think that Mark..." Maggie trailed off, too upset to finish her train of thought.

Luke's back tensed and he sat up straight. Mark! Luke let go of his sister and clenched his fists. If it hadn't been for Mark, Dee wouldn't be afraid to love. Their connection that night was genuine. He was sure of it. She was happy. Luke would even say that she was excited, which was evident by the way she flirted with him. She showed no fear. Had his letters pushed her over the edge, or had Mark?

Luke's thoughts flooded with his knowledge of Mark. So far, he knew that Mark was unpredictable. Though Mark hadn't shown up since the break up, last time he did show up it was out of the blue. He was also possessive and violent.

Did Dee flee because of him? Had he threatened her again? Had he visited, like last time?

Luke's blood began to boil at the thought of Mark's hands on the woman he loved. Every muscle in Luke's body grew tense and his jaw locked with rage. If Mark had even touched her, Luke would make him pay. Maggie stared at her brother, as anger and revenge gripped him. Jumping up, he headed for the door without saying a word. Enough was enough. If Mark had anything to do with Dee's disappearance, Luke would put an end to it.

Dee silently paced the length of the nursery, rocking and soothing a colicky baby. While the other babies slept or quietly stared at their mobiles, this one howled uncontrollably and refused to be consoled. This one was tiny, the smallest baby in the nursery. Some locals had found her in a shoebox in an alleyway. They had no idea how old the baby was, but she couldn't be over a month old.

Dee made a shushing noise in an attempt to calm the inconsolable child. She held her against her shoulder and leaned her head against her, gently shushing in her ear. Walking along the row of cribs, Dee stopped at the end and stared at the blank wall. Silent tears flowed as she empathized with the baby. She too felt alone and devastated. She let the baby cry, wishing that she could howl and scream like that. Instead, she stood there, silently bottling up her emotions, with no one but a newborn baby to share her pain with.

The child eventually began to calm down. Dee rubbed the tiny back until the sobs ceased. Exerted, the baby succumbed to sleep, interrupted by the occasional hiccup. Dee wished that something as simple as a soothing touch could console her. Her thoughts flooded with memories of Luke's strong arms that had held her and comforted her. Tears flowed as she ached for the loving touch that she could never experience ever again. She knew a silent depression was invading her, but she didn't know how to fight it. She spent her lonely nights rocking children to sleep, praying for wisdom or assurance, but God remained silent. He seemed distant, as if He were too far away to hear her prayers. Dee was losing hope and sometimes she found herself wondering if He heard her prayers but for some reason refused to answer them. She felt torn. She admired how Luke persistently prayed for the same thing for almost six years. She wanted to be like that, yet didn't know how. Every time she tried, she felt depressed and discouraged. Sometimes she felt like Jonah, a coward who ran away. Other times she wondered if God was trying to refine her through adversity. After all, Luke had warned her that it would be tough. She had a million questions but no answers. She knew that Luke deserved some sort of explanation, but God refused to guide her in what to say. She knew that God commanded his disciples to be truthful, assuring his believers that the truth would set them free. Dee wanted to feel free, for she felt bound by fear and deception, but she knew that if she told Luke the truth, he would take the risk. By telling him the truth, she would be gambling with his life, and she didn't trust God enough to take that gamble. Perhaps that was why God seemed so distant; because of her feeble faith.

Dee kissed the baby's soft forehead and murmured the nursery song her mother sang to her as a child, "Our God is so big, so strong and so mighty, there is nothing our God cannot do for you." Dee sighed, wishing she could believe such words.

A rusty screech interrupted Dee's dismal thoughts as the old door swung open. Dee turned and watched as a soldier walked in. Though he didn't seem armed, Dee felt her pulse quicken. She stared at his camouflage pants and his blackened military boots. He seemed tall and imposing as he stood there, looking around. Her uncle had warned her that the rebels protected the orphanage, but she didn't realize that they came and went as they pleased. Dee put the sleeping baby down in an empty crib and prayed for her protection. The soldier looked at her and said, "I'm looking for Lupita."

Dee turned and crossed her arms. She hated how he affectionately called Lupe "Lupita". Lupe grew up in the orphanage and rather than running away to become a prostitute, like most girls, or hiring herself out as a maid, Lupe stuck around and worked at the orphanage in exchange for room and board. She was young, about eighteen, and beautiful and Dee feared the reasons why this soldier would be looking for her.

"She's not here," Dee lied, wanting to protect the young girl. "She went into town."

Rather than leaving, the rebel stood there and eyed her curiously. A whimper rose from the crib and Dee turned her attention to the infant. Rummaging about, she retrieved a soother from underneath a blanket and popped it into the baby's mouth, willing her to stay quiet. Dee could see out of the corner of her eye that the soldier was approaching her, but she refused to look up.

"I never thought you would come back." His voice was closer than she expected and startled her.

Dee turned and studied his face. Though his eyes were warm, his rough features made him seem imposing. His nose was crooked, obviously once broken and not straightened before it healed. As well, a long thin scar stretched from his forehead to his left temple. Such battle wounds made him look both insolent and aggressive. His square jaw seemed to dare you to challenge him. Though he seemed to recognize Dee from her last visit, when she was sixteen, she did not recognize him. Back then, all the children were cute, cuddly and playful. This resilient young man didn't resemble the energetic and hopeful children that she remembered, though a lot could change over nine years, especially if he was involved in guerrilla warfare.

"You don't remember me?"

Dee shook her head, not sure if she wanted to.

"Esteban," He offered his name as a clue and looked at her hopefully, afraid that she might have entirely forgotten about him. By the way that her eyes lit up, he knew that she recognized his name, and when a blush gently crawled into her cheeks, he knew that she remembered everything. Though her blush made her look young and girly, her face remained sad.

"You're a..." Dee drifted off. She couldn't bring herself to say it. Lupe had mentioned that her brother was still around, but she never said that he became a militant. What happened to the young boy she met so many years ago? She thought of the chubby eight-year-old she met on one of her family's annual visits. Each year she had looked forward to going back to see her old friend. When Dee last visited, she couldn't believe how much he had matured and their friendship quickly evolved into a teenage crush. Last time Dee had seen him, he was eighteen and was no longer short and chubby. He was tall and muscular and the best soccer player that she had ever seen. He was also a flirt and Dee loved how confident he was around her. He wasn't afraid to tease her and was always kidding around. Now here he was; no longer a playful teenager, but a hardened man whose scars proved that he was accustomed to violence and more than willing to fight.

Esteban picked up on the sadness in her voice. He wished that he could have become more, but that just wasn't a possibility. Everyone in Saravena was poor, and those who weren't were educated. Esteban had to face reality. They didn't educate orphans. His only options were begging, stealing or joining the movement. He was too proud to beg, to honest to steal, and though FARC wasn't ideal, it was his best option. "What did you expect?"

Dee nodded, well aware of his limitations. "What about the military?"

Esteban snorted at the idea of the joining the government's military. "You have to be educated and from a well to do family." The elite military demanded that he had to be somebody, and in their eyes, he was a nobody.

Dee's heart became heavy with disappointment. She wasn't disappointed that he joined FARC, she was just disappointed that he had no other option. She wished that she could help him, but knew that there was nothing that she could do. "Are you happy?"

Esteban smiled. He had hoped that she would understand. "*Sí*," was his sole reply. He was taking care of those that the government ignored. He knew that their way of doing it was not ideal, but it was the only way that he could ensure the safety of his loved ones.

When he smiled, his hardened features softened. Beyond the tough facade, Dee could see a bit of the playful teenager that she had liked so much.

"I heard you were in a serious relationship. Is he here?" Esteban thought it was an innocent question, yet for some reason Dee's eyes grew dark and sad.

Dee looked down. She wished she wouldn't feel so ashamed admitting the mistakes of her relationship with Mark. Yet, she felt embarrassed for making such an awful decision. "I'm single," she mumbled. She knew Esteban wouldn't pry, but she still felt uncomfortable.

Esteban watched her squirm in front of him. He knew that living together was a normal thing in the United States but he was sad to hear that Dee was living with a man, especially one who didn't marry her eventually. Giving her the benefit of the doubt, he spoke as if it were a matter of fact, "That's too bad. You deserve better." He noticed that her shoulders relaxed a bit and decided to change the subject. "How long will you be staying?"

Dee shrugged her shoulders. "It's indefinite."

"As in you might stay?" By stay he meant permanently live here, but Dee caught his drift.

Dee tried to act nonchalant. "Yeah, maybe. We'll see."

"Why would you want to live here?" He understood why people would come for short term missions. They came to offer relief. In return, they felt better about themselves. But he never understood why anyone would choose to live here, such as her aunt and uncle had chosen almost twenty years ago.

"DC's not all it's cracked up to be. This place has always been a bit of a haven for me."

Esteban looked at her incredulously. A haven? "But it's so dangerous."

Dee looked at him straight in the eyes and squared her jaw. "I'm safer here than I was at home."

Esteban thought about the explosions and raids he had witnessed as a child. He grew up in a country full of threats and murders, yet Dee felt safer here than she did in the land of milk and honey. What did her boyfriend do that was so terrible?

"Was your boyfriend a bad man?"

Dee stared at him. "My *ex-boyfriend* is a very dangerous man." The edge in her voice warned Esteban to drop the matter. Though he wanted to know more, he decided not to press the subject.

Luke raced into his office and quickly punched his password into his computer. Impatiently he waited for his computer to load. The muscles in his neck were taut with tension and were pulling the skin across his forehead tight, creating a headache. Luke rubbed the back of his neck, desperate to loosen the tension, but as his mind raced at a mile a minute, the anxiety grew and provoked his headache even more.

Pulling up the Kensington/Cairns file, Luke was disappointed to see how little information it held. Nothing was current. Terrorists were under constant surveillance and every move they made was recorded. But with civilians, it was different. Luke groaned and dropped his head. He had hoped for a police report of some sort, but it appeared that Dee left without filing anything.

Juan popped around the corner and smiled, "Romeo! What are you doing back so soon?"

On the way home Luke had raced through his report. Though thorough and detailed, he didn't want to waste time going to the office to complete it. While the other soldiers relaxed and unwound, Luke concentrated on work. They teased him, but he didn't mind. It was all worth it. Or so he thought.

"I need a favour, Juan."

The edge in Luke's voice caused Juan to stop smiling. He had a thousand jokes ready to tease Luke, but now seemed like an inappropriate time. Pulling up a chair, Juan sat down and leaned forward. Luke also leaned in and whispered, "Dee's gone."

Juan's eyes widened and he sat back, surprised. "What do you mean *gone*?"

Luke rubbed his forehead, frustrated and overwhelmed. "I don't know. She just packed up and left." The lost look in his eyes conveyed how confused he was.

"Did you check her file?"

Luke nodded. "Nothing. No report or anything. I need to find her. Could you pull up her credit card?"

"I dunno man." Luke knew he was asking for a huge favour. "Pulling up a police record is one thing. That's practically public news to us. But a civilian's credit card, that's personal. It's an invasion of privacy."

Luke's heart sunk. He knew what he was asking for. "I know, but I need to find her and make sure she isn't in danger."

"Did she say anything to your sister?"

Aches ripped at Luke's heart as he thought of his tearful sister. "Just a note."

"Well, what did it say?"

"That 'things spiralled out of control'. It's got to be her ex."

Juan scratched at the stubble that was beginning to line his neck. "I'll do some digging. See if I can pull up some info without touching her banking."

A vein in Luke's temple throbbed but he ignored it. "I'll take the fall for you, if this gets out."

Juan nodded and stood up. "I know." He then turned and walked away.

Chapter 13

Juan grabbed the printout and rushed over to Luke's desk. Luke's eyes were apprehensive. Though hopeful, Juan hated to see how stressed his friend looked. Worry lines etched around Luke's eyes, which were dark with concern and fear. Juan had known Luke the three years that they served together in Afghanistan and he had never seen his friend like this. He was calm and composed as war raged around them, but this was different. It was personal and hit home.

"I called the hospital and there was nothing. So I called the officer who handled the case between Dee and her ex to see if there were any pending reports that just haven't been filed onto the system yet. He denied knowledge of any recent occurrences. I had no choice but to pull up her credit cards."

Luke watched Juan as he pulled a chair up next to him and leaned in. Handing Luke a piece of paper, he whispered. "She spent a night in a hotel. The next day she booked a one-way ticket to Arauca, Columbia."

Luke grabbed the paper and read for himself. "One-way?"

Nodding, Juan confirmed. "A one-way ticket. I contacted the embassy and they confirmed that she registered upon arrival. She's staying at a place called "Hope's Haven" in Saravena. It's an..."

"Orphanage," Luke finished for Juan.

"You've heard of it?"

Luke nodded. "Her aunt and uncle run it. She used to visit there all the time."

"So maybe she just needed a holiday?"

Luke rubbed his temples wishing that it was just that. "But a one-way ticket?" Already he felt permanently separated from her. Juan shrugged, wishing he could offer hope and comfort to his friend. Luke continued, "When did this all happen?"

"She stayed in the hotel January first. Flew out the next day."

Luke's stomach tightened as he realized it all happened immediately after he expressed his true feelings towards Dee. Could it be that his letters were too much? Juan could see the wheels turning in Luke's head. He knew that look on his face; it was the look of Luke internalizing everything and heaping all the blame on his own shoulders. Luke did the same thing when Wayne disappeared. Not only did he blame himself, but he had spent the last two years trying to find him.

"There's one more thing," Juan offered, trying to stop Luke's thoughts from going in that direction. "I pulled up Mark's file...you know just in case. On January first he made a purchase on his credit card that was cancelled immediately."

Luke straightened up, "What type of purchase?"

"It took place at a pawn shop near his house. I called to see what the nature of the transaction was. Mark had tried to purchase a gun, but when he found out that he would have a criminal background check done, he cancelled the transaction. The store clerk filed an unusual transactions report and I had him fax it to me." Juan handed Luke another piece of paper, describing the strange behaviour that took place.

"Do you think Mark got a hold of a gun, illegally, and threatened Dee?"

"I don't know. The one thing that I do know is that this *chica* of yours is in a far more dangerous place. Just last week a Red Cross van was looted. The driver and two aid workers were executed on the side of the road. FARC doesn't seem to appreciate aid workers coming into their territory, and she is smack dab in the middle of it."

Dee adjusted the load she was carrying back from the market. Though the box was light, it was bulky and awkward to hold. It was a parcel sent from a church that sponsored her aunt and uncle, and by the large size but light weight, Dee suspected it was full of baby clothes and blankets. Next to her, Lupe seemed to prance along, carrying a couple handmade bags full of groceries. The young girl was so light on her feet, seeming care free and untouched by the burdens of the world. Lupe hummed to herself softly, unaffected by the sweltering heat or the thick, muggy air. With such humidity, they were in store for a storm sooner than later.

Esteban laughed quietly as his sister continued to skip along. His long strides matched her short, quick strut, and despite the heavy box of books that he carried, he had no trouble keeping up. Other than his sister's soft hum, their entourage was silent. Every now and then Esteban would point out something, such as a flower or a bird, but Dee remained silent. She thought that by coming here she would be able to leave everything behind. Last time, she came to escape her step-father and it worked. But this time was different. This time, she couldn't escape. Dark, brooding thoughts refused to let her forget or ignore what she had left behind. Depression seemed to run through her blood and drain all the energy out of her. Everyday she woke up and helplessly watched her strength dwindle. She came to heal but found herself deteriorating instead. She spent her nights sleepless, begging God to help her. Feeling lost and confused, she desperately begged for his guidance, but every time she prayed, she couldn't help but picture Jesus looking sad and turning away. She knew that He was disappointed with her feeble faith.

When they turned the corner, the orphanage appeared and children who had been playing around the gate ran up and greeted them. One small girl wrapped her arms around Dee's leg and looked up with the sweetest smile Dee had ever seen. It warmed Dee's heart and helped push her depressing thoughts aside. Putting her box down on the ground, Dee patted the small head, crowned with thick curls much like her own. Another girl ran up and handed Dee a rope and insisted that she twirled it so that the little ones could jump. As they played jump rope, Esteban rounded up a couple of boys and had them carry Dee's box inside. Lupe followed them inside and Dee remained in the street while other girls lined up for their turn to jump. Beautiful voices filled the air as the girls chanted their silly songs. Dee didn't recognize any of the chants, but enjoyed hearing the clever rhymes.

They had hardly gotten started when her aunt flew out of the orphanage and hustled into the street. Dee had never seen her aunt move so fast and the look on her aunt's face concerned her. Though she didn't look angry, she did not look impressed at all. Esteban quietly followed her aunt, looking quite worried. Dee handed her end of the rope to another girl and left the cheerful chants to join her aunt.

"Is everything okay?" Dee asked. She knew it was a stupid question, but she had to ask.

"A soldier came by today. He was looking for you." Her aunt tried to keep her voice down so that the children wouldn't hear, but rather than whispering, she hissed her words. Her aunt was a bossy woman who had a no-nonsense rule, and her tone worried Dee.

"A soldier..." Dee looked up at Esteban, wondering what a member of FARC would want with her, let alone know about her.

Her aunt continued, dismissing the look exchanged between Dee and Esteban. "An *American* soldier."

Dee looked at her aunt and realized why her aunt was so upset. If the rebels found out that an American soldier visited their orphanage, it could cause some serious trouble. She also felt confused. "What did he want?"

"He delivered this." Her aunt shoved a letter-sized envelope into her hand. "He said it came in their mail, directly from a base in the United States."

Dee looking it over and saw her full name typed on the front. The return address held no name, just an address in DC. Perplexed, Dee opened the envelope and a business card fell out. Flipping it over, she read, *Lieutenant Luke Barden*. Dee's mouth felt dry and she quickly shoved the card back into the envelope. Her aunt began to rant, but Dee ignored her, trying to figure out how Luke found her.

A gentle touch on Dee's shoulder pulled her away from her thoughts.

"Your aunt is right," Esteban said.

"What?" Dee asked. She hadn't been listening and had no idea what they were talking about.

"If you are in cahoots with the U.S. army it'd be best that you leave now. You have no idea what kind of trouble you can cause if *they* find out."

"I'm not in cahoots with anybody," Dee defended herself.

"I'm serious Deanna," her aunt ordered. "You stay away from those soldiers."

Dee squeezed her eyes shut and tried to think. She hated when people used her full name to chide her. She needed to get away so that she could read the letter in privacy. She wondered what Luke had to say. Was he mad at her? Or even worse, was he hurt? Dee could feel a lump grow in her throat and began to fear the contents in the envelope. Would Luke offer her a solution or would she feel worse for what she had done to him? Looking up, she saw Esteban watching her, full of concern as he tried to decipher her thoughts. Backing up, she turned and walked away without a word. She needed to be alone because she had a feeling that no matter what Luke had to say, she would be upset.

When Dee got to her room, she closed the door, thankful that Lupe was elsewhere. Though Dee didn't mind sharing a room with her new friend, right now she desperately needed some privacy. Tugging the letter out of the envelope, Dee apprehensively unfolded it and began to read. She recognized the tight cursive handwriting. Though scrawled out, it was personal, unlike the typed envelope that seemed professional and impersonal.

Dee,

I have so many things to say, yet I can't seem to coherently express my thoughts, so please bear with me.

First of all, I miss you and I am so worried about you.

I know you must be wondering how I found you. Obviously, my job is not as it seems, and I know you've had your suspicions about it. I still work for the U.S. Army. My job is to track down and find missing soldiers and prisoners from the war in Afghanistan. Once I find them, I lead a special tactics unit to rescue and retrieve them. I used these skills and resources to track you down. I'm sorry if that upsets you, but I needed to know that you were okay.

I don't know why you left. Millions of scenarios keep playing through my head. I know that if you wanted me to know, you would have told me, so I'm not going to ask why you left. I know you will tell me when you are ready, so I won't push. But I will tell you how I feel. I cannot help but feel responsible. Dee, I am so sorry if I pushed you away when I revealed my true feelings for you. Perhaps my journal was too much. I know you are apprehensive about relationships, so I should have been more considerate and taken things slower. I am sorry if I pushed too hard, or tried to force things onto you. I care about you more than anything. We were friends first and we will always be friends, if that is what you want. I am a big enough man to respect your feelings and push my desires aside. I would do anything for you. So, if you want me to back off, I will back off. If you need space to breathe and collect your thoughts, that is fine. I will respect that, but don't feel that you have to run away. D.C. is your home where friends and family love and need you. I know that the orphanage has always been a sort of haven for you, but don't feel obliged to hide there. You belong here with us.

I cannot stress how dangerous that area is. I know that you are well aware of the stronghold that FARC has, but things have recently heated up. Over the past few months numerous aid workers have been beaten, kidnapped and even executed. So please be careful and lay low. Do not go out alone. If anything happens, call me. I've included my business card. If you get into trouble of any sort, let me know. I will do anything to keep you safe, and because of the nature of my work, I have the contacts that enable me to help.

Please don't stay away for too long! We all miss you. I would love to hear from you, whether it be a phone call or an e-mail. I could even come visit you. As well, please e-mail Maggie. She misses you so much and is just as worried as I am. I won't tell her where you are, but she deserves to know that you are okay.

I apologize if my words aren't well articulated. There is so much going through my head. I just need you to know that I care about you. I always will. I'm not mad. I'm not angry. I'm just sad and worried and I miss you so much. I'm praying for you and whatever you are feeling and thinking. I hope you find what you are looking for. Please be careful and come home soon.

Love,

Luke

Tears flowed endlessly, forcing Dee to pause and pull herself together before she could read on. Enclosed was a picture of her with her "loved ones", Luke, Maggie and Jeffrey on the day of Maggie's wedding. The wedding party looked their finest. Though they were all smiling, Dee could see the sadness in her eyes, reminding her of the trauma Mark had inflicted on her the night before. Luke's letter was so genuine and sincere, tempting her to pack her bags and run back into his arms, but this picture reminded her of Mark and why she had to leave. With that thought, more tears flowed and her head began to pound from crying so hard. Gathering up the letter, business card and picture, Dee walked over to her dresser and opened the middle drawer. Under a pair of jeans lay the bundle of letters that she had kept. She added this letter to the top and closed the drawer. Looking into the mirror, Dee felt repulsed at her reflection. Her eyes were dull and hollow, surrounded by dark circles. Her cheeks were thin and gaunt. She looked as lifeless as she felt.

Though it was only mid afternoon, Dee crawled into bed with no intentions of ever getting out. She stared at her Bible that rested on her nightstand and doubted that it would have any answers for someone as weak and pathetic as she. She was tired of asking for answers and only receiving silence. Wallowing in her dark thoughts, she let the depression seep in and take over. She was too tired to fight it; too discouraged to hope. She didn't even know what to hope for.

Dee stared at the morning sunshine that bore through her window. Beams of light illuminated her bed, warming her sheets and reminding her that she should get up. It was almost noon, and already her aunt and Lupe had both come in to check on her. Though she got away with hiding in bed all day yesterday, there was work to do. The night had been a restless one. When Lupe came to bed, Dee managed to stifle her sobs, but sleep eluded her. When she did manage to drift off, the sleep intervals were too short to make her feel rested or relaxed. Now, with the bright sun bursting through, Dee knew any chance of a nap would be impossible. Yet she had no desire to crawl out of bed. Her head throbbed from all the tears that she had shed. She wished that she could just turn off all the emotions that she was feeling. She was feeling too many at the same time to understand them. She felt overwhelmed, and like a coward, she wished that she could crawl into a hole and hide until they stopped nagging at her.

A gentle rap at the bars on her window dragged her away from her depressing thoughts. Dee always found the windows in the orphanage strange. They were holes in the wall and didn't have any window panes. Instead, they had metal bars, much like a prison gate, to keep the intruders out but let all the bugs in. She never understood why they didn't put up a screen to keep the bugs out. Another rap followed. Dee sighed and swung her legs over the side of the bed. She had slept in her clothes and her t-shirt from the previous day was terribly wrinkled. Her hair probably looked like a tornado from the all the tossing and turning she did all night. Standing up, she pulled her hair into a low ponytail in an attempt to tame the curly mess. Smoothing her shirt, she pushed the curtains aside. Expecting to find a child waiting for her to come and play, she was surprised to see Esteban standing there.

The look in his eyes confirmed what she suspected: she looked like a mess.

"Lupe said you're upset."

Dee shrugged her shoulders. She didn't want to talk about it. Esteban ignored her shrug and continued, "Come on then, let's go." He beckoned her with his hands.

"Go where?"

"For a walk."

Dee sighed and rubbed her temples. She didn't want to be rude. "I don't want to go for a walk."

A bossy tone took over and Esteban stared her straight in the eyes. "Of course you don't. You're upset. You just want to hide in bed. But a walk will make you feel better." When Dee didn't budge, he continued, "I won't talk, and you don't have to talk. You just have to walk. I'll just walk with you to make sure that it is safe." Again, he beckoned her with his hands.

Dee took a deep breath and dropped her hands from her face. "Fine," she said, as she headed for the door.

"Not that way. Your aunt is waiting at the end of the hall. She's pretending to play with the kids, but she is really waiting for you."

The thought of having to talk to her aunt caused tension to rise in her shoulders and neck. Turning back, Dee unlocked the iron gate that protected her window and crawled out. Esteban offered her a hand, and she took it as she hopped down into the back alley. Esteban then turned and led the way, expecting her to follow.

He continued to march for about ten minutes, leading her outside of the town. Once they reached a dirt road, he slowed down and began to walk beside her. True to his word, he didn't speak. Dee stared at the wild grass that bordered the road. Further up, trees began to emerge and beyond them Dee could see the outline of the mountains. They could only be seen on a clear, sunny day. Dee wished the sunshine would melt away all of her confusion and pain. Silently, they walked along the road until Esteban pointed to the tree line and led her down a rough path into the sparse jungle. Leaving the grasslands behind, the trees surrounded them and various plants and flowers began to pop up. Every now and then Esteban would stop and pick a flower, which he would hand over to her. After an hour or so, Dee had a handful of exotic flowers and the trees grew so dense that she could no longer see the road or the farms that lined it. Finally, Esteban stopped and sat down on a brick ledge. Dee eyed up the manmade bricks that invaded the natural vegetation. They were piled about five high and ran in a circle, collecting the rain and forming a small pond. Dee sat down and tried to follow Esteban's eyes. He sat there silently, staring into the trees. She eventually tracked a colourful bird that he was watching. She set down her flowers and searched the trees, spotting three more.

"Do you feel a bit better?" He cautiously asked.

Dee shrugged. "A bit," she mumbled. It was true. The walk had helped clear her headache and push aside some tension, but everything else still oppressed her.

"I come here a lot, to clear my head." Dee nodded, wishing she could come here everyday. Though they didn't see anyone on their way there, she knew it would be too dangerous to come alone.

"What do you need to clear from your head?" Dee asked, hoping that this conversation would turn her away from her own thoughts.

"Mostly work. If it weren't for this place or Lupita I think I would lose my mind."

Curiosity rose up inside of Dee, causing her to wonder which aspects of his job bothered him so much. "Being a soldier, have you ever had to kill someone?"

Esteban gently laughed, surprising Dee a little bit. Shaking his head, he continued to chuckle. "I'm a mechanic, not a mercenary." Dee felt embarrassed for assuming the worst.

"Then what is it that bothers you so much?"

"I'm good with my hands. I'm good at fixing things. But sometimes I fix a truck and they..." he paused and changed what he was going to say. "I can't be responsible for what they do with the trucks I fix, but sometimes I feel responsible. Like last week..." Esteban cut himself off, not wanting to finish his sentence.

Dee waited, and when he did not continue, she asked, "Are you talking about the Red Cross workers?"

Esteban looked up and she could see sadness in his eyes. "You know?" He asked.

She nodded. "My uncle warned me the second I got here."

Esteban lowered his eyes, "I didn't want to scare you."

Dee shrugged. "You can't take responsibility for other people's actions." As soon as the words were out of her mouth, she wished that they applied to her situation. Guilt began to twist her gut and she felt like a hypocrite.

Esteban slowly looked up and stared at the trees. "My sister says that all the time. But she has to say that; she is my sister." He paused and turned to Dee. Gently squeezing her hand, he continued, "It feels good to hear it from someone else." He then let go of her hand, but continued to stare at her intently. "Do you want to tell me about your letter?"

Dee folded her arms and stared at her lap. "I thought I didn't have to talk."

She could feel his eyes on her, observing her reaction. "I'm not like your aunt. I won't pry. I'm just saying if you want to talk, I will listen. If you don't, that's fine. I'll respect that."

A long silence followed. Dee felt awkward, positive that he was still watching her. She sighed. As much as she did not want to admit her cowardice, she felt compelled to confess. "I ran away. I needed somewhere to hide, so I left without saying good-bye or telling anyone where I was going. I just disappeared. My best friend was really worried." Not wanting to tell the complete truth, she began to lie a little bit, "Her brother is a soldier, so she got him to use his contacts to track me down. She just wanted to make sure that I was okay." Dee dropped her hands into her lap and stared at them. Her chest felt heavy and she didn't feel any better. The thought of Luke writing that letter brought tears to her eyes. She left to protect him, yet all she did was inflict him with pain and confusion. Dee bit her lip, trying to control her emotions. She didn't want to fall apart in the middle of the jungle with Esteban watching her.

"What makes your ex-boyfriend so terrible that you must hide from him?"

Dee trembled at the thought of Mark pressing the gun's cold barrel into her throat. She despised the fear she felt and her tone became bitter. "The best way to hurt someone is to go after their loved ones."

"Why didn't you go to the police?"

"The police can't do anything until he breaks the law. I wasn't willing to wait for that to happen."

"You left to protect them?"

Dee nodded as the tears flowed. "If I stay away, he will leave them alone."

"That's a big sacrifice to make."

His sympathetic statement sent her over the edge. No longer able to control herself, sobs broke free and her shoulders shook with anguish. "I had no choice."

Esteban wrapped his arm around her and rubbed her shoulder in an attempt to soothe her. When her sobs began to subside, he stood up and offered her his hand to help her up. "Let's walk it off," he offered. Dee took his hand, got up, and followed him as he headed further into the jungle.

When Dee returned from their walk, it was mid afternoon. The orphanage was quiet with everyone sleeping except for the older kids. The boys played soccer in the street and the girls sat on the curb gossiping and giggling. With the halls empty, Dee managed to sneak into her room unnoticed. Quietly closing the door behind her, Dee pulled out her laptop and lounged on her bed. Logging onto the internet, Dee patiently waited, forgetting how slow the internet was. She felt slightly refreshed from her walk. Even though she kept most of her thoughts to herself, Esteban's caring nature encouraged her. Luke was right; Maggie deserved to hear from her, and quite frankly, Dee missed her friend. She could use a word or two of encouragement. Entering her password for her e-mail, she was surprised to find her inbox full of messages, mostly from her mother and Maggie. Responding to her mother first, Dee assured her that she was fine and told her that she just needed a change of pace and decided to travel for a while. Dee was surprised that her Aunt Janet hadn't told her sister-in-law what Dee was up to, but appreciated it. Though Dee's mom loved this orphanage as much as she did, her mother would worry way too much.

The next e-mail was much harder to write. Every one of Maggie's messages brought tears to Dee's eyes. The first one was full of delight as Maggie told her about the child they were expecting. As well, it was full of concern, begging Dee to come back where they could talk things through face to face. Words of love echoed throughout each message, warming Dee's heart and encouraging her. Dee was afraid to respond, but loved her friend too much to remain silent. Much like the e-mail to her mother, Dee remained vague, telling Maggie that she was travelling, visiting old friends and making some new ones. Lying, she assured Maggie that the trip was refreshing and exactly what she needed. The truth was, Dee didn't know what she needed. She congratulated Maggie and Jeffrey on their pregnancy, then thanked Maggie for her words of love and told her friend how much she loved and missed her. When she finished the note, Dee read it over. She found her words cold and distant but didn't know how to touch it up. As long as Dee was hiding the truth from her friend, the letter would be neither warm nor genuine. Dee did the best that she could and then sent it before she could change her mind.

She then stared at her list of contacts and pulled up Luke's name. As the page loaded the new message screen, Dee tried to think of something to say, but all the words that came to her mind seemed blunt and harsh. How could she gently say, *Thanks for putting your heart on the line one more time, but you'd be best to forget me and move on.* Should she lie and say, *I don't love you and I never will.* Would she be doing him a favour? She knew it would break his heart, but at least it would get the point across. One day he would heal and move on. One day he would find a nice girl and marry her. Dee's heart ached at the thought of Luke with another woman. He deserved someone else. Someone with less baggage. Someone less complicated. Dee just wished that she could be that girl. Her self-esteem dwindled as she imagined Luke falling for a girl who was much prettier than she was. She'd be smarter and funnier. The second Luke saw her he would forget about Dee and would be much happier. He would fall in love, but Dee would be lonely and miserable.

Dee ran away so that he would be safe and sound. It seemed like the courageous thing to do, yet she felt like a coward. Rather than sending him a message, she closed her e-mail and logged off of the internet. Pushing her laptop aside, she rubbed her temples in frustration. She was too afraid to tell him the truth, yet too weak to blatantly lie to him. She felt pathetic.

Chapter 14

As Dee finished up the last of the dishes, she could hear loud voices coming from the dining hall. Opening the door a crack, she could see Esteban pacing the room, running his hands through his short hair in frustration. Dee could hear Lupe pleading with her brother, but couldn't make out her words. Dee paused in the doorway, unsure if she should go in and try to help calm them down, or if she should return to the kitchen and let the siblings work things out themselves. When Esteban reached the end of the tables, he spun around and paced back. Looking up, he spotted Dee peering around the edge of the door. Turning on his heel, he stormed out of the room, slamming the door behind him. Lupe began to cry and Dee stepped out of the kitchen. When Lupe saw Dee, she jumped up and ran over. Grabbing Dee's hand, Lupe dragged Dee to the outside door.

She began to plead with her, "Talk to him Dee. He won't listen to me anymore!" She then pushed Dee out of the door without offering an explanation. Looking into the courtyard, Dee saw Esteban rush past the gate. By the time she reached the gate he was already in his old, beat-up truck. Playing with the ignition, he coaxed his engine to start. The engine whined but refused to start on the first try. This bought Dee some time as she dashed up to the side of the truck. Reaching through the open window, Dee tugged on his sleeve to get his attention. Esteban turned as if to say something, but caught himself when he realized that it was Dee standing there. His face looked hard and angry, but in his eyes Dee could see guilt. Letting go of his ignition, he lowered his face.

Dee opened his door and beckoned him out. When he refused to move, she offered, "How about a walk?" When he refused to look up or say anything, she quoted him, "You don't have to talk. You just have to walk."

Turning, he slid his hand along the frame of the door and climbed out of his truck. Dee couldn't believe how much his hand trembled. Rather than closing the door behind him, Esteban wrapped his arms around her shoulders and leaned in. Holding her tight, Dee could feel his body shake and a tear escaped from his cheek and ran down her shoulder. Sinking one hand into her mess of curls, Dee could feel it slowly regain control. Steadying himself, he began to calm down. When Dee felt that he had regained his composure she pulled back and looked him in the eye. He avoided eye contact and mumbled, "I didn't know."

Dee nodded in an attempt to assure him, though she had no idea what he was talking about. Turning, he began to walk and she joined him. His strides were long and fast and Dee struggled to keep up. Reaching the corner, Dee turned to go left, but he caught her hand and pulled her back. "Not that way," he said. His tone was full of grief and Dee wondered why he avoided the route he always took. Complying, Dee turned and followed him in the opposite direction. When they reached the edge of town, Esteban found a fallen tree in the ditch and sat down on the trunk. He leaned forward, with his elbows on his knees and stared at his hands. Dee sat next to him. She remained silent for a while, giving him the chance to talk if he wanted to. After a long time, she broke the silence.

"What happened?"

A long silence ensued. Dee patiently waited, not wanting to push. She watched as his shoulders began to slightly tremble. After a while he responded.

"They attacked some aid workers. Stole all of their medicine. They killed one of them. The one girl..." his voice broke and Dee waited for him to continue, "She was so young. She couldn't have been older than Lupita."

Dee thought of Esteban's teenage sister. That was young for an aid worker. He continued, "She's just a kid, trying to help. And they beat her..." He refused to finish his train of thought.

Dee waited to see if he would say more. When he remained silent, she asked, "Were you there?"

He slowly shook his head, "I fixed their truck. They needed it right away. I knew something was up, I just didn't know what."

"It's not your fault. You didn't do this to them."

"I just keep thinking if I had taken longer to fix the truck, perhaps this wouldn't have happened."

Dee reached over and rubbed his back. "You can't blame yourself, Esteban. You had no way of knowing."

He looked up and rested his chin in his hands. "But I'm enabling them. If I didn't fix the trucks for them..."

"Then somebody else would. And the same thing would still happen. You can't take responsibility for their actions."

Esteban slowly nodded and stretched his arms in front of him. "I know. I know. My brain keeps telling me that. But my heart...my heart..." he paused, unable to find the right words. "I wish it never happened."

Dee continued to gently stroke his back. "Of course you do. You're not cruel. You're compassionate. That's what sets you apart from the men that did this to them."

Esteban turned and a slight smile tugged at the corner of his lips. Patting her knee, he thanked her. Dee smiled back and asked the question that had been bugging her for a long time. "Why do they attack aid workers? I understand why they would steal their supplies, but why are they killing them?"

"We've been fairly peaceful for the past few years. A few months ago, our commander was killed and Jorge filled his position. He has a personal vendetta against them."

"But why? They are only trying to help."

Esteban turned to face her. "Years ago, probably before your aunt and uncle built their orphanage, some missionaries came here. They weren't like your aunt and uncle. They were religious fanatics. Jorge's mother was a witch doctor in a neighbouring village. These missionaries thought she was demon possessed and tried to beat the demon out of her. She died from her injuries a few days later. Jorge is targeting anyone he suspects of trying to convert the locals. Last week, the Red Cross workers were executed because he found some New Testaments in a bag. They were just looting the van, but it soon turned violent. Today's mission was just supposed to be a raid. They were just roughing them up, but when Jorge saw that the one volunteer was wearing a gold cross around her neck, he lost it and beat her to death."

Dee's eyes widened as she began to realize the actual danger that surrounded her. "Then why does he leave my aunt and uncle alone?"

"Your aunt and uncle are very quiet about their faith. Their first priority is to protect the children and give them a healthy home to grow up in. As well, so many of us grew up in the orphanage. Your aunt and uncle are unintentionally raising soldiers for him. If Jorge went after your aunt and uncle, he'd probably have a coup on his hands."

"What about me?"

"As long as you keep quiet and mind your own business you will be fine. Besides, you're with me." Esteban winked at her in an attempt to reassure her. Luke's warning echoed in the back of her mind. She ran away to escape the dangerous wrath of her ex, only to insert herself in the middle of guerrilla warfare. She was beginning to wonder if she unintentionally gravitated towards danger. Pushing her thoughts aside, she patted Esteban on the back.

"Feel a bit better?"

Esteban sat up, put his arm around Dee and pulled her close. "How could I not feel better? I've got a beautiful woman taking time out of her day to chase after me and put up with my mood swings."

Dee blushed at his compliment. For the past couple of weeks, she sure didn't feel beautiful. She felt pathetic and cowardly, frustrated and exhausted.

Esteban tilted her chin up and studied her face. Her reaction wasn't what he expected. Though she blushed, she didn't smile or act coy. Instead, her eyes became sad and her face looked stressed. Again, he tried to make her smile. "I mean it. A girl like you sure makes a man feel special."

His efforts were futile. Her face fell even more and he feared that she would cry. "What is it?" He gently asked.

Dee straightened her back and bit her lip in an attempt to control her emotions. "I just don't feel so special. Ever since my Mark and I broke up, my life has been on a downward spiral. And God..." Dee stopped herself. She never intended to blurt out such personal thoughts.

But Esteban pushed on, "What about God?"

Dee shrugged and let out a deep breath. "He just seems so distant. I beg Him for guidance and He remains silent. I keep trying to do the right thing, but it never feels right. I can't help but feel that He is so disappointed with me that He is ignoring me."

"Why would He be disappointed with you?"

"Because I am a coward. Rather than trusting in God I give in to my weak faith. I honestly thought that by coming here, things would get better, but they are not."

"You just got here. Some things take time."

"I just wish He'd tell me what to do."

"That makes two of us."

Dee looked at him surprised. "How so?"

"When I first joined the rebels, things were quiet. We were just there to protect the community, but when Jorge took over, things changed. Drug trafficking started up, locals are being taken advantage of, and aid workers are being killed. I keep asking God, 'what do I do?' Do I defect or do I wait it out? For months I've been asking this, but God hasn't told me what to do. So, I figure I'll stay where I am until He tells me otherwise. Perhaps it's the same for you. Now that you are here, perhaps you just have to patiently wait until God tells you otherwise."

"But don't you feel like God has turned his back on you?"

"All the time. Lupe thinks God is using his silence to test my faithfulness. He wants to see how long I will stick it out for."

"I don't feel tested. I feel punished."

"Why would God be punishing you?"

"Because my fear outweighs my faith."

"I think you should wait it out. Jonah was a coward. God put him through a huge ordeal, but in the end, God told him exactly what He wanted."

Dee studied his face, surprised at how insightful he was. "You think I should tough it out?"

Esteban smiled. "You look tough. I think you can handle it."

"I wish it were easier."

Esteban nodded. "Don't we all?"

Chapter 15

Dee stared at her e-mail, contemplating whether she should open up the new message from Maggie. Every time she heard from her best friend, she was filled with both delight and sorrow. Mustering up her courage, she clicked on the message and read:

Dee!

How are you? How are your travels going? With you being so secretive, should I even bother asking where you are? You're missing a ton of excitement at home! Yesterday Jeffrey and I had our first ultrasound. We are having a baby girl! And I absolutely insist that you come home when she is born, at least for a short visit. Since you are practically family, it only makes sense that you come home to see your first niece!

As you already know, we've rented our basement out to a girl named Ashley. She's fallen head over heels for Luke.

She's such a sweetheart and they get along great! He's been so moody the past few months. He's working way too much. Now that she's here to provide him some company, perhaps he won't feel the need to work so hard. Anyways, Ashley and I have been spending the past few weeks planning a huge birthday party for him. She's added all the personal touches needed to make the party perfectly suit him. She's perfect for him! I hope he realizes this sooner than later. I would love to have her as my sister-in-law.

Anyways, not much else is going on here. I wish you could be here for the party. Enjoy yourself wherever you are and I can't wait to see you in the fall. (We won't take no for an answer.)

Love,

Maggie

For days Dee had been watching the calendar, anticipating the arrival of March 12. She wanted to e-mail Luke and wish him a happy birthday. She wanted to show that she still cared but knew it wouldn't be fair. She didn't want to lead him on. So instead, she remained silent and tried to ignore his approaching birthday. For the past couple of months, Dee had been praying for Luke, hoping that he would find healing. Now it appeared that he had found Ashley and was able to move on. Dee wanted to be happy for him, but jealousy struck and she missed him even more. Closing her laptop, she buried her head into her pillow. She wanted to scream. Why was everything so confusing? Why did it have to be so hard if she was doing the right thing? She knew this day would come, yet nothing prepared her for how much it hurt.

Dragging herself out of bed, Dee headed down the hallway and entered the kitchen. Noisy chatter filled the dining hall as the kids impatiently waited for breakfast. Washing her hands, Dee helped Lupe fill a basket full of fruit. Lupe silently watched Dee but didn't say anything. Though they had become quite good friends, Lupe recognized Dee's bad days and graciously gave Dee the space that she needed. Unlike Dee's aunt, Lupe didn't pry.

Once the basket was full, Lupe carried it over to the counter. Dee followed with an armful of cereal boxes. Setting them next to the milk, Dee could hear her uncle saying grace. When he finished, the children stormed the buffet line, helping themselves to cereal and fruit. Dee followed Lupe into the dining hall and helped the younger children pour milk into their bowls. When all the children had been served, Dee helped herself to some food and sat down at a table full of girls. She remained silent, listening to their endless chatter. They told jokes and teased the younger girls. Dee half-heartedly smiled at their antics. Though the children were a source of joy, Dee still felt empty inside. Finishing her breakfast, she gathered up her dishes and headed into the kitchen. Her feet felt heavy. Already the sink was heaped with dirty dishes. Dee began to wash them and stack them on the counter next to her. She could hear footsteps behind her but ignored them.

Continuing to wash the dishes, she was surprised to see Esteban standing next to her with a towel in his hands. Silently, he began to dry the mound of bowls, stacking them in the cupboard. He smiled at her gently, but left her to her thoughts. When the dishes were done, he turned to Dee and handed her the towel.

He watched as Dee dried off her hands. "Lupe said you are sad today."

Dee tried to shrug, not able to acknowledge nor deny it.

"Another e-mail from home?" He tried again.

Dee nodded. She didn't really want to talk about it. She had spent all this time, pushing Luke away from her, and now that he was moving on, she wanted him more than ever. Part of her felt tempted to return to DC and try to rekindle what they once had. But as long as she stayed away, he'd be safe; and by the looks of it, happy.

Esteban studied her face, trying to read her thoughts. He wondered who it was that she missed so much. Was it really Maggie? Or was it her ex? He knew many girls that seemed to fall for the "bad-boy" and he wondered if she still had feelings for Mark, despite how terrible he had been. Determined to make her forget about Mark, he continued, "I'm taking Lupe into town. You should come with us."

Dee looked around the spotless kitchen, wishing she could find some sort of excuse to stay behind. When nothing came to mind, she resigned and nodded. Tossing the towel aside, Dee followed him into the yard to find Lupe waiting by the gate. As they walked into town, Lupe pranced beside them, swinging a basket of goodies that she made for her sweetheart. Once they reached the *zócolo*, Lupe dashed off to the butcher's shop. When she reached the door, she turned and waved and then went inside. Neither Lupe, Dee, or her aunt were allowed to go into town unless they were escorted by Esteban or her uncle. With her uncle being so busy, Lupe desperately depended on her brother to take her to see her boyfriend, Carlos, the butcher's son. Recently it seemed that they were making more trips into town.

Sitting on the steps that led up to the fountain that adorned the town's square, Dee watched the vendors set up their makeshift shops. Esteban sat down next to her and stretched out his long legs.

"Lupe seems really happy," Dee commented.

Esteban smiled and nodded. "He loves her. Came and told me himself. It's just a matter of time before they get married."

"Then what are they waiting for?"

Esteban let out a low laugh. "For Carlos to muster up the courage to propose."

Dee laughed with him. Carlos was a strong boy, but was extremely shy. She wouldn't be surprised if Lupe had to force the words out of him. "I'm happy for them."

Esteban grew serious. "Are you really happy?"

His blunt question caught her off guard. She didn't know how to answer it. Was she really happy? She tried to work it out. "Sometimes I'm lonely and confused, but I'm lucky to be here."

"Then why do you look so sad?"

Where to start? Dee thought to herself. "Maggie's having a baby and wants me to come home when she is born."

"Home is where the heart is."

"I don't know where my heart is."

Esteban paused before he asked the question he had wanted to ask for a long time. "Is it still with your ex?"

Dee snorted. Her "no" was extremely straightforward.

"Then perhaps with another man?"

Dee paused. Her heart no longer belonged to Luke. Ashley's heart belonged to him now. She shook her head.

"Then maybe it belongs here."

"I thought this was my new home. Then I got an e-mail from Maggie and I no longer know what to think."

"Will you go visit her?"

Dee shook her head.

Esteban leaned forward and propped his elbows on his knees. Folding his hands together, he became serious. "As much as I want you to stay here, perhaps this is God's way of telling you to go back and make things right. It doesn't mean you have to stay."

"A short visit is tempting, but I'm too afraid."

"God doesn't want us to be afraid."

"But if my ex finds out, he'll..."

"You can't be responsible for other people's actions. At least, that's what you keep telling me."

Dee sat back, stunned at his rebuke. "If someone threatened Lupe, wouldn't you do everything in your power to protect her?"

Esteban nodded and sat up. Staring Dee straight in the eyes, he replied, "But the only thing I could do to ensure her safety is to trust that God will protect her."

"You think I should go back and hope that God will keep them safe."

"Not hope – believe."

"I don't think my faith is strong enough to actually believe such a thing."

"Well, the baby isn't coming for a few more months. That should be enough time to work on it."

Dee leaned forward and rubbed her temples. She could feel all of her stress mounting into a headache. She knew that Esteban was right, but refused to acknowledge it.

"Why did you break up with your boyfriend?" His tone was soft and curious, no longer authoritative and admonishing.

"There was another woman.

"So let me get this straight. He leaves you for another woman yet he still threatens you?"

"As long as I'm miserable, he's happy," Dee stated.

"After you broke up was there ever another man in your life?"

Dee thought about Luke but kept a straight face. Shaking her head, she lied. "No, there was no one else." There was no sense acknowledging her feelings for Luke anymore. His heart belonged to Ashley. The sooner she accepted that, the sooner she could move on.

Esteban leaned forward and picked a small flower that managed to grow between the cracked cobblestone road. "Well then, I see no reason for you to be unhappy. You can be happy here. Your ex will never know." Tucking the beautiful, white flower behind her ear, he cupped her chin and looked straight in her eyes. "Who knows what kind of happiness you might find here."

Dee blushed and turned her head, pulling away from his intimate embrace. He leaned back and watched her react. "I know you remember."

Dee blushed even more. She thought back to the last time she sat at this fountain with Esteban. She was sixteen and he had been her first kiss. Back then, when it was safer, her uncle let her go to the market with some friends from the orphanage. Esteban managed to sneak her away from the crowd and took her to see the fountain. He was such a flirt and had obviously kissed a girl before. Between his charisma and his gently whispered words of endearment, Dee was smitten. She had never been called beautiful before. She felt awkward and didn't know how to respond, but it didn't matter because Esteban took control of the situation and kissed her before she could say anything. Dee smiled at the memory of how giddy she felt afterwards. She was a silly schoolgirl who thought she had fallen in love.

Esteban watched her as a smile crept across her face. He hadn't seen her smile so genuinely since her arrival. He loved seeing the effect that he had on her. Though she was a grown woman, she still blushed like a teenager. "That's the first real smile I've seen since you got here. Who knew I was such a good kisser," he teased.

"Of course you were a good kisser," Dee retorted, "with all of your expertise."

A smug smile spread across his face. "What expertise?" He asked, trying to sound innocent.

Dee didn't fall for it. Calling him on it, she asked, "How many girls have you kissed in front of this fountain?"

Esteban tried to look serious, but his smug smile remained. "Only one that mattered."

"And why was that?"

"Because if your uncle found out, he'd kill me!"

Dee burst out laughing and playfully swatted his shoulder. Getting up, she stood ready to go back to the orphanage. Standing next to her, Esteban held her hand and playfully looked into her eyes. "See how much happiness a simple kiss can create. Next time you're sad, just let me know. I'll make you smile again."

Dee rolled her eyes at his cheesy come-on and laughed. "I'm not falling for your charm this time."

Esteban raised an eyebrow and challenged her. "Oh yeah?"

"Yeah. If you try to kiss me, I'll tell my uncle."

Dee turned and began to walk away. Esteban stood there smiling and called out, "I'm not afraid of your uncle anymore."

Dee laughed and called over her shoulder, "We'll see about that!"

Chapter 16

Dee absentmindedly watched the preschool children draw pictures with crayons. She stared down at her blank sheet of paper. Spring had come and the rainy season had hit, soaking everything outside. The children were becoming rowdy and impatient, needing a place to run around. Dee laughed as she watched Jose hoard all the green crayons to himself. His abstract scribbles offered so many shades of green that she could envision it in an art gallery. He claimed that it was a dragon, though no shape of a dragon was evident. Dee then complimented Sophia's drawing of a cat and stared down at her blank paper.

The never-ending rain was getting to Dee as well. Much like the children, she felt imprisoned. She needed to break free from the confining walls of the orphanage where her thoughts plagued her day and night. Ever since the day at the fountain, Esteban's words had bothered her. She knew she shouldn't take responsibility for Mark's actions, yet she felt entirely responsible. She wondered if Esteban was right. Did God want her to go home and make things right? If so, what was there to make right? According to Maggie, things were heating up between Luke and Ashley. Sure, she could confess the reality of her situation to Maggie and Jeffrey, but was there any point in telling Luke? If he had moved on, who was she to interfere with his happiness?

Dee tried to bury her thoughts. She felt bitter, knowing that Luke was moving on and finding happiness, while she was locked up in an orphanage, lonely and depressed. She wished the rain would stop. She needed fresh air and a chance to stretch her legs. She felt like running; running until her legs felt like they would collapse beneath her.

Staring out the window and watching the rain pour down, Dee's thoughts immediately returned back to Luke. She had left because she feared for Luke's life. Once she left, she was too afraid to tell him the truth. She was afraid of so many things: that he would take the risk, that he would be so hurt that he would never heal, that he would become so angry that he would hate her and never forgive her, or that he wouldn't understand. Now she was filled with a new fear: a fear that it was too late. He said that he would wait and Dee was afraid that she made him wait too long. What if Ashley was the real deal? What if she made Luke happier than Dee ever could? Perhaps he was better off with Ashley? That is what Dee feared the most.

Fear, fear, fear. That was all she felt and it was driving her crazy. She wished she could be more like Esteban, patient and trusting in God. The rebels were getting out of control. Lately it seemed like there had been daily instances of abuse or crime. Local farmers were having their land stolen from them. Drug use surged in their tiny town and many people were either kidnapped or disappeared entirely. Esteban didn't agree with the route his commander was taking, but he wasn't going to do anything drastic until God told him to. He was so sure God would answer his prayers and petitions. Unlike Esteban, Dee was convinced that God no longer listened to her. Esteban kept encouraging her, telling her not to give up, but she wondered what the point was. God had better things to do then to listen to her petty prayers.

Dee picked up a purple crayon and began to draw a flower. Little Jose picked up a green crayon, reached over and began coloring in the petals for her. Dee smiled at the green flower in front of her. By the time she finished her picture, the rain had let up and she let the kids outside. They rushed out and attacked the mud puddles. Dee put on her shoes and followed. Though they were creating a mess, they were expending energy that had been bottled up and driving them crazy. Soon the sun broke through the thick clouds and the air turned muggy and unbearable. Dee could feel the damp curls on the nape of her neck curl even tighter. Flowers that were flattened by the harsh rain stood up and stretched towards the sun, drinking in its warmth and sunshine.

Finding the biggest puddle in the entire courtyard, Sophia and two friends began to play jump rope, with each jump landing in the middle of the puddle, soaking everyone. Some younger girls began to play imaginary hopscotch, for their hopscotch lines were either washed away by the rain or buried beneath puddles. In a matter of minutes, each child was soaked and filthy.

Esteban soon pulled up in his truck, and quickly drove through a large puddle, splashing a group of older girls. They shrieked with delight, obviously enjoying the attention Esteban paid to them. Dee smiled as she watched her friend get out of his truck. Carlos got out of the passenger seat and went to see Lupe. The girls immediately swarmed Esteban, flirting and giggling. With the constant rain, Dee hadn't seen Esteban for over a week. She had missed him. He was both an encouragement and a distraction. Breaking free from the entourage of pre-adolescent girls, Esteban turned and jogged into the courtyard. Spotting Dee, he hurried over and presented her with some wild orchids that he had found. He was always showing up with gifts for her. Usually they were flowers, though the one day, dared by some of the boys, he gave her a box full of frogs.

Dee smiled and accepted his simple gift. Returning her smile, he asked, "Can you sneak away for a bit?" His words were rushed and he sounded impatient.

Caught off guard, Dee stuttered back. "I...I suppose so." Catching Lupe's attention from across the courtyard, Dee motioned that she was leaving with Esteban, and Lupe nodded, signalling that she understood and would watch the children.

Walking towards his truck, Esteban's stride was long and hurried. Dee hustled in order to keep up with him. Opening the passenger door, Esteban helped her inside and shut the door. Running to his side, he jumped in and pulled away. As they drove, he nervously tapped his steering wheel. Dee noticed that his shoulders looked tense.

"Is everything alright?" She asked.

Instead of responding, he just drove faster. When they reached the path that led to the pond, he pulled over into the ditch and hopped out. Dee let herself out and followed him down the path, practically jogging to keep up. The trees were still damp from the rain and sparkled in the sunlight. Occasionally a fat drop would fall to the ground. A few sounds in the jungle startled Esteban and Dee wondered what made him seem so uneasy.

When they reached the man-made pond, he paced back and forth. Dee watched him with curiosity. Finally, he stopped, grabbed her hand and pulled her down to sit next to him on the brick ledge.

"It's bad Dee," he started. Dee questioned him with her eyes but he continued before she could ask. "This morning, they came to me with a bunch of trucks. They want me to weld cages onto the box. It's to hold prisoners. They've been extorting the local farmers, saying that if they don't pay, they will kill their families or destroy their land. Some farmers have refused, so they are going to arrest them tonight. Who knows what they will do to them. I can't do it Dee. If they hadn't told me, I would have assumed it was for cattle, but now that I know, I can't do it."

Dee nodded. She didn't blame him. "What are you going to do?"

Esteban took a deep breath. "I have to leave. Jorge is coming back at supper time and when he finds out that I haven't started on his trucks, he's going to be furious. If I'm not out of town by the time he finds out, I'm dead! Carlos is taking Lupita out of town to keep her safe. I need you to come with me!"

"Go with you?!" Dee stood up shocked.

Esteban stood up and cupped her cheeks in his hands. His eyes were warm but serious. "I know this isn't how things are done. I know that we should date first, but Dee, I care for you too much to leave you behind. And I am afraid that they will come after you, knowing how I feel about you." Kneeling, he plucked a beautiful pink orchid from its stem. Rising he tucked it into her hair and sweetly murmured "Te quiero." He gently stroked her cheek and watched her reaction. Dee felt overwhelmed and confused. Continuing, he promised, "You are my best friend, Dee. I love you too much to live without you."

Dee opened her mouth to respond, but no words came. Esteban eagerly searched her face for an answer, caressing her cheek with his thumb. Sliding his hand from her face, he reached down and played with her long, blond braid. "When I kissed you at the fountain," he murmured, "I knew you were someone special. I just never dared to dream that you would come back into my life."

Again, Dee fought for words. She had no future with Luke, but she knew that she couldn't settle for a marriage with Esteban. She lowered her eyes, sad that once again she was hurting someone she cared for. Before she could respond, a loud crack sounded from the jungle behind her. She could hear footsteps and turned to find a rifle trained on her. The man who held it was short and ugly and looked old for a soldier. One after another, a dozen rebels emerged from the jungle's brush, dressed in camouflage and heavily armed.

273

They circled around Dee and Esteban, pointing their weapons at them. Dee turned to face Esteban. Fear seized his face and he froze in his spot.

The ugly old man spoke up. "She's a beautiful woman," he acknowledged, keeping his gun trained on Dee. "But beauty is deceiving. It can brainwash you. Make you believe things that aren't true and turn you into a traitor." Turning his attention to Esteban, he continued, "They come preaching God's love and forgiveness, but they are really here to mislead and betray you. It takes a pathetic man to fall for their lies. We are revolutionaries, not converts!"

Esteban stepped forward, about to say something, but before he could a rebel came up from behind him and struck him in the back with a pipe. Esteban fell to the muddy ground, winded and unable to get up. Dee turned and shrieked. She knelt to help him up, but before she knew it, the butt of a rifle struck her in the back of her head, knocking her out.

Dee's head pounded and her mind was thick and foggy. She tried to push herself up, only to find her hands and feet bound by a thick rope. Rolling onto her side, she forced her eyes to focus. The room was dark and shadows swirled into blurry images. Dee squeezed her eyes shut and tried to concentrate. Pushing up, she managed to sit herself up and leaned against a cold cement wall. She tugged her arms and found that they were tied to the wall, as if she were a dog on a leash. Leaning back, she could feel the blood draining from her head and the fog began to lift. She heard her name and froze, searching the darkness. The voice was close, but she couldn't see where it came from. Again, she heard her name. Turning to her right, she stared into the darkness, concentrating. Soon her eyes began to adjust and she made out the form of a man sitting in the opposite corner, tied up the same way she was. He strained against his ropes, trying to inch his way closer to her.

Giving up, he sat on his knees and stared at Dee. Her head throbbed and she closed her eyes. She felt so sleepy. The fog began to thicken again. Dee could hear him calling her name, but she didn't have the strength to respond. Giving in, she allowed the thick fog to envelope her, caressing her mind and carrying away her consciousness.

Again, Dee woke up to the sound of a man calling her name. This time there was no fog to cloud her mind. Only pain was present, shooting through her head and down her neck. Still seated against the wall, a dim light began to trickle into her cell from behind the iron bars that enclosed them, signalling either dusk or dawn. Across from her sat Esteban, watching her desperately. Dee stared at him, wondering how long she had been out. Minutes, hours, perhaps even days?

Now that he had her attention, he refused to look away. Staring into her deep, copper eyes, he tried to determine the amount of pain she was feeling. Dee returned his stare and noticed that he had accrued more injuries than she remembered. His face was bruised, his lips fat and swollen. His one eye was black, the other red and puffy. Blood had run from his rose and dried onto his face, forming a crusty layer. As if forgetting that he was tied to the wall, he tried to crawl towards her. When the ropes prevented him, he angrily jerked against them, like a wild animal in captivity. When the ropes refused to give, he gave up and leaned against the wall. He wanted to be brave, but he could see no way of escaping the nightmare that lay before them. Desperation clung to his emotions and tears escaped from his eyes. "Lo siento," he murmured as he hung his head. "I'm so sorry Dee. I never meant for," he paused and looked around, "*this*."

Dee nodded and looked away. She couldn't stand to look her friend in the eye. His injuries were too much. Looking down, she mumbled, "I'm sorry too."

Esteban opened his mouth to say more, but stopped when he heard voices from around the corner. Three soldiers appeared and stood before the iron bars. Opening the gate, two soldiers entered and approached Dee. Esteban shouted and madly fought against the ropes that confined him. The third soldier entered their cell and began to beat him mercilessly. The other two soldiers undid the rope that held Dee to the wall and yanked her to her feet. Ruthlessly, the one shoved her so hard that she flew out of the gate onto her knees, scrapping them on the cold cement floor. They then grabbed her by the arms and dragged her away. The third left Esteban, closing the gate behind them. As they dragged Dee outside, she could still hear Esteban's shouts, pleading for them to leave her alone.

Luis raced into the kitchen, searching for any sign of Janet or Rick. A small boy, sneaking some food out of the fridge, stared at the soldier with large, startled eyes. Without saying a word, he pointed down the hall. Luis raced down and found them in the office at the end.

Bursting in, Janet and Rick stared at him in amazement. It had been two years since Luis ran away from the orphanage and joined the rebel movement. They hadn't seen or heard from him since.

"They arrested them!" He blurted out, catching his breath from the long run.

Rick offered Luis a chair, which he gladly collapsed into. Before Lupe had left, she told them that Esteban was defecting. Rick urged her to hurry away with Carlos, but was surprised that Dee would go with Esteban. He knew that they were growing closer together, but never realized that they

277

cared for each other that much. Letting his wife take the other chair, he leaned against the computer desk.

"Who, Luis? Who did they arrest?"

Luis sucked in a deep breath. "Esteban and your niece."

Janet moaned with alarm and began to cry. Rick ignored her and tried to concentrate. Dee was his only niece and he would do anything to help her. "Are they still alive?" He asked.

Luis thought back to the image he had witnessed, the ring of soldiers beating the small white girl in the middle of their camp. When they had finished, they dragged her back to her cell. She was alive, but suffered a great amount. He nodded in affirmation.

Rick continued, "What are they going to do?"

Luis shrugged his shoulders. "Right now they are in the holding cells, but," he paused and looked at Janet, unsure if she should hear the rest. Rick urged him to continue, so he did, "They have these things called sweat boxes. They are tiny jails placed directly in the sunlight. Lately they've been putting prisoners in there. Either they starve to death or suffocate."

"You think Jorge will use those on Dee or Esteban?"

Once again, Luis shrugged his shoulders. "It's hard to tell. He's really got it in for her, being a Christian and all.

When he's this mad, either he instantly executes them or tortures them. Since she's still alive..."

Again, Janet moaned and Luis stopped. This time Rick acknowledged his wife and patted her hand. "If so," he pried, "how long would she have?"

"If it's hot, only a few days."

Rick nodded. "Luis, thank you for telling me. Now you better get back before they notice you are gone. I'll see what I can do."

Luis nodded and then bolted out of the office, eager to get away before someone caught him there. He knew the great risk he was taking, but he felt that he owed Esteban, who had always been like a big brother to him.

Dee crumpled to the ground as another blow struck her across her back. The scorching sun dried up the week's worth of rain, making the ground hard and dried out. Blood poured from her mouth and sank into the cracks in the dehydrated ground. Another blow knocked her onto her side and she moaned with pain. She could hear them taunting her, but her ears were ringing so bad that she couldn't make out their words. Dee gagged on the acrid taste of blood and spit out a mouthful. She then felt two sets of arms pick her up and drag her back to her cell. That was enough for today. She'd see them again tomorrow. That is, if she managed to survive the night.

Rick left the desk and knelt before his wife. Taking both of her hands into his, he forced her to look him in the eyes.

"I'm going to the embassy. Hopefully someone will still be there. I need you to go through Dee's stuff. See if you can find a contact number for her friends at home. We need to contact someone."

Janet nodded and feebly asked, "What about Rita?"

Rick felt his heart sink even further at the mention of his sister-in-law. "I'll call her when I get back. I'll tell her, but I want to try to get some good news first."

Dee collapsed the second the soldiers let go of her. The cement floor was cold and soothed her swollen face. Sweat dripped into her cuts, stinging her forehead. The soldiers didn't even bother to tie her up, knowing she was too injured to move. She forced her body to roll onto her side. Her aching muscles screamed at her, but she needed to see if Esteban was there. She searched the room and found him huddled in his corner, staring at her horrified. Though he had endured his own beating earlier, it appeared that they left him alone since the last time she saw him. She fell onto her back and stared at the ceiling, no longer able to hold herself up. A dim light trickled in. Night was descending upon them. Dee lost track of time, unsure of what day it was.

"How long have we been here?" She asked.

Esteban's voice was quiet, but calm. "Since yesterday afternoon."

Dee sighed. It felt like longer, but she was sure that he was right. Pain crawled through her abdomen as cramps seized her muscles and organs. She squirmed with pain, but finally gave up. There was no point fighting it. The more she squirmed, the more it hurt. Tilting her face towards Esteban she sighed and gave in. *If this is the end, then so be it*, she thought. She was tired of running and hiding. She was tired of fighting and worrying. She was just plain old tired.

Sighing she stared at Esteban. If this was her last night, she'd make it a truthful one. Taking a deep breath, she let the damp, stifling air burn her lungs. "I lied to you," she admitted. Esteban looked at her, about to ask, but Dee continued on before he could. "There was another man after Mark. When Mark found out, he threatened me, saying if he ever saw me with him again, he'd kill him. So, I left. I thought that eventually I would forget about him, but I love him too much. Even now, despite all my fear, I can't forget him." She looked at Esteban and confessed, "I couldn't go with you, because I love him too much."

She knew her words hurt more than the physical pain he was enduring. She felt bad, but didn't regret what she said. She didn't want to lie anymore. She didn't have the strength to. Esteban's eyes grew sad, but she didn't see any trace of anger. "I always suspected," he murmured, "but I didn't know why you came alone. Why didn't he come with you?"

Dee felt tears rise to her eyes. She thought of Luke's gentle smile and his strong shoulders. "He would have, but I wasn't willing to gamble with his life. I left without telling him, because I knew he would take the risk."

"Then you must have really loved him," Esteban acknowledged.

Sobs erupted from Dee's throat, causing her whole body to shudder with pain. "I'm sorry if I hurt your feelings." Her apology felt pathetic, but at least she said it.

Esteban nodded and then lowered his eyes, too sad to respond.

Janet opened Dee's laptop, hoping to find an address book of some sort, but was locked out by a password that protected Dee's privacy. Putting the computer aside, she began to dig through the chest of drawers. Most drawers were bare; emptied when Lupe left with Carlos. The bottom two drawers contained all of Dee's clothing. Rooting around, she found nothing and opened the next drawer. Pushing aside a set of jeans, she was surprised to find a journal wrapped in a pink ribbon. Resting on top was the strange envelope that the American soldier delivered the one day. Opening the journal, Janet found more letters. She wasn't aware that Dee was corresponding with anyone during her stay at Hope's Haven.

Sitting on the narrow bed, Janet opened the top letter and began to read. She raised her eyebrows as this man, who was not Mark, professed his love for her. In her own opinion, it seemed a little too soon for Dee to be moving on, so early after her break up. She finished his letter and put his business card aside. She would have Rick call him when he got back and see what this Luke character could do. Personally, she had a feeling that it would be a waste of time. She doubted that he had the connections or the skills that he claimed to have.

Moving on, she began to read the next letter. Within the first few lines, she knew that these were extremely personal letters, but she couldn't help herself. She continued to snoop, admiring him for the amount of love he professed, yet disliking him for being too cowardly to admit it. If he was too afraid to tell her of his love, what would make him brave enough to save her from militants? Janet continued to pour through the letters, noting the dates. She had a suspicion that their relationship continued, despite Dee's relationship with Mark. That would explain the abrupt break up.

Rick suddenly came into the room. Janet checked her watch, surprised that he was back so soon. She questioned him with her eyes and he sadly responded, "There was no one there. I'll try first thing tomorrow morning."

Janet nodded and handed him Luke's business card and his most recent letter. Rick read it over and as Janet watched, she could see hope rising in his eyes. She hated to get his hopes up. She seriously doubted this character. When Rick finished the letter, he eyed the rest of the letters, scattered about the bed. "What are those?" He asked.

"More love letters," Janet replied nonchalantly. She then narrowed her eyes and put her hands on her hips, "You don't think that they..."

Rick cut her off. "It's none of our business. You shouldn't have read those. I'm going to phone Luke. You better have those put away by the time I am done this call."

Rick left the room without another word. Janet scowled, hating how her husband chided her. She gathered together the letters, not caring if they were in order or not.

Chapter 17

Luke stared at the silly scribbles, trying to make out some sort of image.

"Come on, Luke," Ashley whined, "It's so obvious!"

Luke continued to stare at the board, but nothing popped out at him. Not that he really cared. He wondered how he managed to get dragged into this. He knew his sister wanted him to spend more time with Ashley and get to know her, but he wasn't interested. All he was interested in was getting Dee back. Her silence was driving him mad. Scenario after scenario kept him up at night, each one getting more and more dramatic and disheartening.

The buzzer went and Ashley dropped her marker. "It's an ostrich!" She exclaimed over-dramatically. Luke stared at her scribbles, still unable to see an ostrich in the mess she made. She flopped down next to him and patted his knee. "Your turn!" He couldn't tell if she was always this annoying or if she was just trying to impress him.

Luke scowled at her contact and reached for the Cranium dice. He didn't want to play, but it gave him an excuse to escape her awkward touch. Rolling the dice, he grunted when he realized that he had to act out a scenario.

"I love charades!" Ashley squealed like a thirteen-year-old. Luke rolled his eyes. Picking his card, he stared at it, obviously not impressed. He groaned, stood up and handed it to Maggie and Jeffrey who cuddled on the other couch. It was one thing to join them for supper. They were family and he hadn't seen them much lately. He was feeling guilty, afraid that he was missing too much of Maggie's pregnancy. Then he found out that Ashley was joining them. He knew that he should be able to handle it, but he couldn't. After all, Dee joined them all the time, ensuring that he wouldn't feel like a third wheel, but it was different with Dee. He enjoyed spending time with her. He liked her and he didn't like Ashley, despite his sister's attempts to set them up. This last attempt was not subtle at all. Playing a game was one thing, but pairing him up with Ashley was another. He tried to get out of it, insisting on making it a battle of sexes. Perhaps if he was on Jeffrey's team he would be having more fun. Instead, he was stuck with Ashley, who acted like a teenager and insisted on sitting too close to him.

Everyone waited expectantly. Luke thought back to his card, having no desire to act like Britney Spears.

"Ready?" Maggie asked as she reached for the timer. Luke shrugged his shoulders, but right when she reached for the timer his cell phone began to ring. Thankful for the interruption, Luke dashed for his phone as it vibrated against the coffee table. He looked at the caller ID, not recognizing the number. Either way he didn't care. "Sorry guys," he explained, "I have to take this."

"Luke!" Ashley whined, but he ignored her and opened his phone.

"Luke Barden," he answered in a professional voice.

"Luke," an unfamiliar voice responded, "This is Rick Cairns calling. We've never met, but I'm..."

Luke's face grew serious as he recognized the name. "No," Luke interrupted, "I know who you are. Just a second."

Everyone stared at Luke. Maggie and Jeffrey looked concerned, picking up on his serious facial expressions. Ashley just looked bored, wishing that he would pay attention to her instead of his stupid phone call.

Racing out of the room, Luke went through the dining room and into the kitchen. He kept his back to the entryway and lowered his voice. "What happened? Is Dee ok?"

The deep sigh on the other side of the phone unsettled him. "She's been kidnapped. We found your letter and business card and thought that maybe you could help."

Luke sank down onto a stool at the island. He was afraid that this would happen. Of all the scenarios that played through his head, this was one of the worst ones.

"When did they take her?"

"Yesterday afternoon."

"Do you know if she is still alive?" As soon as the words were out of his mouth, he realized how grave they were. It was protocol to ask such questions. He had done it a hundred times, but never had it affected him like this.

"A rebel confirmed that she is still alive. They're torturing her. He said she'd only have a couple of days."

Luke hopped off of his stool and raced around the island. Opening Maggie's junk drawer, he pulled out a pen and a scrap piece of paper. He began to take notes.

"Do you know why they took her?"

Her uncle hesitated, not too sure how much he should tell Luke, given that they seemed to have an intimate past.

Luke continued, "I'm going to help you, but I need to know everything."

Her uncle sighed. Now was not the time to lie. He had to trust that the truth would save Dee. "She had grown quite close to an old friend. He was a mechanic for FARC, but decided to defect. He asked Dee to run away with him, but they arrested them before they could get away."

Luke's heart sank and jealousy began to fill him. Who was this man, and did Dee love him? "What is this mechanic's name?"

"Esteban Vargas."

Luke wrote down the name, simultaneously embedding it into his memory.

"How well do you know him?"

"He's like a son. He grew up in our orphanage."

Luke considered Rick's response. "What are the chances that he was using Dee? Perhaps they will try to extort money out of her family?"

Rick's response was immediate. "Esteban truly cared for Dee. They've been friends since they were children. He would never do such a thing. Now his commander; I wouldn't put such a thing past his commander."

"Do you think that Dee refused to go with him and that is why they kidnapped her?"

"I don't know where Dee's heart is. She is a very private woman. Not once did she mention feelings for anyone. Not her ex-boyfriend, Esteban or you."

Luke squeezed his eyes and tried to concentrate. He knew he was getting off track. "I'm just trying to determine what their motive might be. If it's extortion, then negotiations might be a possibility..."

Rick immediately cut Luke off. "Jorge doesn't negotiate with anyone. If you rub him the wrong way he will execute you on the side of the road."

Luke thought of the murdered Red Cross volunteers and knew that Rick was right. "Who's Jorge?"

"Jorge Acosta? He's the commander. He's the one that ordered their arrest."

"Have you reported the arrest to the local authorities?"

Rick sadly chuckled, "FARC is the local authority. I went to the embassy to report it, but they were closed for the night. I'm going back first thing tomorrow."

Luke nodded, even though Rick couldn't see him. "Good. Report it first thing tomorrow, but whatever you do, don't mention our phone call. FARC has a huge stronghold in your community, perhaps even in the embassy. The last thing I need is news of our phone call made public. It might make Jorge do something rash."

"Can you help us?" The desperation in Rick's voice softened Luke's already tender heart.

"I will do everything in my power to make sure that Dee is safe."

"Thank you, Luke." Luke then took down Rick's contact information and hung up.

Immediately he dialled another number. "Juan," he almost shouted the instant his friend picked up, "I need you to meet me at the office."

"Why, what's up?"

"I'll explain when I get there." He then hung up and grabbed the piece of paper full of notes. Shoving it into his pocket, he headed into the living room and grabbed his coat out of the closet.

"I'm sorry guys. I have to go."

Maggie looked at him concerned, trying to read the mass of emotions written all over his face. "Is everything alright?"

Luke nodded. "Just an emergency at work."

"Work?" Ashley pouted, "You work way too much!"

Luke ignored her and tugged on his jacket. Heading over to Maggie, he bent over and kissed her on the cheek. "I'll be back in a few days." He then patted Jeffrey on the shoulder and left without acknowledging Ashley.

When Luke reached the office, no one was to be found except for a few cadets monitoring the surveillance networks. Logging onto his computer, he pulled up everything he could regarding the military station set up in Saravena. Printing out detailed maps of known rebel camps in the area he tried to pinpoint which camp would be holding Dee. His frustration mounted as the unfamiliar territory confused him.

Unlike Afghanistan, he didn't recognize names of common areas. The latest report detailed the murder of an aid worker at the zócalo, but no where on the map could he find a place called "zócalo". Luke threw down the maps in frustration and reached for his coffee cup, only to find it empty.

Right then Juan strolled in and pulled up a chair. He watched his friend, silently noting the vein in Luke's temple that throbbed with aggravation.

"What is a zócalo?" Luke asked impatiently.

"It's a town square, but you won't find one in Afghanistan." Juan set a cup of coffee in front of Luke and picked up the maps that he printed off. After a quick glance, he raised his eyebrows and looked at Luke over the tops of the sheets. "However, you will find one in Colombia. Are you going to go see her?"

Luke face was grave. "She's been kidnapped."

Juan let out a low whistle. He understood the gravity of the situation, but he also understood the impossibility of Luke being able to do anything. "And you're going to go save her?"

Again, Luke nodded.

"Are you going alone?"

This time Luke shook his head. "I'm going to assemble a team."

"A team?" Juan almost spit out his coffee. "There's no way the Colonel will approve that. Our district is Afghanistan, not Colombia."

"I know, I know," Luke admitted, digging through the pile of papers that he already accumulated. "That's why I need you to help me design a fool-proof plan that he won't be able to say 'no' to."

"Let me get this straight: you're going to plan a mission, pitch it and hope that the Colonel agrees to spend tax-payers money on a region the U.S. government is barely interested in."

Luke nodded, causing Juan to roll his eyes. "Think about it Juan. How many aid workers have been killed or assaulted over the past four months? Dozens! And it's all in this one area. Other towns don't have the same problem. Dee's uncle said it's this one commander that's causing problems. He has a personal vendetta against aid workers. So, we go in on a peace-keeping mission, take care of this guy, save some American citizens and re-establish stability in this town. As well, we prove to the world that the United States of America will not tolerate terrorism of any sort. No matter how big or small."

"Wait a minute," Juan interrupted, waving his hands. "You're getting your information from Dee's uncle. What does he know?"

"He knows that his niece has been kidnapped and tortured by FARC. Other than that, I don't know how reliable this guy is. That's why I need you to call this Lieutenant," Luke dug for a piece of paper with some contact information for the base in Saravena, "and see if his information adds up." Luke handed the paper over to Juan. "As well, I need you to try to find out which camp is holding Dee. We aren't taking on all of FARC, just one camp. There are still four Red Cross workers unaccounted for and I have a feeling that if they are still alive, they will be in the same camp as Dee. It's led by a Commander named Jorge Acosta. They should know all about him."

"So let me get this straight. You are going to save Dee, but hope that there are others in order to justify this mission?"

Luke turned from his computer screen and stared at Juan. "I will do anything to save Dee. And if that's what it takes to sell my pitch to the Colonel, then so be it."

"How sure are you that the other aid workers will be in the same camp?"

Luke shrugged his shoulders. "If Dee's uncle is right, ninety percent. That is, if they are still alive. Check with our base in Saravena. I have a feeling that they will share my suspicions."

Juan nodded and stood to go to his desk. "You know it's a long shot, right?"

Luke nodded gravely. "A long shot is all I have."

Pain shot through Dee's back, making sleep impossible. Throughout the night, she had drifted off here and there, but for the most part sleep eluded her. Sunlight was starting to trickle down the stairs that led to her cell, signally the beginning of another day. She looked over at Esteban, who managed to sleep in the corner. His injuries, though significant, were not as extensive as hers. The pain that Dee felt was so overwhelming that she could not determine if any bones were broken or not. Not that it mattered. Dee had a feeling she would die in this cell. It would take a miracle to get out of there, and right then she didn't feel like she deserved one. Her life was a mess. She couldn't even indulge in "if only" thoughts because she had no idea of how she could have done things differently. She thought of Luke. If she could have one wish, it would be that Luke knew that she died loving him, but perhaps he was better off not knowing. Dee closed her eyes, too tired to try to sort out her confused feelings. He could think what he wanted to think, and if that comforted him, then so be it.

The sunlight grew and stretched further into her cell. Already she could feel the stifling heat of the day approach.

She could hear voices outside, signalling her fear to return. She silently hoped that they would leave her alone, even if that meant starving to death in her rancid cell. Starvation seemed preferable to the beating that she endured yesterday.

Much to her dismay, footsteps began to descend the stairwell. Two soldiers entered her cell. Esteban remained asleep and they ignored him. Picking her up off of the floor by her armpits, they dragged her out. Dee didn't make a sound, not wanting to wake Esteban. She knew that if he saw them taking her, he would draw attention to himself, which would surely lead to another beating.

As they yanked her up the stairs, Dee tried to make her feet move. Once outside, she stumbled along, unable to keep up with their fast stride. They didn't go far, dragging her to a tiny tin building. They pushed her inside and locked the door behind her. Dee stared at her surroundings. Though the floor was dirt, the walls were tin and already warm from the rising sun. The gaps between the tin roof and its walls were large enough to let the sun in, but too small to air the place out. Already it was hot and stuffy. Dee felt claustrophobic and found herself gasping for air. Her deep, frantic breaths made her dizzy and she collapsed onto the cool, dirt floor.

Luke watched expectantly as Juan approached his desk. Taking a seat, he leaned forward and spoke in a hushed voice.

"Ok, so you weren't that far off." Luke felt a glimmer of hope and let Juan continue. "Lieutenant Malloy wasn't available, so I spoke to a man named Sergeant Farrow. He confirmed not only the actions of Commander Jorge Acosta, but also the location of his camp. Most of the camps you printed out are abandoned. His camp is the only one within twenty-five miles."

"How big is it?"

"I was just getting to that. Farrow said the camp held about thirty to forty rebels, but only half are actual soldiers. The rest are labourers, such as your mechanic friend, Esteban. Those that are not actual soldiers are not armed. As well, he confirmed the likelihood that the other Red Cross workers are still there. Apparently, whenever someone dies, he either dumps them in a ditch or leaved them in the middle of town to set an example for everyone. Since no bodies have been recovered, he's pretty sure they are still alive."

"Anything else?"

"Oh, there's more, lots more. The night that Dee was arrested, there was a huge raid. They arrested and captured not only local farmers but also three more volunteers. One is a U.S. citizen, serving as a doctor at the local clinic. The other two were nurses, one from Canada, the other from England. Your chances of getting this approved are getting better by the minute."

"What are the troops in Saravena doing about it?"

"Nothing."

"Nothing?" Luke couldn't believe what he just heard.

"Since the rest of the region has been relatively cooperative, Lieutenant Malloy has decided to stand down for the time being. Though incidents in his region have increased, he hasn't received any pressure from the government to respond. Until then, he isn't willing to do anything. Apparently, they lack the man power."

Luke groaned at the realization that the base lacked both skills and man power. He hoped that he would be able to depend on their expertise. "What do you think?"

"I think it's possible." Luke assessed Juan to see if he was serious. Juan continued. "Think about it. We're taking on twenty rebel soldiers, maximum. You send down a team of five or six to cooperate with Lieutenant Malloy's men. Our expertise will make up for their lack of experience. We've taken on more men, with less help. The benefit: we walk out of there with approximately eight hostages. We've sent more men to rescue one person. The best part is that there's no one else around. By the time the other FARC camps hear about this, we'll be long gone."

Luke nodded, seeing where his friend was coming from. "Ok. Where is this camp exactly?" Juan began to spread maps across Luke's desk and together they began to design a rescue mission. Hours later, they completed an initial attack plan and Luke sent Juan home to catch some sleep. Luke stayed at the office though, typing up a missing persons report and finalizing details for the mission he would propose to the Colonel as soon as he came in.

Dee could feel a ray of sunshine sneak through the cracks and settle on her skin. Immediately its hot rays began to burn her shoulders. She shuffled to the side, trying to escape its direct exposure. Too sore to sit up, she curled up into a ball, careful not to brush against the piping hot walls. The shack was small, about five feet by five feet, and Dee's aching muscles screamed to be stretched out, but the room did not allow such a thing. She managed to get her entire body out of the direct sunlight, except for her feet. Those she dug into the hard ground and covered them with dirt. She would be fine, for now, until the sun moved some more. Her mouth was dry and her lips cracked from the heat and dehydration. Her stomach rumbled and Dee tried to remember the last time she ate, but the heat kept her from thinking clearly. It made her feel faint and weary, and she gladly gave in to sleep.

Luke finished his report hours ago and waited for the Colonel to show up. Around ten o'clock he strolled through the door with a coffee and bagel in his hand. Jumping up, Luke gathered all of his reports and raced over to meet him outside of his office.

"Morning, Lieutenant." The Colonel opened his door and gestured for Luke to go in.

"Sir," Luke acknowledged, heading in and taking a seat.

The Colonel sat down and began to unwrap his breakfast bagel. "You look like you've been here for a while," he commented.

Luke nodded. "All night, Sir." The Colonel raised his head and studied Luke. Wrapping his bagel back up, he set it aside.

"Must be important then?"

"Yes Sir." Luke handed him the initial report and allowed him to peruse it.

"Colombia," he commented as he read on. Luke remained silent, watching his supervisor's face for an indication of opinion. Putting down the report, the Colonel looked at Luke directly. "Very interesting, and I agree with you. Our country has zero tolerance when it comes to terrorism, and we need to enforce it. But why Colombia? We have more hostages in Afghanistan and North Korea."

Luke nodded. "It's personal, Sir. Dee Cairns is a close friend of the family. Her uncle called me and reported her disappearance directly."

"And you just decided to leave that out of your report."

"That is a professional report to be filed."

"And the fact that she is a good friend has nothing to do with it?"

Luke stood his ground as the Colonel grilled him. "She has everything to do with it," he boldly confessed. "I took this job to protect the ones that I love. I told you that from day one. I made it very clear that the only reason that I took this job was to find my friend Lieutenant Wayne McCabe. Though my motives are personal, I have remained objective, professional and extremely effective. Just because the target has changed does not mean that my focus has."

The Colonel began to wave his hands, bringing Luke's speech to a halt. "I get it, Luke, I get it. And I'm sorry about your friend. I wish I could help you, but the fact is that I can't. It's out of my jurisdiction."

"I am well aware of that Sir, but can't you call in a favour from somebody. The military base in Saravena is unable to respond, due to lack of personnel. Perhaps you can loan out our expertise, much like you do when we cooperate with the officials in Afghanistan."

The Colonel assessed Luke's face, watching for any signs of emotion. "Shouldn't you be focusing on Afghanistan?"

Luke nodded. "We have a surveillance team working around the clock, but no new leads. Until we get a new lead, there's nothing we can do."

"You think I should loan out my battalion and risk losing some of my best soldiers to help out some dumpy little town, just because we don't have any new leads?"

"Yes, Sir."

The Colonel sat silent for a minute, contemplating his alternatives. Tapping his pen on his desk, he replied, "I'm sorry about your friend, Luke. I really am. I'll see what I can do, but I'm not making any promises."

"I know, Sir. Thank you, Sir!"

Though the heat made Dee groggy, she found it impossible to sleep. Her stomach wretched and she heaved in the one corner. Cramps assaulted her abdomen as Dee stared at her vomit. She hadn't eaten for days. How could she manage to throw up? A headache ransacked her brain, preventing her from thinking. She could feel her body turning against her. Was this what it felt like to starve to death?

She scuttled away from the vomit, careful not to touch the scorching hot walls. The stench immediately overtook her tiny cell, making it even harder to breath. Each breath was laboured, as she desperately drunk in the thick, sticky air.

She heard sounds outside as someone unlocked her door. A soldier opened the hot door, wearing gloves to protect himself from being burned. Immediately fresh air invaded her cell, thinning out the thick, damp air. Dee wanted to lunge towards the door and inhale as much air as possible, but her body refused to budge. Instead, she lay there, watching everything with her eyes. She now recognized their commander. He was the short, ugly one who led her assaults and barked out orders. He stood in the doorway. Poking her with a stick, he saw her eyes flicker and he smiled a malicious smile.

"Still alive?" He asked, obviously not expecting a response. "Don't you think that if your God truly loved you, he would have finished you off by now?"

Unable to respond, he let out a menacing laugh and motioned the soldier to shut the door. His laugh continued as he walked away, echoing in Dee's mind with increasing horror. She tried to force such sounds out of her head, but she couldn't. At times she would drift off, but the unsettling cackle haunted her, even in her dreams. She became delirious, but was unable to do anything about it.

Chapter 18

Luke spread out a large map on top of a table and the troops gathered around him. He had begun to lose hope when the Colonel didn't get back to him immediately. It took almost twenty-four hours for him to obtain permission to move ahead. Adding sixteen hours to collect his men and fly to Saravena, Luke was afraid that time was running out. When they arrived at the base in Saravena, he quickly realized that Juan was not exaggerating. The base was small and the numbers were few. Though they had the equipment, many of the soldiers did not have adequate experience in the field.

Using the map as a guide, he began to lay out the details of their mission. Having arrived in the morning, the troops would wait until midnight before they set out. Lieutenant Malloy was helpful and extremely thankful for the expertise that Luke's men were bringing to the mission. His knowledge of the area helped them refine their plan. Luke then reviewed it to make sure that everyone was on the same page.

When they finished, Luke dismissed them and headed to the bunks for some rest. It took a while for his mind to stop and succumb to sleep. For over an hour he laid there, exhausted but unable to stop worrying about Dee. He knew his mission inside and out: to rescue Dee and save the other aid workers. He wasn't worried about that. He was worried about what would happen after. Assuming that Dee was still alive, would she return home with him or would she remain in Colombia with Esteban? He couldn't blame the mechanic for falling in love with her. It only took minutes for Luke to realize that Dee was one of a kind. But did Dee love him? She professed to have feelings for Luke, but how strong were they? Perhaps he was just the rebound after her messy break up. He knew this mission would prove how much he loved her, but was his love what she wanted?

Luke pushed that thought away and rolled over. He said he would love her as a friend or more, and he meant it. He had just hoped that if she chose the friend route, she would be close enough that he could see her on a regular basis. He breathed another prayer, begging God to make this mission a success and then let his thoughts drift to sleep.

Dee could feel hands lifting her up, but didn't have the energy to move. She tried to force her eyes open, but her eyelids were too heavy and refused to budge. Listlessly, she let whoever it was roughly pick her up and carry her outside. She knew she was outside because it was cooler. She gasped for air, but her lungs refused to cooperate. Instead of gulping in the air, her breaths were shallow and unsatisfactory. She could hear people talking, but her ears acted as if they had earmuffs on. Words droned on but they were quiet and slurred together.

Esteban sat in his corner, horrified, as he watched a soldier carry Dee down the stairs. While another soldier opened the gate, he entered and carelessly tossed her into the far corner. Her body was limp and lifeless. She didn't move and he studied her hard, trying to see if her chest was rising with breaths of life. As he carefully scrutinized her, a malevolent laugh broke his concentration. Jorge stood behind the bars and continued to laugh.

"She's not dead," he assured Esteban, "but she will be soon. I want you to watch her die and then it will be your turn."

Esteban was too tired to act brave. Tears broke free and streaked his dirty face. Jorge laughed at his pain, but Esteban didn't care. All he cared about was Dee. Was it too late to hope for a miracle? He felt torn. Part of him dared to hope for a miracle, the other part prayed that her death would be as painless as possible. Jorge continued to laugh as he walked away.

Dee could feel the cold floor through her flimsy tank top and wished that she could roll over and cool her face on the chilly surface, but her muscles retaliated and refused to budge. Despite the comfort of the cool floor, heat burned through her veins and her body continued to sweat. Her heart raced, causing her to sweat even more. She became delirious as hallucinations of someone crying echoed in her ears. She wanted to curl up in a ball and cover her ears, but her body failed her, unable to move at all.

Luke stopped and signalled for Juan's team to pass him. Crouched in a ditch, he waited for them to settle. Eddie and one of Malloy's men continued on towards the camp. Their task was to take over the two sniper towers. Meanwhile, Lieutenant Malloy was leading a team around to the north side of the camp. Once the snipers were taken out and Eddie gave him the go ahead, Malloy's team would storm from the north, Luke would lead a team from the east, and Juan's team would cover off the west. With those being the only exit points, Luke felt confident that no one would escape past them.

An hour later, Malloy confirmed his position at the north side and Juan soon followed. Giving Eddie the go ahead, the two snipers went to take over the watch towers. Luke waited patiently. About a half hour later, Eddie confirmed that they had seized the towers and were watching from above. Luke breathed a sigh of relief, glad that they had overtaken the towers so silently. No gunshots had gone off to alert the rest of the camp. Giving the signal, the three teams began to move in, silently and stealthily.

Surrounding the one cabin, Luke left the two cadets outside to guard the windows and led the rest of the team inside. A panic filled the cabin when Luke turned on the lights. Many young boys jumped out of bed startled, but remained unarmed. Some raised their arms in surrender, others knelt on the ground, signalling to Luke that they were not soldiers. Their immediate compliance helped neutralize the situation. Two soldiers began to handcuff them and searched the room for weapons. When none were found, Luke and the two soldiers left, leaving the other two to guard the cabin. Lieutenant Malloy and his men would deal with them later. Entering the next cabin, Luke found it empty. From the north, he could hear gunfire and knew that Malloy had come into contact with some armed rebels. Ripping the screens out of the windows in the cabin he was in, Luke and the two soldiers prepared to open fire. Sure enough, armed rebels soon emerged from the tree line and began to hurry towards the north. Luke and his soldiers began to shoot. The militants turned and dove behind trucks. They began to open fire on the cabin Luke hid in, unaware that there were soldiers closing in from the West. Juan and his team quickly appeared and took the militants out from behind. Soon gunshots from the North ended. Luke signalled for his men to follow him and they went out into the courtyard where Juan and his men began taking a body count. They counted twelve and knew that the majority had been taken care of. Malloy soon appeared and signalled that the North had been both neutralized and searched. Luke then radioed for the trucks to move in. He would need them to transport the hostages back to the base.

Dee could hear loud bangs and wondered if she was delirious or if they were actually occurring. She had never heard an actual gunshot and wondered if that was what it sounded like. If so, were they executing prisoners outside? She could hear someone calling her name. Though the sound was muffled, she was unable to acknowledge it. The explosive noises became louder and louder. Dee tried to block them out, but they continued, rapidly increasing until they blurred into one constant sound. It soon became unbearable. Dee felt like her ears were going to explode. The longer the noises continued, the more convinced Dee became that she was facing death. Gasping for air, she feared that each breath would be her last. Though she expected to die in this rank cell, she never realized that death would be so loud. More than ever, she just wished that she could die in peace.

Esteban woke up to the sound of gunfire. Standing up, he strained to see out of the window. The gunfire grew closer, and he knew that whoever was raiding the camp was winning. Believing that a miracle had come to save them, he began shouting Dee's name, trying to gain her attention, but she remained still. He crawled as close to her as he could and listened. Throughout the night he could hear her laboured breathing. Occasional gasps would wake him, reminding him that she was still alive but barely hanging on. Now, with the gunfire so close, he couldn't hear her and shouted even louder. He begged her to tilt her head towards him, but she didn't move. When the gunfire halted, he listened, but foreign voices outside prevented him from hearing her. He began to shout hysterically, calling for help. Immediately, two American soldiers appeared at the base of the stairs.

With all the rebel soldiers neutralized, Luke called the soldiers and began to disperse them in teams to search for prisoners. The trucks arrived and Luke ordered the cadets to organize the prisoners when they appeared, putting the locals in one truck and the foreign hostages in the Jeeps. Lieutenant Malloy would take the locals to town where they could either stay or pack up and leave. The Jeeps would take the hostages to the base where they would be air lifted to a safer location.

With all the soldiers dispersed except for Juan, Luke turned to him and said, "I need you to translate for me. There's a cabin back there with militant prisoners. I need you to ask them what they have done to Dee."

Juan nodded and they began to head for the cabin when they heard shouts coming from the tree line nearby. Walking through some brush, they soon found some small underground barracks that were not located by their satellite surveillance. A man continued to scream for help hysterically. Radioing for backup, Luke broke down the door and went downstairs with his gun drawn. Turning on his flashlight, he scanned the small underground compartment. Behind an iron gate, a young man frantically tugged against the ropes that bound him. In the other corner lay a crumpled body. Rushing into the cell, Luke hurried over to the frail woman. Juan shone his flashlight on her, exposing her beautiful blond curls, now bloody and matted. Crouching, Luke checked for a pulse while the agitated man continued to shout. Hey body was hot and feverish and Luke struggled to find a pulse. Eventually he found one, and was surprised at how shallow it was. Brushing back her hair, he studied her injuries while the man continued to shout.

"What is he saying?" Luke asked aggravated, as he gathered Dee into his arms.

"He wants to know if she is dead," Juan responded as he cut the man's ropes. The man pushed Juan aside and raced over to Dee. Cupping her swollen face into his hands, he began to whisper. His words were interrupted by his sobs as he gently caressed her face. Luke felt jealousy rise as he watched this man intimately hold the woman that he loved.

"He's begging her to open her eyes," Juan explained.

Luke nodded, feeling the same way. "Ask him what they did to her."

Luke listened helplessly as the young man explained their situation to Juan in Spanish. Eventually Juan responded. "They beat her and put her in a sweat box."

That explained the fever that she was sweating out. Lifting her up, Luke stood and carried her out of the gate into the cool, midnight air. The fresh air caused her to stir and she buried her head into his shoulder, whispering, "Te quiero." Luke recognized the term of endearment from the limited Spanish lessons that Juan gave him in Afghanistan. For years he dreamed of being able to profess his love to Dee in the foreign language she fluently understood. He finally had the chance, yet he faltered, wondering who she spoke those words to. Did she know it was him or did she think it was Esteban? Chocking back his jealousy, he whispered back, "I love you," and laid her down in the back seat of a Jeep. The young man then rushed up and pushed Luke aside, desperate to get closer to Dee.

Jealousy surged inside of Luke. Pulling him away from Dee, Luke slammed Esteban into the side of the Jeep and tightened his grip. "Esteban?" He questioned in an intimidating tone.

The young man froze and nodded, confused at how an American soldier would know his name. Luke could feel Juan's hand on his shoulder.

"Let go of him, Luke. It's not worth it."

Luke ignored his friend's advice. "Ask him," he barked out, "ask him if she agreed to run away with him."

He waited impatiently as Juan translated. He watched Esteban's reaction and knew from the miserable look on his face that it was a "no". When he sadly shook his head, Luke knew that he was telling the truth.

"Satisfied?" Juan asked him.

Luke loosened his grip but his tone remained stern. "Then tell him that he needs to get onto that truck," he pointed to his right. "It will take him into town. He then needs to go tell Rick and Janet that Dee is safe and that we are taking her to the hospital in Bogota and that I will call them when I have an update on her condition."

Juan translated to which Esteban responded. Juan nodded and motioned to the Jeep. "He wants to say good-bye." Reluctantly, Luke let go and watched as the rebel crawled into the back on the Jeep.

Crouching on the floor, Esteban crept next to Dee and began to stroke her face. She turned her head and sighed. Whispering, he gained her attention. Though she couldn't open her eyes, she began to murmur.

"I smelt him...It was so real...so real that I could smell him..." she faltered and tried to catch her words, "Am I dying?"

Esteban sadly smiled, "No, sweetheart," he whispered, "You're not. You're going to be fine."

Dee sighed, too exhausted to respond. He leaned forward and kissed her on the forehead, sadly saying his good-byes. He then obediently crawled out of the Jeep and got into the truck that Luke pointed to.

Already the other soldiers had loaded hostages onto the other trucks. Lieutenant Malloy approached Luke and reported. "I believe that is our eighth hostage, accounted for and alive," he gestured towards Dee. "My men will stay here and take care of the prisoners and clean-up. I've radioed the base and asked them to have the choppers ready to go. By the looks of it, most of the hostages need immediate medical attention. Our medic is on standby at the base and will airlift them to a hospital in Bogota."

Luke nodded, glad that all went according to plan. Shaking the Lieutenant's hand, he crawled into the backseat with Dee while Juan climbed into the driver's seat. Propping her head on his lap, he began to stroke the blood crusted curls that framed her face. Juan handed him a canteen of water and he gently tilted her head up, urging her to take a drink. Water slowly trickled into her mouth, but she sputtered, unable to swallow. Luke rested her head back onto his lap and Juan started the truck.

"The sooner we get her to the base, the better," Juan acknowledged, driving out of the camp.

At the base, the medic waited for them. Being the last truck to arrive, the rest of Luke's team had already loaded the hostages onto the three helicopters. Their propellers spun, ready for take off. Pulling a stretcher up to the truck, Luke got out and carefully placed Dee on it. The medic quickly checked her pulse and opened her eyes. Feeling her forehead, he stated what Luke already knew. "That's a serious fever." The medic went inside and soon returned with an IV, a few towels, a First Aid kit and a large bottle of water. Feeling for a vein, the Medic expertly inserted a needle and hooked up the IV, hanging it on the edge of her stretcher. Handing Luke the towels, medical kit, and water, he quickly instructed as he pushed the stretcher towards the furthest helicopter.

"The IV is to try to replenish her fluids. There is no medication in it. Wet the towels and use them to cool down her skin. There is an ice pack inside the First Aid kit, use it for her eyes, they are extremely swollen. Do whatever you can to keep her fever from rising."

Reaching the helicopter, the medic collapsed the stretcher and had Juan help him load it into the aircraft. Luke stared at the medic in disbelief, "You're not coming with us?"

The medic shook his head. "I'm going with the doctor. His condition is much more critical."

"What about the nurses?" Luke asked, referring to the nurses that were kidnapped with the doctor.

The medic sadly shook his head. "Those girls are in no condition to tend to anyone."

Shaking hands with Juan and then Luke, the medic turned and got onto the middle helicopter. The first two choppers took off, leaving Luke standing there with his jaw hanging open.

Juan patted his friend on the shoulder, in an attempt to encourage him. "It's okay man. We're specially trained in survival skills. We'll get Dee through this."

Luke nodded, hoping that Juan was right. Climbing into the helicopter, he found Eddie waiting for them with two other hostages that had been rescued. Juan took a seat next to Eddie and Luke settled down next to Dee's stretcher. Giving the signal, the pilot nodded and took off. Luke wet down a towel and began to wipe dirt and dry blood from Dee's face. Beneath the filth lay bruises that shocked Luke. The doctor must be seriously injured to have a condition considered worse than Dee's. Patiently and diligently, Luke continued to clean her face with the cool cloth. He leaned forward and felt her forehead, surprised at its burning temperature despite his efforts. He swallowed a lump that formed in his throat, feeling inadequate and discouraged. He had saved her from the rebels, but could he save her from death? He felt his hope beginning to dwindle and hated feeling so useless.

Juan watched Luke as he tended to Dee. As Luke's face fell, he realized that his friend was beginning to feel discouraged. Getting out of his seat, he knelt on the other side of the stretcher and tried to encourage him. Picking up the First Aid kit, he began to rummage about. "Keep wiping her down," he urged Luke, "All we can do is try to keep her as cool as possible." Pulling out some antiseptic wipes, he began to swab the small cuts that covered her face, in an attempt to clean out any bacteria or infection.

Grabbing a clean towel, Luke began to wipe down her shoulders and arms. Checking for broken bones, he carefully felt his way down her limbs. Satisfied, he lifter her arm and wiped underneath. Cleaning her hand, he found her knuckles cut and bruised and wondered if they were defensive wounds. Did she have enough gall to fight back? Is that why her injuries were so much more severe than Esteban's? Luke gritted his teeth at the thought of the Colombian man. Why did Dee suffer so much more than him? He got her into this mess, so why did she have to pay for his actions?

Juan noticed that Luke had stopped and feared that his friend was losing hope. "How about we switch?" He offered, handing Luke the antiseptic swabs. Luke put down his towel and took them. Moving back up to her head, he began to carefully wipe a nasty cut that lined her left eyebrow. Juan cleaned out the wounds on her elbows and knuckles and then began to clean her badly banged up knees. "She knows it's you," he continued, trying to offer Luke a glimmer of hope. The way that Dee's body burned beneath his hands had even Juan concerned, but he wouldn't let on.

Luke felt his throat tighten. "How could she," he mumbled, "she's unconscious."

"Just because she can't respond, doesn't mean her senses aren't working. She can smell you." Luke stopped cleaning her eye and looked up, trying to determine if Juan was only offering him a false hope.

Juan continued, "I'm serious. I heard her tell Esteban that."

Luke pondered what Juan was saying. "Do you think she can hear me?"

Juan nodded, "Even better. She can feel you."

Luke looked at her body, so still one would think that she was dead. Completely battered, he was almost afraid to touch her, not wanting to inflict any more pain on her. Leaning forward, he carefully kissed her forehead. Eddie stared at him curiously, but he didn't care. Tears welled up in his eyes and he wiped them away. So what if he fell apart in front of his comrades! If he didn't show emotion at a time like this, then he wouldn't be human.

Pulling himself back together, he broke open the ice pack, wrapped it in a towel and rested it on Dee's severely swollen eyes. Opening another swab, he began to clean a gash along her hairline. He carefully pushed aside the matted curls, which were no longer spongy and lively. They used to be thick and soft. Now they were crusty and flat, weighed down by dirt and blood.

By the time he had finished cleaning that cut, Juan had finished cleaning her knees. Returning to his seat, Juan left Luke alone with the woman that he loved. For the rest of the flight, Luke tenderly wiped her down with cool cloths, urging her fever to go down.

For two days Luke commuted between the U.S. base in Bogota and the hospital. Having filed his reports, he now waited for Dee to recover enough so that he could transport her home. All the other hostages were treated and had already returned home, except for Dee and the doctor. Badly beaten, the doctor was still in critical condition and it would be quite some time before they could airlift him back to the USA. Dee was slowly recovering. Her swelling had gone down, but the fever remained. She was no longer unconscious, but too exhausted to do anything but sleep. Every time Luke visited her, she laid there lifeless. He longed to wake her up, just for a minute, so that she would know that he was there for her, but he was afraid he would wear her out, so he just sat there, clasping her hand, silently praying.

On the third day, her fever went down and the doctors agreed it would be safe to airlift her back to DC. All of the soldiers had already left, except for Juan, who stayed with Luke to offer support. Escorting her to the chopper, Luke felt relieved that Dee was finally able to come home. He knew once Maggie was by her side she would recover quickly. As much as the medical attention helped, what she really needed was loved ones nearby to encourage and support her.

Loading the aircraft, Luke settled in his seat and leaned his head back. The doctor assured him that the worst was over. Now all he had to do was be patient and wait for her to slowly recover. He glanced at Dee's stretcher, surrounded by medical equipment. A heart monitor steadily beeped, notifying them of her shallow, but regular heart beat. An oxygen mask covered her delicate face. Though she didn't rely on it, they put it on as a precautionary method. An IV kept her medicated and hydrated. Though she didn't have any broken bones, her ribs were severely bruised. The bruises were so deep that the doctor could make out the tread of a boot as a footprint discoloured her back.

Dee woke up to a gentle, rhythmic whirling noise. Glancing about her, she recognized the medical equipment though she did not recognize the small, cramped quarters that housed them. A doctor sat nearby, but he was fair and not dark like the Colombian doctors and nurses that had tended to her.

Slowly turning her head, pain throbbed as her neck rebelled against her movement. On her left sat two soldiers dressed in full uniform. Their heads were tilted towards each other and they quietly whispered as they went over certain documents. Dee's chest grew tight as she recognized Luke. For days she had dreamt of him, but when she woke up in the hospital alone, she knew it was ridiculous to think that he had

321

come for her. Yet, here he was, sitting next to her. She squeezed her eyes shut, wondering if it was another dream, but when she opened them, he was still there. The throbbing pain proved to her that it was no dream. Guilt began to rise inside of her. As much as she longed for his arms, she knew that she didn't deserve them. She felt ashamed that he had come all this way for her. Especially after all that she put him through.

Luke whispered with Juan, careful that the doctor didn't overhear them. The details that they were going over were case-sensitive. Their conversation was interrupted by the gradual increase of beeps coming from Dee's heart monitor. Staring at the screen, Luke saw activity increasing, denoting stress or strain on Dee's cardiovascular system. The doctor got up and checked the paper printout and furrowed his brows. Luke began to get nervous and looked over at Dee, only to find her lying there and staring back at him.

Hurrying to her side, he saw tiny drops of sweat form on her brow. The look on her face unsettled him. It wasn't ridden with pain. Instead, she looked horrified. Coming over, the doctor studied her face. "Something's got her worked up," he commented, as he fiddled with her IV, "I'll give her something to relax."

Luke stared deep into Dee's eyes, wondering if he was the cause of her anxiety. Gently stroking her thick curls, which were now clean and soft, he began to murmur, "Its okay, Dee. You're safe now. I'm here for you. I'll take care of you."

Her face began to soften and her breathing became deeper. Relaxing beneath his touch, the doctor injected a sedative into her IV and soon she was back asleep.

Chapter 19

Dee picked at her Jell-O, not really in the mood for food. She wasn't in the mood for anything. The white walls seemed dull and depressing as they closed in around her. Setting down her spoon, she pushed away the small tray of food.

She had been back in DC for three days now and was bored and depressed. As soon as she could think clearly, she requested no visitors—not even family. She told herself that she needed time and space to think and sort things out. She tried to convince herself that she had to figure everything out before she could explain it to others, but she knew that she was really just using that as an excuse to hide. She didn't want to face her problems, let alone the loved ones who were affected by her problems.

Dee remembered Esteban's words. He thought that Maggie's invitation was God's way of saying He wanted her to return to DC and make things right. She wasn't convinced, but now that she was miraculously rescued and brought back to DC, there was no doubt that God brought her here. She felt ashamed of how her fear of Mark held her captive. It had such a strong hold over her that it caused her to doubt God. God had saved her from the rebels, but was He going to save her from Mark? She knew that He could, but would He?

She thought about the sinful life she had led with Mark. She gave him everything and some of it she would never get back. Maggie assured her that God forgave her, but wouldn't there be repercussions for her sinful behaviour? Now she not only feared Mark but she feared God too. She was afraid that God wanted her back in DC to face something. She wasn't sure what it was, but she had a feeling it wouldn't be easy.

Dee let out a huge sigh, sick of worrying. It wasn't getting her anywhere. She had pretty much recovered. There was no trace of a fever and since she had no broken bones she really didn't need to be in the hospital anymore. The bruising was bad, the fatigue even worse, but it was obvious that Dee would be fine. Her doctor encouraged her to stay for another day or two, to let her body rest and heal some more. Dee gladly accepted his advice since she had no where else to go.

Dee shifted her weight. Though she was healing, every bone ached. Her joints and muscles screamed every time she moved, but she ignored them. She had bigger issues to deal with. Soon she would have to leave the hospital, and then what? She couldn't stay in DC and she most definitely couldn't go back to Colombia. She felt homeless; homeless and alone with nowhere to go and no one to help her.

Dee stared at the clock and the second hand quietly ticked away. Closing her eyes, she laid back but knew that she wouldn't sleep. She could only sleep so much in a day. Guilt nagged at her as she tried to imagine Maggie's growing belly. Her friend was six months pregnant and she hadn't even seen her. A nurse told her that Maggie had visited and delivered a bouquet of flowers on her behalf. The note was filled with love and concern, upsetting Dee even more. She wished that they had taken her to a hospital in any city but DC. Unfortunately, assuming that home was best, they brought her here.

Her thoughts drifted to Luke, handsome as always, in his uniform. She wished that his presence in the helicopter was a dream, but she knew that it was foolish to think so. He had rescued her, like a knight in shining armour, and here she was, hiding in the hospital like a coward.

The sound of Dee's door opening drew her away from her thoughts. Opening her eyes, she expected to see a nurse, but was surprised to see Luke standing there, once again dressed in his uniform. He stood there awkwardly, unsure of himself. He wished he could read her thoughts. He wondered why she looked at him like that, surprised, yet remorseful. She had nothing to be sorry for, yet there she was, looking guilty and uncomfortable.

He lifted up a duffel bag and beckoned towards it with his head. "Your aunt sent Maggie your stuff. Maggie packed a few things she thought you might need."

Dee nodded and he placed the bag on the floor, out of the way.

"How did you..." Dee started.

"Get in?" He finished for her. A sly smile spread across his face. "I told the nurse I needed to ask you a few questions about what happened in Colombia."

"Is that why you are wearing your uniform?" Numerous times Dee had witnessed Luke rush off to work, but she never saw him in his uniform.

Again, he smiled and pulled a chair up close to her bed. "Had to make it look official," he confessed. Deep down inside he also hoped that it would impress Dee.

"But you're not here to talk about Colombia." Dee wasn't stupid.

Luke leaned forward. "Not exactly." He could see Dee's eyes cloud as she avoided his gaze. He wondered what she had to hide and was here to find out. Continuing, he stated his intentions. "I just wanted to know why you requested no visitors."

Dee nodded. It was a fair question. She just wished that she had a fair answer. Struggling to articulate it, she responded, "I just needed to clear my mind and figure things out for myself before I tried explaining everything to everyone."

Luke nodded. "That makes sense. You can't really explain what you don't understand."

Dee lowered her eyes even more. She hated how understanding he was. It made her feel even worse for everything that she had done to him. Luke watched her as she avoided his eyes. "Perhaps you can practice by telling me what you're feeling and together we can try to figure it out." He watched as she uncomfortably shifted her weight. She continued to avoid him. Taking her hand into his, he could feel her trembling. He lowered his voice and spoke gently, "You don't have to go through this alone, Dee. I'll help you."

"You've already done enough."

Her comment was like a slap in the face, but he could take it. Snorting, he replied sarcastically, "You're right, now that you are on home soil, my job is done." Changing his tone, he softened and genuinely replied, "Dee, I'd do anything for you. Including helping you through whatever you are going through." When Dee continued to avoid him, he pressed further. "Do you trust me?"

Dee nodded. Of course she trusted him. He flew halfway around the world and saved her from death. Taking her hand into his, he held it tightly. "Then trust me," he whispered.

Dee turned and stared at him. She couldn't believe how unbelievable he was; so patient, so giving, constantly mirroring God's love. No matter what she did to him, he continued to forgive her.

Luke returned the stare. He could see tears in her eyes, but they refused to spill over. Glad that she finally acknowledged him, he coaxed her. "Let's start at the beginning. Why did you leave?"

A single tear finally spilled over. He felt her hand tremble and he closed it in with his other hand, trying to comfort her.

"It's complicated," she responded, trying to dodge the question.

"So is organizing a rescue mission in Northern Colombia. I can handle complicated," he assured her.

"You wouldn't understand." She tried again.

"Maybe not," he acknowledged, "but at least I would know where you are coming from."

Dee tried changing the subject a little bit. "Thank you for saving me."

Luke patted her hand. "I told you I'd do anything for you."

Dee nodded. She knew that was true. That was what she was afraid of. "You shouldn't have," she started. "After..." she paused, not knowing where her words were going, "I didn't deserve it."

Luke stared at the woman he loved. In his opinion, she deserved everything. He wanted to ask *why not* but decided it would be best to go a different direction. "There are lots of things that I do not deserve, but that doesn't mean that I will give up and stop fighting for them. That's why I won't give up on you."

Tears flowed more rapidly. "You should," was all that she could sputter out.

Grabbing her chin, he gently tilted her head so that she couldn't avoid his eyes. "Give me one good reason why," he challenged her.

Dee stared at him, astounded by his challenge. Any wise man would have given up on her a long time ago, yet here he was, willing to fight to the end. Everything within her wished that she could be with him, but she knew it couldn't be so. She stared back at him, as if challenging him. As if saying he couldn't handle her.

He seemed to read her thoughts and reminded her, "Trust me."

Dee thought back to her words last New Years Eve, when she said, *"If I can't trust you, then there is no hope for this world."* Everything in his eyes dared her to trust him. "It's not a matter of whether or not I trust you," she confessed. She trusted Luke. That wasn't the problem. The problem was that he would do anything to be with her, and Mark would do anything to keep them apart.

"Okay," he pondered. It didn't make any sense to him, but at least he was making some progress. "Perhaps the problem is that you trust me when you need to trust God." By the look on her face, he knew he hit a sore spot, but he wasn't here to preach. He was here to help her. Changing direction, he continued, "But you have something on your chest that you need to get rid of. You need to tell someone, and if you can't tell me, who will you tell?"

Dee knew that he was right. She needed to tell someone, but if she told him, would he trust her enough to leave her alone? Or would he take the risk and fight for her? Fear rose as she considered the outcome. She wanted to protect him, yet she desperately needed to clear her conscience and tell him the truth. Staring into his eyes, searching for strength to confess the truth to him, she took a deep breath.

Opening her mouth, she was about to begin when the door opened. Mark's head peered around the edge of the door and Dee quickly yanked her hand free from Luke's.

Luke was startled by Dee's reaction but soon understood why. Watching Mark saunter into the room, his blood began to boil. Clenching his fists, he reminded himself of his vow to protect Dee.

"Mark..." Dee began but was cut off by Luke.

"What are you doing here?" Luke growled. She had never heard such a hostile tone come from him before.

Mark saucily smiled, obviously impressed with the reaction he was getting out of Luke. "Can't a man come see his girlfriend," he casually responded.

"Ex-girlfriend," Luke barked as he rose out of his chair.

Mark's smile gave Dee shivers. The more upset Luke got, the more chilling Mark became. "How did you know I was here?" She asked.

"It's all over the news. Quite the heroic rescue." Mark tossed a newspaper onto her bed. Dee reached forward and grabbed it, seeing her picture on the front page.

"And how did you get in here?" Luke challenged Mark.

"Probably the same as you," was Mark's simple response.

Dee began to tremble, fearing what Mark's reaction would be. He made it very clear what he would do if he ever saw them together. She needed to take control of this situation before it escalated. Gathering all her courage, she tried to remain cool. Controlling her voice, she casually replied, "Luke works for the military. He stopped by to ask a few questions about what happened in Colombia. But we've finished and he was just about to leave." Dee added. The sooner she got Luke out of there, the sooner she could try to diffuse the situation.

Luke stared at her as if she had gone mad. He couldn't believe her. After all he had done for her, she was still standing up for her ex. "No," he began, "I'm not..."

Dee interrupted before he could finish and spoke sternly. "Luke, could you please leave. There are some things I need to talk to my..." she paused and stopped herself before she said *partner*. "There are some things I need to talk to Mark about. I would appreciate some privacy."

Luke's face turned red and Dee could see the rage inside of him. She felt terrible, especially after he once again spilled his heart out, but she needed to get him out of there. She would explain later, if she had a later, but right now she needed to get Luke away, safe and sound. Luke turned and faced her. As much as she hated to see so much anger and frustration in his face, she was glad that Mark couldn't see it.

"I'm not going to ask again," she said, staring coldly at him. "There's the door."

Dee knew that was the final straw. Loosing his cool, he turned and stormed out of the room. How could he protect her when she constantly kept putting herself in such dangerous situations? Slamming the door behind him, as if to wash his hands of her senselessness, he walked away. If she wanted to have her heart broken again, then fine! He was tired of laying it all on the line, only to be rejected for a dirtbag like Mark!

Staring at the closed door, Mark let out a low whistle and laughed. "He didn't take that so well."

"Can you blame him? After our history, it's no wonder he doesn't trust you."

"That wasn't a man who doesn't trust me. That was a man spurned by love."

Dee felt her mouth go dry and tried to think of a way to draw attention away from Luke, but before she could, he continued, "I always knew he had a thing for you, but I was never worried because I thought you would never fall for a guy like that." His voice changed. The edge in his tone gave Dee chills, "I guess I was wrong."

Dee tried to defend herself. "I never fell for..." but Mark's laugh cut her off. His laugh was low and disturbing. Mark watched her reaction, obviously enjoying how uncomfortable he was making her. He was beginning to resemble Jorge, both being men who got a thrill out of the discomfort of others.

Sitting on the edge of her bed, Mark stared at her and shook his head, making a quiet tsking sound. He looked her straight in the eyes and Dee couldn't believe how blank his eyes were. Though they seemed calm, they lacked emotion. They didn't look human. Instead, they seemed eerie and unearthly. Dee inhaled deeply, trying to control herself and keep her hands from trembling. As he spoke, his voice remained flat. Such composure seemed weird for what he was saying. "Now I can't have the love of my life falling in love with another man."

His words were direct. Dee didn't dare argue that they had broken up a long time ago. His composure frightened her. How could one utter a threat so calmly? He was so disconnected; Dee wondered if he even knew what he was saying. Taking her hand, he gently stroked the top, careful to avoid the IV, "But don't you worry. I'll take care of it." Getting up, he tipped his head towards her and turned to leave.

"Where..." she began, afraid to ask and risk setting him off, "where are you going?"

His smile was instantly disturbing, "To go pay your friend a visit."

All the color drained from her face. Mark noticed and anger flickered across this face. Pacing the room, he began to rant. "I knew it! I knew it!" With each word he became more agitated, but he wasn't making any sense. Turning on his heels, he swiftly left the room, leaving Dee horrified and frightened.

The door swung shut and Dee tried to rack her brain. Realizing that she didn't have time to think, she impulsively reacted. Reaching over, she pressed the call button, summoning a nurse.

Dee leaned forward and watched the door, impatiently waiting for someone to arrive. She didn't have an action plan. She just needed to leave and get to Luke before Mark did. Then she would warn him and...and what? Dee closed her eyes and pushed her palms against them. She could get him out of town, but what if Mark found out? Would he go after Maggie instead? The situation deepened into a bottomless pit that had no resolution. Dee had to face reality. The law was useless. A restraining order only works when someone adheres to it, and Mark considered himself above the law.

Dee shook her head. She didn't care. She had to try. She couldn't just sit back and let Mark—she cut herself off, not allowing her thoughts to go there.

Finally, a nurse showed up.

"I want to check out," Dee stated, hating how she made the hospital sound like a hotel.

The nurse was young and just stared at her. Dee became agitated, frustrated by the nurse's incompetence. "The doctor said I could leave whenever I wanted to and I want to leave NOW!"

The nurse's eyes immediately widened and she silently looked over Dee's medical chart. Reading the doctor's comments, she began to nod and replied as if she were apologetic, "I just need the doctor to sign these discharge papers. Then you can go." Taking out Dee's IV, the flustered nurse grabbed her medical papers and rushed out of the room.

Getting up, Dee grabbed the duffel bag that Luke had brought and rooted around for clothes. She got dressed and impatiently paced the room, too worked up to think rationally. When the nurse returned, she nervously asked Dee to sign a wavier. Dee signed it, grabbed her bag and left without a word, leaving the nurse gawking at her.

Heading for the pediatric ward, Dee searched for Jeffrey's office. Finding his door closed, she knocked, praying that he would be there. When he answered the door, he was surprised to see her standing there.

"Dee," he replied stunned, motioning for her to come in, "Good to see you up and about."

Dee glanced at his desk and saw a half-eaten sub. She turned and faced him directly, ignoring his chit-chat. "I need to borrow your car."

He stared in surprise. He knew Dee vowed to never borrow a vehicle ever again. "You're leaving already? Are you sure you are feeling well enough."

Dee ignored his concern. "There's something I need to take care of immediately. It's an emergency. I need your car!"

Picking up on the urgency in her voice, he nodded and walked around to his desk. Opening his drawer, he fished out his keys, but before he handed them over, he hesitated, asking, "Are you sure you're okay? I can call Maggie and get her to go with you."

Dee shook her head and insisted, "I'm fine."

Jeffrey sighed and surrendered his keys. "Maggie will be expecting an explanation later."

Dee nodded, grabbed his keys, and raced out of his office without another word. Taking the elevator to the main floor, Dee leaned against the wall, already exhausted. Sweat beaded along her forehead and she wiped it in an attempt to cool down. Ignoring her fatigue, she hurried out to the parking lot directly below Jeffrey's office. Reserved for surgeons, Dee quickly found his BMW and hopped inside. Making her way out of the hospital parking lot, she got onto the freeway and began to take deep breaths, trying to calm down and focus. She looked at the clock and sped up. It seemed like the nurse had taken forever and if Mark went directly to Luke's house, she might be too late. Rummaging through the console, Dee checked for a cell phone, hoping that Maggie might have forgotten hers there. Looking back up at the road, Dee straightened the car and continued to dig. When she failed to find one, she scrunched up her forehead. If she had paused for one second, she might have thought of calling Luke first, or asking Jeffrey for his cell phone as well. Slamming the console shut, she sighed and stepped on the gas. Soon her exit appeared and she hurried off the freeway and drove into the familiar suburban neighbourhood. Refusing to slow down for a yellow light, Dee sped up and ran it right when it turned red. Usually a careful driver, Dee no longer cared. She only had three blocks to go and she wasn't stopping for anything.

Catching a flash in the corner of her eye, she looked in the rearview mirror and found a police car signalling her to pull over. Looking ahead, she knew she only had two more blocks to go. Rather than pulling over, she turned right onto Luke's street. Up ahead she could see Mark's black Mercedes parked, with Mark standing next to it. Luke's garage was open and she saw Luke walking around his SUV. Unaware that he was being watched, Luke turned his back to Mark and began loading things into his hatch. Mark lifted his one arm and Dee could see the metallic gleam of his handgun. Hammering on the gas, she sped up, ignoring the police cruiser behind her. She raced up until she was aligned with

Mark's car and slammed on the breaks. Mark was so focused on Luke that he didn't see her coming. Pulling the trigger, a loud bang erupted and her passenger side window exploded, showering her with shards of glass. Screaming, Dee ducked.

The second Luke heard the loud noise he instinctively lunged behind his workbench. Catching his breath, he tried to calm his racing heart. Though the noise sounded like a gunshot, Luke knew that it couldn't be so. Not in his neighbourhood. Leaning back his head, he considered the possibility that his military duty was getting to him. Was this a bout of PTSD? Peeking around the corner of his workbench, he saw an unfamiliar black car, Jeffrey's car and a police cruiser. A man stood next to the black car, but his face was blocked by the BMW.

Dee undid her seatbelt and slid open the driver's side door. Crawling out, careful to avoid the glass, she sunk to the ground, unhurt but terrified. Huddling in front of the tire, she peeked underneath the car and saw Mark's feet only steps away from her. She could hear the police officers shouting, but her ears refused to make out their words.

Luke peeked around the corner again, unable to see the driver of Jeffrey's car. Soon the door cracked open and Dee slid to the ground. He couldn't tell if she was hurt or just frightened. She huddled next to the wheel, with her knees drawn up tight to her chest, like a small child. Immediately Luke realized that he was not losing his mind. An actual gunshot had gone off. Staring at the black car, he tried to see what make it was. Mercedes? Though he had never seen it before, he knew that Mark drove a Mercedes, and if that was Mark standing there, ignoring the cops, then Dee was in trouble. Scurrying around his SUV, Luke made his way to the other side of the garage. Crouched in the corner, he stuck his head out and tried to get Dee's attention. The man yelled back at the police, ignoring their commands. Though Luke couldn't make out their words, he knew that they were serious. The police stood behind their car doors, with their guns drawn.

Dee could make out a shadow and knew that it was Luke crawling around in his garage. She saw him peer around the corner, and when the police officer began barking orders at Mark, he began to crawl along his hedge. Looking underneath the car, Dee saw Mark's feet pointed towards the police officers and she knew that he didn't see Luke leave the garage. Though he was hidden by the bushes, she wished that he stayed in the garage, where there were walls to protect him.

The police officer stopped talking and waited for Mark to comply. She heard his low laugh and began to tremble.

341

Looking underneath the car, she noticed that he had backed up and now stood over the hood of her car. As well, his feet were pointed towards the house, ignoring the two police officers. Looking ahead, Dee saw part of Luke peering from behind the bushes and knew that Mark saw him too. A slow click echoed through her ears as Mark pulled back the hammer on his gun. Panicking, Dee jumped up and rushed towards him screaming for him to stop, but it was too late. The gun fired and a searing hot pain ripped through her body.

Luke watched helplessly as Dee's delicate body crumpled in the middle of the street. Multiple shots rang through his ears as the police officers opened fire on Mark. His body collapsed behind the BMW, hidden from Luke's view. As the police officers approached Mark, Luke rushed into the street and pushed Dee's limp body onto her back. Applying pressure to her wound, he begged her to hang on, but her lifeless body was unable to respond. He could hear a police officer request an ambulance. No matter how hard he pressed, blood continued to run onto the pavement, forming a large puddle before help arrived.

Chapter 20

Luke vigilantly watched Dee's shoulders rise and fall with each laboured breath. Though the doctors assured him that her surgery was a success and that she was expected to make a complete recovery, Luke had his doubts. The shock that her body had endured over the past few weeks was too much for anyone to endure. He knew that Dee was a fighter, but one could only take so much, and he feared that this was too much. Gripping her hand tighter, he prayed the same prayer that he prayed the past two days as he anxiously waited for Dee to recover. The doctors kept her heavily medicated, for fear of an infection, and Dee slept peacefully while Luke continued to replay the moments that led up to such dire circumstances. Nothing made sense. There were so many questions, with no one able to answer them.

Luke heard a gentle tap at the door and Juan's head popped around the corner. For the past two days, Maggie and Jeffrey took turns visiting, but Luke refused to leave Dee's side. He tried to be strong enough to encourage his sister, but when Juan was with him, he let down his guard. Taking a seat next to Luke, Juan genuinely asked, "How are you doing?"

Luke shrugged his shoulders. Physically he was fine, but mentally and emotionally, he was a wreck. Juan cupped his shoulder and reminded him, "The doctors said that she will be fine."

Luke nodded, wishing he could completely believe them. "But look at her," he whispered, "She doesn't look fine."

"She looks like she is doing better," Juan observed. "She's got some color in her cheeks."

Luke nodded half-heartedly. He had witnessed men recover from gunshot wounds that were much more critical than this, yet his fear remained. He knew that she would be fine; he just wanted her to be fine immediately.

Juan pulled out a folder and handed it to Luke. "I want you to take a look at this." He knew that Luke took time off to care for Dee, but he felt that this was too important. Luke opened the folder and stared at a picture of his lieutenant and friend, Wayne McCabe. Though he had aged and his hair and beard were wild and unkempt, there was no question that this was his friend who disappeared before his tour ended. For almost three years Luke had been searching for him and this was the closest he had come to see seeing him.

"Where did you..." Luke began.

Juan reached over and flipped the page. "Recognize this guy?" Luke stared blankly at the unfamiliar face and shook his head. When Juan said his name, it didn't ring a bell, so Juan continued. "Two days ago, this guy's house was raided on allegations that he was running a child sex film industry. Amongst numerous pornographic videos, authorities stumbled across a demands video that he had filmed. It seemed that porn didn't pay well enough so he had to get a second job filming for terrorists."

"Are they still holding him?" Luke dared to ask.

Juan smiled. "Yup. But wait, it gets better. In return for some protection, he's agreed to cooperate. He gave us information about the video he shot and its whereabouts."

"Was his information any good?"

"Incredible!" Turning the next page, Juan showed Luke a map. "Recognize this road?"

Luke recognized it for sure. "We've driven by a hundred times and have never found anything."

"That is because everything is underground." Pulling out a new stack of papers he handed Luke an armful of satellite surveillance photos. "Once we knew where to look, we found everything that we have been looking for."

Luke flipped through the photos, recognizing high profile terrorists and fellow comrades that they had been searching for. He couldn't believe what they had found. He felt like a child being handed the keys to a candy store.

"The Colonel is organizing a team right now. He wants you to lead it."

Luke looked up and studied Juan's face to see if he was serious. He then looked over at Dee.

"Luke, she's going to be fine. This is three years of work, practically handed over to us. It's exactly what you've been looking for. One more mission and we're done. You can retire from the army, get a normal job and marry her."

Look looked back at the stack of evidence. "Did the Colonel send you here to convince me?"

Juan nodded. "We need you, man. Wayne needs you. His wife's been waiting for him for three years. His baby is in preschool..."

Luke nodded, cutting him off. "When do you leave?"

"As soon as I get you there."

Luke stared at Dee, afraid to leave her side. "What if..."

"She'll be fine," his friend assured him. He knew Juan was right. Dee was strong and she was fighting through this. He felt torn, wanting to be there when she woke up, yet needing to save his friend and restore him to his old life. Nodding, Luke handed the file back to Juan and pulled a pad of paper out of the drawer next to Dee's bed. Quickly writing a note, he explained his departure, assured her of his love and promised a return as soon as possible. Leaving it next to her bedside, he stood and turned to go. Right then Maggie and Ashley walked in. Putting down a basket of fruit, Maggie placed her hands on her hips and stared at Juan and his uniform. Turning to Luke, she asked the obvious, "You're leaving?"

Luke nodded and Maggie immediately responded. "Hallway," she ordered. Luke stood surprised. He had never heard his sister speak with such authority. Following her into the hallway, Juan snuck by and said, "I'll bring my car around front."

Maggie glared as Juan walked away. "I can't believe you are leaving!"

"It's an emergency," Luke tried to explain.

Maggie waved her hands, dismissing any possible excuse. "This is an emergency, Luke! My best friend—our best friend—was just shot by her ex! How can we expect her to stick around if we aren't around to help her?"

"I know, I know," Luke apologized. "Maggie, I wish I could explain, but right now I can't. I will when I get back, but until then I need you to trust me." He took her hands into his, attempting to calm her down. "You know I wouldn't leave if it wasn't important."

"How long will you be gone?" Her words had an edge that cut at him.

"I don't know. I'll be back as soon as I can," he promised.

"This better be good."

Luke leaned in and kissed his sister on the cheek. "It is. Trust me." He turned to go, and then stopped himself. "Don't worry too much, Maggie. Everything will be fine. Just worry about the baby, okay?" When she threw her hands up in frustration, he took on his big brother tone. "I mean it." Maggie scowled at his bossiness and stormed into Dee's room.

Ashley looked around the sterile room and pouted. She had no desire to visit some ailing woman, who, quite frankly, was tearing apart Maggie's life and endangering Luke's. The only reason she agreed to come was because she knew Luke would be here. He had been here for two days straight, refusing to leave Dee's bedside. Flopping into a chair, she stared at the still body of the woman that had obviously caught Luke's attention. She didn't see what was so spectacular about her. Yes, she was slim and somewhat pretty, but her hair was an uncontrollable mess of curls. Quite honestly, it was probably all the drama that roped Luke in. She was pretty sure that if someone tried to hurt her, she'd have Luke's attention. He was just that kind of guy. He had a hero complex. He needed to be needed and wanted to feel like the knight in shining armour.

Glancing over, Ashley caught sight of a piece of paper on the bedside stand. Curious, she reached over and opened it. Seeing Luke's signature scribbled on the bottom, she couldn't help but read it. She didn't care if it was an invasion of privacy. First of all, no one would know, and second of all, why would she respect the privacy of a woman that she did not respect.

Dee,

I always knew that I would do anything to protect and take care of you. I never realized that you would do the same for me. I know I've said this before, but I love you. I always have and always will. We have so much we need to talk about. I wish I could be here for you—to help you recover. I need you to know that I wouldn't leave you for any small reason. We've found Wayne, and I firmly believe that this will be my last mission. If anyone understands, I know it will be you. Take care of yourself Dee. Don't rush your recovery. I'll be home as soon as possible. And PLEASE do not run away until I have a chance to talk to you!

Love,

Luke

Ashley crumpled up the letter and stuffed it in her purse. She hated how naive Luke was being. Couldn't he see that this woman was destroying his life? Men! Sometimes they were so blind! But she would see to it that he didn't fall for any more of this woman's traps. He may think that he loves her, but he'd be much better off without her. In her opinion, the sooner Dee left the better.

Dee stared at the boring, white walls, anxious for a new setting. Though she wasn't awake for the first two, this was her third day in the hospital, and she was already sick of it. Maggie sat next to her, making small talk. They were waiting for Jeffrey to get off duty, and then he would join them. Dee knew she was in for a big talk. Maggie's growing belly had made her both motherly and confident. She knew that Maggie wouldn't rest until she knew everything. Unfortunately, Dee had no desire to talk about things until she saw Luke, so she continued to ask questions about the baby, which Maggie ecstatically responded to. The more they talked about the baby, the more she hoped that Maggie would get distracted and forget to pry.

Unfortunately, Jeffrey showed up determined to keep his wife on track. As they exchanged glances, Dee knew that they had an agenda that they were sticking to.

Maggie cleared her throat and began her well rehearsed speech. "Dee, we know that you've been through a lot this past year, and we don't want to push, but now that you are feeling a bit better, I think it's time to talk about it."

Dee nodded. She couldn't blame them. They were her closest friends. How could they not be confused or curious?

Maggie continued. "Why did you leave without telling us what was going on?"

Dee took in a deep breath. She wanted to tell them, she really did, hoping that it would help clear her conscience, yet she felt that she ought to talk to Luke first. Unfortunately, she hadn't seen him and had no idea if he would even visit. Was he avoiding her?

"Mark got to me." She replied. She knew her response didn't really explain anything, but she didn't care.

"Then why did you just leave? Why didn't you get help? Go to the police or at least tell us what was going on?"

"Look at what happened! What would the police do? They can't stop him."

"But they did," Maggie argued.

"Yeah, for now," Dee muttered underneath her breath.

"Dee," Jeffrey interrupted, "Mark's never going to be a problem again. You don't have to worry about what you say or do anymore. So why don't you move on in life. You don't need to hide anymore."

Dee sucked in a deep, frustrated breath. "Move on to what? Yeah, okay, so Mark will be arrested and go to jail, but one day he will get out of jail and this will start all over again."

Maggie gasped and whispered, "You don't know?"

"Know what?" Dee asked crankily.

Jeffrey took a deep breath. "I'm sorry Dee. We thought that the police told you." He paused and looked at his wife for support. "Mark was shot and killed on the scene."

The police had visited her earlier that morning and taken her statement. They mentioned that Mark was shot by a police officer, but she just assumed that he was recovering, much like she was. They never mentioned his death. Dee stared at them, unsure of what to feel. For a man that caused so much grief in her life, she was beginning to feel sorry for him.

Maggie reached out and grabbed her hand. "It's okay to feel upset. You shared part of your life with him."

Dee nodded. She felt sad, yet relieved at the same time. They gave her a moment, but when she didn't say anything, Jeffrey continued, "I guess what we really want to know is why all this took place in front of Luke's house."

Another valid question. Of course they would be wondering that. Carefully choosing her words, she cautiously responded. "I don't want to hide anything from you. You're right. I need to move on, and I can't keep secrets from you.

However, that is something I need to talk to Luke about before I can talk about it with you."

Maggie opened her mouth to protest, but Jeffrey stopped her by gently rubbing her knee. "I think that is fair enough and we will respect that, on one condition: that you promise to talk to us about it as soon as possible."

Dee nodded. Though she promised, she really wasn't looking forward to it.

"You're in luck, because Luke is out of town and who knows when he will get back," Maggie commented, obviously unimpressed that she would have to wait before she got any answers.

Dee looked up surprised. She had wondered why she hadn't seen him. She assumed he was upset, but if he was just out of town, perhaps there was a chance of receiving forgiveness. But then, perhaps he left so that he wouldn't have to deal with her. Immediately, numerous possibilities flooded her brain and she no longer knew what to think, let alone hope for.

After Maggie and Jeffrey left, Dee reached over and lifted the well-worn Bible off the nightstand. She flipped it open to a verse she had memorized when she was in the Mountains over Christmas. "'For I know the plans I have for you,' declares the Lord, 'plans to prosper you and not to harm you, plans to give you hope and a future.'" Ever since she ran away to Colombia she doubted that there was any hope of a future. Never bothering to read further, she read the next verse, "'Then you will call upon me and come and pray to me, and I will listen to you. You will seek me and find me when you seek me with all your heart.'"

Dee groaned, wishing that she had read that verse before. For months she doubted, uncertain that God heard her prayers. Yet here it was, in black and white, promising that he listened to prayers. She knew that she had been foolish and asked God to forgive her. Then she promised to seek him with all her heart, for she truly wanted to find the Lord.

Feeling comforted, she asked, knowing that God was listening, for a chance to make things right with Luke. Confessing her love for him, she earnestly prayed that the hope and future that God planned out for her was one with Luke. When she finished praying, she leaned back and smiled, knowing that God heard her.

Dee threw the last of her clothes into her suitcase. Her recovery had been longer than she anticipated, and she was more than ready to get out of this place. Besides the dreary white walls and the dreadful food, she was anxious to move on to the next phase of her life. Finally able to leave, Maggie insisted that Dee stayed with them rather than a hotel. Dee agreed upon one condition: that Maggie took her apartment shopping the next day. Though she appreciated Maggie's generosity, she was anxious to establish her independence and had no desire to share a living space with Ashley.

As Dee packed the rest of her belongings, Maggie checked the bathroom to make sure they weren't forgetting anything. Ashley, who came with Maggie, stood by the door sulking and didn't offer to help. Dee was sure that Ashley was a nice girl, but every time she looked at her, she felt a pang of jealousy and wondered what Luke's relationship was with her. Maggie made it sound very serious, yet Luke flew halfway around the world to save her. Was he torn between two women, or had Maggie misconstrued their relationship? Or was she the one that had misunderstood?

Dee had enough thoughts to confuse her. Asking her mind to stop, she looked at Ashley. She would be pretty if she didn't pout so much. Dee was sure that she was nice, but she felt uncomfortable around her.

Satisfied, Maggie emerged from the bathroom and led them down the hall. Once they reached the first floor, Maggie slapped her forehead. "I forgot! I have to drop something off at Jeffrey's office. I'll just be a minute. You two wait here."

Leaving them in the hall, she went back up on the elevator. Dee stood there uneasily. She wondered what Ashley was doing there, considering that they had never met before. At first, she thought that Ashley came to help carry the suitcase, considering Maggie was six months pregnant and Dee's one arm was in a sling, but she made no offer to help, so Dee carried it herself, managing fine on her own. Perhaps Maggie wanted them to be friends, but couldn't she introduce them under better circumstances? The hospital was not the classiest place to establish a new friendship.

Any hopes of friendship were kyboshed the moment Ashley opened her mouth. "Luke's not really out of town," she stated. Dee looked up at her surprised. "I know Maggie told you that he's out of town, but that's because she didn't want to hurt your feelings. The real reason why he hasn't come to visit you is because he's done with you."

Her statement felt like a slap in the face and it stung. "Oh," was all that Dee could manage to mutter.

Ashley watched as Dee lowered her eyes and stared at the floor. Impressed with the effect that she was having, she continued, glad to see that Dee believed her. "We had a nice long talk about it last night. He was pretty worked up. It took a while, but I finally calmed him down. I think it'd be best if you gave him some space. Maybe one day down the road he'll feel differently."

Dee nodded and stared at the ugly tiles, urging her eyes not to cry. So that was why he stayed away. That was what he wanted. She was beginning to understand the relationship that existed between Luke and Ashley. Dee felt silly. For a moment she had hoped, with Mark's death that...

"Ready?" Maggie asked. Dee looked up surprised. She didn't even know that her friend was back already. Nodding, she lifted her suitcase off of the floor and lugged it out of the hospital.

Chapter 21

Dee placed her last shopping bag on her kitchen table and sunk down into a chair. She looked around her apartment, proud of all the progress she had made that day. Having her furniture delivered that morning, it no longer looked lonely and empty. Stretching her shoulder, she stared at the sling that she had carelessly tossed onto the counter. Though she should have left it on, she found it easier to haul her newly purchased dishes from her car to the kitchen without it. Again, she stretched her aching shoulder and began to lift her kitchen essentials out of their bags.

Finding this apartment was easy. Furnishing had taken a bit longer than she expected, but she looked forward to being independent and settled. It had been nice of Maggie to offer for her to stay a bit longer, but with Ashley around, things felt both awkward and uncomfortable. Ashley made no attempt to hide her scowls and Dee couldn't help but wonder how upset Luke was at her.

Dee stared at her new cell phone. She had tried calling Luke a couple times, but he didn't answer. Finally, she gave up and left a message, expressing her regret but also making it very clear that she would like to apologize in person. She tried to be patient, but after a few days she needed to be alone, so she moved out and began camping in her empty apartment, slowly purchasing furniture and buying her daily essentials. Now that her bed had arrived, she would no longer have to sleep on an air mattress on the floor. Perhaps after a good night's sleep her shoulder wouldn't ache so much.

Opening up a shopping bag, Dee pulled out a set of dishes. Now that she had dinnerware, she would no longer have to depend on take-out. Her shoulder gave up as she tried to open the box. She had overdone it carrying the heavy bags up the stairs. Pushing the box aside, she slumped in her chair, frustrated. As her irritation mounted, her thoughts floated back to Luke. Loneliness weighed in, even heavier than before and she sighed. She moved out of Maggie's because she wanted to be alone, but now that she was alone, it was driving her crazy. It wasn't so much the solitude. She knew that if she called Maggie, she'd be over there in a flash. What truly bothered her was the fact that she was apart from Luke. She didn't want to spend time with just anybody; she needed to spend time with him. Even if he didn't want to be associated with her, she needed to tell him the whole story and get things off of her chest. Then he would know, and if he didn't like it, fine! That would be his choice, but at least she would have tried.

Things just didn't make sense. This wasn't like Luke. He was a man of reason. Even if he didn't want to talk about it, Dee thought he would be considerate enough to hear her out. The fact that he remained silent worried her and it was driving her crazy. She knew he would be upset. Of course he would be upset. Her ex tried to kill him. She just figured that he would react differently. She never expected him to avoid her.

A loud knock interrupted her depressing thoughts and Dee got up to answer the door. Opening the door, she was shocked to see Luke standing there.

"You look surprised," he casually commented.

"Well, yeah..." Dee admitted, beckoning him in. It had been over a week since she left him a message. With his growing silence, the last thing she expected was for him to show up at her apartment.

"I got your message," he commented, looking around her new living room. "I must admit, it left me a little perplexed. Didn't you get my note?"

Dee watched him as he remained calm and cool. This was nothing like what she had expected. Where was the anger and frustration that Ashley described? She shook her head. She began to speak cautiously, not wanting an argument to erupt. "I hope you don't mind me calling. Ashley told me you would call when you felt ready to, but I just needed you to know..."

"Ashley?" Luke asked, confused as to what she had to do with anything.

Dee nodded. "She told me about your talk. About how upset you were."

"Ashley did?" He asked again. Dee could see that he was getting worked up. She lowered her eyes, afraid that she said the wrong thing. Perhaps he would prefer it if she left Ashley out of this. Maybe he didn't want her talking to his girlfriend. Maybe he felt it was necessary to protect Ashley from a person like her. He began to pace in her small living room like a caged animal. Frustration mounted as he ran his hands through his short hair.

"I'm sorry," Dee apologized. "I shouldn't have said anything."

Luke looked up at her with such intensity that she began to feel nervous. He closed the gap between them in two steps and stared at her, reading her reaction. Sinking his hands into her hair, he pulled her close. His kiss was long and deep. Dee sunk into his embrace, melting as his lips warmed her own. When he eventually pulled away, he looked her straight in the eyes. With his hands still in her hair, he cupped her face and stared sternly. Dee watched him with wide eyes, feeling unsure, but pleasantly surprised.

"No more lies," he demanded. Dee nodded, but before she could respond, he kissed her again. When he pulled away this time, his gaze was gentler.

Despite his kisses, Dee still felt uncertain of where she stood. Afraid that this would be her only chance to explain, she mustered up all her courage and murmured the truth for the first time in a long time. "I love you."

Luke dropped his hands to her shoulders and tilted his head back laughing. It wasn't the reaction that Dee expected. She felt bewildered, not knowing how to read him. Looking back at her, he played with a curl and replied, "I know that." When Dee's eyes remained confused, he continued, "You wouldn't take a bullet for me if you didn't love me."

Dee began to understand his logic. "Are you mad?" She dared to ask.

Luke studied her face for a moment. Turning he sat down on the couch. Rather than letting Dee sit next to him, he grabbed her hips and pulled her down onto his lap. Drawing her close, he wrapped his arms around her and held her tight.

"Of course not. Frightened? Yes. Worried? Most definitely. But mad? No. At least not at you. I'm mad at

Mark for keeping you away from me, for scaring you and most of all, for hurting you." He drew Dee's head into the crook of his shoulder and rested his head on top of her soft curls. "How about you start at the beginning and don't leave anything out."

Dee sighed and began her long story, beginning with the assault that took place on New Year's Day. Her story was long, and Luke listened silently. He didn't interrupt once, and when she was done, he let out a slow, long breath and kissed the top of her head. Dee waited, unsure of what his reaction would be. He didn't throw her aside, but did he understand?

Speaking slowly, he confessed, "I just wished you told me."

"There was nothing that you could do."

Luke nodded, seeing her rationalization. "I could have gone to Colombia with you."

Dee shook her head sadly. She knew that was exactly what he would have done, if she let him. "But if Mark found out, he would have gone after someone else. He would have gone after Maggie."

Of all the scenarios that went through his head, he never imagined one that would harm Maggie. Immediately the complexity of her predicament dawned upon him. "I still would have liked to know."

He could feel Dee nodding underneath his chin. "I wanted to tell you so badly, but I knew that if you knew, you would take the risk. I wasn't willing to gamble with your life, or anyone else's."

"Do you miss him?"

Dee knew who he was referring to and shrugged her shoulders. "Not really. Perhaps I should be a weeping widow, but I don't really feel like one."

"What do you feel?"

"Honestly?" Dee asked.

"Nothing but the truth," he insisted.

"I feel relief. I feel bad that it had to end this way, but I'm just glad that it is over."

"Me too," Luke whispered as he drew her closer. Kissing her forehead gently, he asked the single question that he had been aching to ask. "Now what?"

Dee pulled back so that she could see his eyes. She needed to be honest. "I love you, Luke, I really do, but if I'm going to be honest, I need you to know where I'm coming from."

"And where is that?" He urged out of her.

"I know you have loved me for a long time, but I'm not ready to get married," she confessed. She knew it sounded bad and rushed on, trying to cover it up. "I'm not saying I don't want to date you. It's just that with Mark I made so many bad choices. And with my mom's terrible marriage to my step-dad, I just want to make sure you are the right guy before I rush into marriage."

Luke let out a low chuckle. "I'm not proposing."

Dee knew she sounded foolish. "It's just that you flew half way around the world and stormed a rebel camp to rescue me..."

Luke cut her off by taking her chin and stared her straight in the eyes. "Deanna Joy Cairns," he began, "I've waited six years to date you and that is exactly what I'm going to do." Dee felt silly and tried to look away, but he wouldn't let her. "You don't think about marriage?"

"Of course I do! But you have to date a woman before you can marry her. Besides, how do I know if you are the one if I haven't dated you?"

"I just thought that after all you've done that you were pretty sure..."

"I am pretty sure, but there are a few things I still need to learn about you."

"Like what?"

"Like...what if you load the dishwasher the wrong way?"

Dee stared at him incredulously, trying to see if he was teasing her. "You would let a silly thing like that keep you from marrying someone?"

"It's kind of a deal breaker," he admitted.

Dee's jaw dropped. "You'll face terrorists and all kinds of threats, but you won't endure a wife who loads the dishwasher the wrong way?"

"I didn't say I wouldn't endure her. If she's worth it, I'm sure I can overlook such a thing."

"I didn't even know there was a wrong way to load it."

"I know," he teased. "I've seen you load one. It's terrible. So much wasted space."

Dee laughed and raised her arm to playfully slap his shoulder, but winced at her sudden movement. Luke looked at her concerned, "Where's your sling?"

"I took it off so that I could unpack."

Luke narrowed his eyes and chastised her. "You shouldn't be unpacking."

Dee's eyes met his and challenged him, "What was I supposed to do? Get your pregnant sister to do it for me?"

Luke raised his arms in surrender and then drew her close again. "Well, you're in luck. Now you have a boyfriend to unpack for you."

Dee snuggled in. "Boyfriend," she murmured. "I like the sound of that."

"I was thinking we could go on a double date tomorrow," he suggested.

"With Maggie and Jeffrey?" Luke nodded and Dee began to tease him. "I dunno. Maggie really had her heart set on one day being Ashley's sister-in-law."

Luke glowed as Dee flirted with him. Nuzzling her nose, he murmured, "I think she'll get over it," and kissed Dee deeply, refusing to pull away this time. Dee sank in, hoping that he would never stop.

Made in the USA
Monee, IL
26 September 2024

66560037R00215